BEST LESBIAN ROMANCE 2009

BEST LESBIAN ROMANCE 2009

EDITED BY
RADCLYFFE

CLEIS
PRESS

Copyright © 2009 by Radclyffe.

All rights reserved. Except for brief passages quoted in newspaper, magazine, radio, television, or online reviews, no part of this book may be reproduced in any form or by any means, electronic or mechanical, including photocopying, recording, or information storage or retrieval system, without permission in writing from the publisher. Published in the United States.

Cleis Press Inc., P.O. Box 14697, San Francisco, California 94114
Printed in the United States.

Cover design: Scott Idleman
Cover photograph: Celesta Danger
Text design: Frank Wiedemann
Cleis logo art: Juana Alicia
First Edition.
10 9 8 7 6 5 4 3 2 1

"Christmas Blizzard" © Teresa Noelle Roberts appeared in *Naughty or Nice: Christmas Erotica* (Cleis Press, 2007); "Finding My Feet" © Shanna Germain appeared in *Wetter* (Alyson Publications, 2008); "In Flight" © Andrea Dale "Sand Castle Queen" © Rachel Kramer Bussel appeared in *Best Lesbian Love Stories: Summer Fling* (Alyson Publications, 2007); "Hide" © Alison Tyler appeared in *L Is for Leather* (Cleis Press, 2008); "Sugar on Snow" © Sacchi Green appeared in *Sex and Candy* (Pretty Things Press, 2008); "Music on the Wind" © Radclyffe appeared in *In Deep Waters, Vol. 1*, (BellaBooks, 2007).

Contents

| INTRODUCTION

R omance is as difficult to define in literature as it is in life. Over the centuries the popular view of the concept has evolved from the grandly defined "heroic quest" to something far more personal, if sometimes just as elusive. Whether thought of as a noun, "an intimate physical and emotional relationship," or as a verb, "to court or seduce," the sine qua non of romance is intense, passionate emotion. Love.

Searching for love, discovering love, and celebrating love are way stations on an emotional expedition that is as varied and complex as we are ourselves, and yet we all recognize those quintessential moments when what we feel can only be love, and nothing else. Sometimes love drives us to distraction and beyond (Potter's "Place, Park, Scene, Dark"), sometimes it gives us the strength to be our best selves (Kallmaker's "Last Call"), and sometimes it haunts us (Graham's "A Ghost of a Chance"). But always, by stirring our deepest wants and desires and needs, love reminds us that we are alive as only the most critical of emotions can. From the excitement and uncertainty of a first date (Bergquist's "Femme Fatale: 1992") to the celebration of enduring passion ("Music on the Wind"), these sensual, erotic stories capture the many shapes of the intimate encounters we call love.

Radclyffe

FEMME FATALE:
1992

Kathie Bergquist

The new underwear was my best friend Gabi's idea. "You can't go on a date with the same old *Jockey for Her* white cotton hipsters you've been wearing for the past three years," she reasoned as we strolled through the lingerie section of Marshall Field's. "You're a new girl, with a new attitude. You need new underwear."

We were shopping before my first post-break-up date. Cody and I, who had been together for three years, were so freshly broken up that we still lived in the same one-bedroom apartment, but tonight I was going on a date with Angel, a poet Gabi introduced me to.

"How will Angel even know what kind of underwear I'm wearing?" I asked.

"What kind of attitude is that! Think positive! *You'll* know you're wearing sexy new underwear. Not those libido killers you usually wear."

"They're comfortable!" I argued.

"This has nothing to do with comfort. This is about getting some action." She held up a black thong.

"I can't wear that!"

"Why not? It's hot."

"I'm not having a string up my butt all night! I'll feel ridiculous."

In the end we compromised. I bought some black lace underwear that covered my whole bottom and a sexy bra that matched.

Gabi also gave me some of these plastic latex squares that dentists use for I don't know what. They were called dental dams. Lesbians were supposed to use them for safe sex. Like, when you go down on a girl, you spread it over her vagina so you don't swap juices, kinda like a lesbian condom. Nobody knew if lesbians could even give AIDS to each other, but the theory behind dental dams was *better safe than sorry*. The ones Gabi gave me were pink and smelled like bubblegum.

My bedroom looked like a helicopter had landed in it. Clothes were strewn everywhere as I paced around in my itchy underwear, trying to figure out what to wear. We were going to a performance art show at a club. I wanted to look stylish but not too dressed up, casual but not like a slob. I also wanted to look kinda sexy but not slutty. I wanted Angel to want to have sex with me.

There, I said it.

I wanted to get laid.

Besides Cody, and rolling around on my futon with Gabi that one time before she deemed us sexually incompatible, by the age of twenty-two my entire sexual history consisted of making out with a few guys in high school and giving one hand job, which was the last convincing I needed that I liked girls. When actually faced with the prospect, I was nervous about the idea of having sex with someone new. How would I know what she liked? What if I was no good?

And not only did I *want* to get laid, Gabi had practically convinced me that I *had* to get laid. "A palate cleanser," she'd said, "so you can move on."

I'd finally decided on a pair of nice jeans with no holes in them and this shiny black satin button-up shirt—something soft to the touch—and (hopefully) to encourage more touching. At first I had the shirt buttoned up to the top, but then I undid one button, and then another. After the second button, you could see a hint of my cleavage. I buttoned it back up. Then I unbuttoned it again.

I checked myself out in various poses and positions in the full-length mirror and decided I looked pretty good. My crazy, curly hair was behaving somewhat with the help of pomade. I don't usually wear makeup, but I put on a little mascara and a thin smear of reddish lipstick.

In the meantime, Cody came home from school. "Wow, look at you! You look sexy."

That's right, I thought to myself. *Too bad for you.*

"Are you coming home tonight?" she asked. She was in the bedroom, examining the stains on her various work shirts.

"How would I know?" I responded coyly. Then, thinking about it, I added, "Probably." After all, no matter what happened tonight, the last thing I wanted was to come home to find my ex-girlfriend with her new brunette "friend" in what used to be *our* bed.

Despite not having a car, Angel offered to pick me up so we could walk the eight or so blocks to Club Lower Links together. The door buzzer rang right on time, to the minute.

Angel looked nice. She was wearing what looked like vintage

men's trousers with a white shirt and a suit coat, and like me, she had some makeup on, too. "How are you?" she asked, kissing me on the cheek. We started walking.

"I'm excited about this show," Angel said. "I love Paula Scott. Have you seen her before?"

"I don't think so," I said. "I know the name…"

"She does all this great performance stuff around town. She's the most famous performance artist in Chicago."

"That's cool," I said.

Performance art was something that I guessed I liked in theory, although I had not actually seen very much of it. To be honest, I'd never even really heard about performance art until last year when the National Endowment for the Arts took back grants that they'd awarded to these four performance artists because they decided that their stuff was obscene. One of the artists put a crucifix in a jar of piss, and another one poured a can of pork and beans over her bare behind. I don't know what the other two did besides just being gay and talking about it. Anyways, since then it seemed that performance art was popping up everywhere. Everyone was doing it. It was about free speech or something.

When we got to the club, they weren't letting people in yet, so we waited in the line outside. We were early enough that we were close to the front of the line. Because it was the middle of summer, it was still light out and warm, even though it was almost eight p.m. Angel took off her suit coat and held it over her arm. A trickle of sweat skidded down my ribcage.

To kill time, I checked out the crowd. People were in their late twenties or thirties. The crowd was mostly women, and mostly white, and a majority were wearing glasses. Cool glasses. I wished I had some cool glasses, despite the fact that I had 20/20 vision.

By the time they finally opened the door, the line snaked around the corner. Angel had bought our tickets ahead of time. She handed me mine, and we shuffled in.

The club was small and dark. The walls were painted black, the floors were black, the chairs and tables: all black. White candles on tables lent flickering light, and spotlights illuminated some artwork hung on the walls. Rectangular-shaped, the room had a bar along one of the sides, a small cleared-out area that made up a stage down at the far end, and bathrooms across the way from the bar. Tables and chairs were scattered with little rhyme or reason.

The rest of the line filed in behind us, the bar filling in our wake.

We took a table near the stage, and then Angel went and got us beers. By now the place was pretty full—the indecipherable murmur of collective voices, the heat of bodies and anticipation, and thickening blue smoke rose up to create a chaos that made the air feel heavy and the walls compressed. A cold sheen of sweat covered my skin. Under my satin shirt, the lace of my bra was making my boobs itch like crazy. I twitched. Angel was taking a long time.

I scanned the throngs clustered around the bar to see if I could spot her. It took a while. Finally there she was, emerging from a group, with a sweating brown bottle in each hand. She was talking with some girl I didn't know or recognize. They laughed. An arrow shot through me.

Then I saw Angel gesture with a beer in my direction. Both Angel and the girl turned to look and caught me gawking at them. Angel smiled, and with a hand still gripping the beer bottle, raised her pointer finger as if to say, "Give me one minute." I faintly returned her smile and nodded.

What was this? Was Angel cruising another girl on our date?

Now, not just my boobs but also my ass was starting to itch. Maybe I should just leave, I thought.

"I'm sorry that took so long." Angel set two Bud Lights on the table. "The crowd at the bar was ruthless."

That's it? I thought. No explanation about the girl?

"That's okay." I picked up my beer and took a swig. It was barely cold. "Thanks for the beer."

"I ran into this girl," Angel continued, "who I haven't seen for a long time."

"Oh?"

"She used to date this guy, Gary, who I know. Then she dumped him for the bass player in that group Struck by Lightning, that dude—what's his name?" Angel looked up as if the answer existed above my head.

Relief washed over me. The girl was straight. Of course! The girl was straight. Sometimes I forget that, statistically speaking, most of the people in the world are heterosexual.

"Whatever, it doesn't matter," Angel concluded. "I always thought she was a bitch. Now I guess she has an album coming out."

"Really?" I looked back to where the girl had been standing, but she wasn't there anymore.

"You girls okay?" A pretty cocktail waitress hovered over us. She had dark hair and lots of makeup on. It was hard to tell how old she was.

"Want another?" Angel asked me. I looked at my beer bottle. It was only half empty.

"Sure," I said.

"Two more," Angel told her.

Club Lower Links was getting more and more crowded. Angel and I were each on our third beer, and there was no sign of the show starting. My new panties were wedged up in my asscrack. I leaned on the table over my folded arms so I could discreetly try to scratch my tits.

Meanwhile, I had also edged a little closer to Angel, or she had to me. We were sitting side by side, out thighs touching, and our faces inches apart. We kept having to talk louder to hear each other over the mounting din. All the noise and smoke was making the space on my forehead between my eyes throb, and the beer had filled my bladder.

"I'm going to try to go to the bathroom before the show starts," I yelled to Angel.

I started to rise but right at that instant a spotlight came up on the stage, and the crowd hushed. I sat back down.

A giant breast came through the crowd, up to the front of the stage. That is, a woman wearing a giant breast costume—papier-mâché or what, I don't know. What she was were skinny legs in pink tights, giant Caucasian breast with round, brown areola, spindly arms, and head.

"Stop staring at my tit," she said, deadpan. The audience broke out into appreciative laughter.

"Paula Scott," Angel said. "She's a trip."

"Thanks for coming out tonight, and for those of you for whom it's relevant, thanks for coming out in general. Ka-boom!" Paula Scott hammed it up, doing some vaudeville-style dance moves.

"Tonight, ladies, and…" she paused and looked out as if scanning the crowd, "…*ladies*…Everyone check your tickets to make sure you're in the right place because this ain't your Friday night church bingo game! If you think it is, you walked in the wrong door! That's down the street! This is *Femme Fatale.*"

Some *woots* erupted in the audience.

"A night of female performance art *on the edge*! We're on the edge, ladies, so fasten your seatbelts! We have a great showcase lined up for you tonight. You'll laugh, you'll cry, you'll want to stick an ice pick in your eye. Now everyone give a big hand for Daphne LaRoche performing 'All Is Vanity.' "

"Woo-hoo!" Angel hooted, along with scattered others in the crowd. Paula Scott stepped off of the stage. A moment later, a bare-chested young woman wearing a ballerina skirt took her place. Her boobs were kind of uneven—one pointed downward, the other one shot out sideways. She stood in front of everyone and stretched her hands out to her sides, revealing brown stigmata drawn on her palms. Closing her eyes tightly, she started reciting. "The words of the preacher, the son of David, king in Jerusalem. Vanity of vanities saith the preacher, vanity of vanities, all is vanities."

"Ecclesiastes," said Angel.

I wondered how she knew that. As for me, I'd had no idea what this topless chick was spouting off about. Furthermore, wouldn't it be "all *are* vanities?" I had this thing about subject-verb agreement.

Two minutes into the performance, and my mind started to wander. Would it be rude to get up and go use the bathroom? I scanned behind me. It would be tough to work my way through the crowd. I glanced down at my third beer, long empty. My mouth was dry and gummy. Angel's eyes were fixed on the performer. Was she into this? I tried to refocus my energy to the stage.

"...I have seen all the works that are done under the sun and behold, all is vanity..."

The woman's arms were beginning to droop a little bit. Her eyes remained squeezed shut.

What if I didn't have sex with Angel tonight? Would that be the end of the world? I mean, this was only our first date.

It wasn't that unusual to *not* have sex on the first date. On the other hand, we did already kiss. Did Angel assume we were going to have sex? I wondered how many people Angel had had sex with. She'd once had a threeway with Gabi and Jamie, so she must be pretty adventurous. Did she just have casual sex all the time? Maybe I was in over my head.

"…And he that increases knowledge, increases sorrow…"

Everyone burst into applause. I snapped to attention. Daphne LaRoche curtsied in her tutu and then scurried off the stage.

"I'm going to try to use the bathroom," I told Angel.

I pushed myself back into the crowd. Paula Scott, now dressed in black jeans and a turtleneck, had retaken the stage and was introducing the next act. When I finally made it to the bathroom, there was someone standing in front of the door.

"Are you in line?" I asked.

"Yeah," she said. "That's the line." She gestured back with her thumb, and in despair I followed the length of the line, which seemed to close ranks; each woman was prepared to defend her position. The line was at least, *at least,* twenty people deep.

"That was quick," Angel said when I returned a few minutes later to my seat.

"The line was too long," I explained. "I can wait. What's this?" I asked, gesturing toward the stage.

Two women were sitting back to back about two feet away from each other.

"Shh…" Angel fluttered a finger up to her lips. "Just watch."

One of the women was speaking in a completely monotone voice. "I want to touch you," she was saying. "My hands shake with passion."

"For your arms to envelop me," began the other, her voice equally flat. She sounded almost robotic. "Your legs wrapped in mine."

"Your breath in my mouth," robot lady number one continued.

At a table across from us, a woman with protruding eyes and frog jowls seemed to be maliciously blowing smoke in my face. Where was the cocktail server? I couldn't believe Angel was into this crap. I now knew what Paula Scott meant when she predicted I'd want to stick an ice pick in my eye. My boobs itched insanely, and I couldn't sit comfortably for the pressure on my bladder and the lace panty wedged up my ass. At that moment it seemed ridiculous that I had purchased this horrible underwear just for this date.

If this kinda thing was what Angel was into, then maybe we were not meant to be. I sized her up. Her eyes were fixated on the action—if you could call it that—on the so-called stage. Minutes of my life ticked away from me.

"Control, alt, delete," both of the robot women said in unison. Then each stood, picked up her chair, and walked off either side of the stage.

Please let this be over soon, I prayed to no one in particular.

"Would you like another beer?" Angel asked over the applause. Suddenly, as if appearing in a vapor, the cocktail waitress had reappeared. "Sure," I said. "I'll get this one." Why not? If my bladder exploded, at least I'd have an excuse to leave.

I dug in my back pocket for the twenty I'd shoved in there, but felt instead something I couldn't identify—something plasticy. I started to pull it out when it dawned on me—the dental dams! Fuck! I quickly shoved them back in and felt around until I had located the lone bill.

"What do you think of the show so far?" Angel leaned toward me as she spoke.

"It's, um…" I scrambled for the word. "It's very postmodern."

"Do you think so?"

"Sure. I mean, I don't really know what that means."

Angel burst out laughing. "Neither do I, but I'm sure you're right. This show is *very* postmodern."

"I think it might even be post-postmodern," I added.

"It's *so* postmodern," Angel continued, "it's practically modern again."

Now we were both laughing, and just like that I felt closer to her again. The cocktail server returned with our beers, which I paid for as Paula Scott announced the next performance. I didn't catch the artist's name, only that the performance was called "Blood Money."

A woman who looked like a librarian in a skirt and tweed jacket walked onto the stage with a satchel. She set the satchel on the ground, reached in it, and pulled out fistfuls of Monopoly money, which she began scattering on the floor. Then she took out a red ketchup squeeze bottle, stood up, lifted her skirt, and held the bottle to her crotch like it was a penis. I couldn't help but observe that she was wearing the same kind of white cotton panties that I usually wore, and that tufts of dark pubic hair stuck out from the elastic around her crotch.

"Oh, no she didn't," Angel said under her breath.

The woman squeezed the bottle. A long stream of ketchup arced out, splattering over the pastel money on the floor. The vinegar-sweet smell of ketchup immediately overwhelmed any other odor in the club.

I glanced at Angel. She looked at me. "Let's get out of here," she mouthed.

"Right."

I was up in an instant. Angel grabbed my hand and pulled me through the crowd, back to the door. We fled outside and took off running down the street screaming and finally stopped after a few blocks, when we were out of breath. Angel put her hands on her knees and was breathing hard. Her sides shook with laughter. She glanced up at me, a grin spread across her face.

"Holy shit," I panted. "I have to pee!" The need became urgent. I was near the point of peeing my pants. We had run deep into a residential area and were surrounded by houses.

"Come on." Angel grabbed my hand again and pulled me into an alley. "I have to go too," she said. "You watch for me and I'll watch for you. You first."

I didn't argue. I dropped my pants and crouched down, barely making it before the dam broke and the pee burst out of me, splashing my shoes. Relief, sweet relief. After giving my rear a quick shake, I quickly stood up and refastened my pants.

Angel went right after me. I made sure not to look, and kept my eyes open for anyone who might be heading in our direction. In a moment she was back next to me.

"Nice panties," she said. "You dropped this." To my utter mortification, I saw that she had the dental dams. "I'll hold onto them," she said, sliding the baggie into her suit coat pocket. "So, what next?"

"What do you want to do?" I asked.

"Whatever you want."

And then she did the most beautiful thing. She stuck out her arms, her head tilted up to the sky, and spun around. "The night is young," she said to the nonexistent stars. "The world is ours!"

CHRISTMAS BLIZZARD

Teresa Noelle Roberts

"Another cancellation," I sighed as I hung up the phone. "Merry fucking Christmas to you too!"

The promise of a "blizzard of the new century" threatening to rival the infamous, deadly Blizzard of '78, here on the far tip of Cape Cod where snow rarely sticks at all, had cleared the few winter tourists out of Provincetown long before the snow actually hit. I'm sure some of the locals were pleased, but it was making for a less than happy holiday at our bed-and-breakfast. We'd been booked full for tonight, Christmas Eve—women who'd decided on a romantic holiday in P-town and either breakfast in bed or a big pajama-clad, family-style breakfast on Christmas morning—but one by one they'd been canceling. The couple who'd just called had been our last holdouts; they'd gotten as far as Providence, Rhode Island on their way from New York City, creeping through a near whiteout, and had decided to hole up in a hotel there for the holiday instead of risking the rest of the drive.

Lucie circled her arms around me from behind. "Look on the bright side. We have Christmas to ourselves! When was the last time we got to spend a holiday, any holiday, without an inn full of guests? And we can enjoy the inn all decorated and pretty instead of hiding up in our little cave." Her hands slid up from my waist to cup my breasts. "What's the point of owning a lesbian romantic haven if we can't enjoy it ourselves sometimes?"

Good point, I thought, as her small, hard hands sent waves of sensation radiating out from my breasts. Our apartment above the garage was the only part of the property we hadn't succeeded in making luxurious, the only part we hadn't bothered decorating for Christmas/Solstice/generic midwinter cheer. But left alone, nothing would stop us from enjoying all the amenities we offered to guests. "Let's start in the Lavender Room," I whispered. "I'd gotten it all ready for the folks who just called."

We all but ran there. We'd had a fire going against the window-rattling gale, and the room was toasty warm, the flames casting dramatic shadows on the lavender walls. We shared a quiet moment enjoying the sensation of pretending to be guests, appreciating the beautiful color scheme we'd chosen, the richness of plump pillows, velvet duvet cover, brocaded drapes. The room smelled delicious, like Christmas cookies (we'd gone crazy baking for the guests and would now be eating gingerbread women and pfeffernüsse for weeks), wood smoke, pine, and, of course, lavender. Yeah, our guests had it pretty good—and today, so did we.

Then clothes began flying everywhere. Soon we were naked and lying in each other's arms on the Oriental rug in front of the fire.

Just long, languid kisses at first, and pressing together, loving how our breasts brushed against each other, how our legs intertwined to allow maximum skin contact. The warmth transmuted into heat and the heat filled me, igniting nipple and clit and pussy and every inch of skin in between. From her movements against me, I could tell Lucie was in the same place. It had been ages since we'd taken the time to just make out like this.

Finally I pulled away, sat up. Lucie's skin glimmered with a fine sheen of sweat. Her nipples were hard, crinkled with excitement, and moisture gleamed between her parted legs. "Beautiful," I breathed. I moved to touch her, but she shook her head. "The floor's hard, and I've always loved that sleigh bed."

If I could have picked her up and carried her, I would have. It seemed appropriate in that room with its Victorian aura. Alas for that fantasy. Lucie, while shorter than I am, does chimney work in fall and winter and landscaping in summer, and she's dense with muscle. So I just gave her a hand up instead and whirled her over to the bed.

It was high and puffy and enveloping, and her café-au-lait skin—Lucie's background includes Cape Verdean, French-Canadian, and Mohawk—looked both darker and creamier against the purple velvet duvet. I dove onto the bed next to her, squealing "Whee!" and for a minute all we could do was giggle. Then I began to stroke her, and the giggles faded into sighs.

Silken skin over firm muscles, and small breasts with prominent, plum-colored nipples, and the tight, black curls that drew my eye to her pussy, just as plum-dark as her nipples and currently juicier than any plum I'd ever encountered—I stroked and kissed my way down Lucie's body to that spot and began to lick.

I've given a lot of thought to what Lucie actually tastes like. The briny sweetness of oysters—Wellfleet oysters, eaten in Wellfleet just hours after they were harvested—always come to mind, but there's a hint of smoke and spice there too, and a fragrance that adds to the mystery. Lucie tastes like Lucie, I suppose, and she's delicious.

She filled my mouth, my nostrils, all my senses. In turn I filled her with two fingers, crooking them to tantalize that sensitive little node that someone unpoetically named the G-spot. Slick and smooth and gripping, she rode my hand and mouth, cooing and mewling to herself. Strangely ladylike noises, as if she was afraid of being overheard. But that was just Lucie's way. At other times, she's outspoken, with the hearty voice of someone who works outdoors a lot. In bed, she becomes deceptively quiet. (For the first year we were together, I tried everything I could think of to make her scream or at least moan when she came. Then I decided it was just the way she was wired, and since it didn't interfere with her enjoyment, I wouldn't let it interfere with mine.) There was nothing quiet or ladylike about the way she was thrashing around, though, or the way she clenched around me.

And even less ladylike was the way she returned the pleasure once she'd caught her breath. She knows I like a little roughness sometimes, and there was something especially perverse about her pinning me down with her body weight and working me over in a lush Victorian space lavishly and sentimentally decorated for Christmas. Love bites on my breasts and fingernails raking my thighs were just the start, enough to make me wet and squirming and loudly excited.

"Onto all fours, darling," she said huskily. It wasn't an order—we're into sensation, not power play. I still rolled over obediently and stuck my ass into the air. Why not? I knew what was coming, and I knew I'd love it.

With a thwack her hand came down on my butt. I jumped at the sudden sting, even though I was anticipating it, but heat blossomed from the impact immediately, spreading from my butt throughout my whole body. I arched my back up, raising my ass to show I wanted more and was promptly rewarded.

The pleasure built as the spanking continued, spiraling from her wicked little hand through my pelvis, right into my cunt. Unlike Lucie, I'm not quiet when I get excited. Pretty soon I was yelping, growling, and occasionally giggling from the adrenaline rush.

And pretty soon after that I was begging incoherently.

"What do you want?" she demanded.

"Please...." This was not the time to ask a girl to speak in complete sentences, but if I couldn't say what I wanted, I certainly couldn't string together a concept that complex.

"Please what? Please stop spanking you?"

She said that just as I grunted out another "Please." It was poorly timed—she did stop spanking me.

That provoked one other word: "Bitch."

"Your bitch, though."

I nodded. Then I raised my ass even higher and managed to squeak out, "Please make me come."

She leaned around me, nibbling my ear in passing. "Hey, that was almost articulate. Can't have that."

Her fingers touched my clit, began to circle. With her other hand, she smacked me again, a little faster and sharper now that I was so close.

I howled as I came.

"Happy holidays," she purred. "Consider this the stocking gift—there's plenty more to follow!"

Later, as the storm hit the Cape in earnest, we headed down to Race Point, bundled in our warmest clothes. We clung to each other as we walked, partly against the force of the wind, but mostly because we love to touch, even when the touch is muted through layers of fabric. The crash of the storm-fueled waves and the roar of the wind combined into a white noise that we couldn't talk over. I love the ocean when it's so wild and dramatic, but big areas of beach have been known to wash away when the seas get so rough—we lost entire buildings during the Blizzard of '78—and Lucie finally dragged me away as the snow began to fall thicker and faster.

It was flying fast by the time we got home, obscuring the Christmas lights that brightened the town and the sliver view of the harbor you can usually see from our apartment, the one saving grace of the cramped space. We stripped out of several layers of clothing (pausing frequently to smooch) and made ourselves hot chocolate (pausing frequently to cuddle up against each other and nibble).

"I'm still chilled," Lucie said after we'd finished our cocoa. "How about a hot shower together?"

That sounded like a good idea, but as I rose to take her up on it, I looked out into the yard and got a better one. Snow fell steady and thick against the twilight. If you could ignore the howling wind, and the fact we couldn't see the house next door despite it being blanketed in a truly scary light display in the shape of a buff Santa waving a Pride flag, it was an idealized Christmas Eve straight out of an old movie. The house and the privacy fence sheltered the back deck from the worst of the wind so it was falling straight down instead of blowing sideways like it was out on the street. "Ever made love in a hot tub in the snow?" I asked.

Lucie grinned. She was already struggling back into her boots before she answered, "Not yet!"

I don't think we'd ever made it downstairs so fast. I made one detour, to turn on the outside speakers so our favorite offbeat versions of holiday classics filled the air, but that took mere seconds since the music mix was already set up.

Certainly we'd never gotten the cover off the tub so efficiently for our guests.

We eased ourselves into the water and melted together, kissing frantically. The snow, a heavy veil around the tub, was searingly cold on my skin at first, but within a few minutes the steam from the tub began to do its work and most of the flakes evaporated before they hit us. Some lodged in our hair, cooled our shoulders and necks, but it was just enough to feel good, to remind us of the power of the storm. The wind break wasn't complete, but as long as we stayed mostly underwater, it was all right.

More than all right. It was downright miraculous to be out here on Christmas Eve in the middle of a storm, buoyed by hot water and surrounded by Loreena McKennitt working her strange magic on "God Rest Ye Merry Gentlemen." All the better to be in the arms of the woman I love.

My hand slipped between Lucie's thighs, finding a slick warmth, hotter than the water surrounding us. I started to stroke, but then had an inspiration and positioned her over a low jet on her hands and knees. She arched her back in pleasure, dancing multicolored lights illuminating her expectant face, her short dark hair spangled with snowflakes. "You're evil," she gasped. "Brilliant, but evil."

"Jets are a girl's best friend—I can't believe you never tried it before."

"Never had a chance. We've mostly used the tub when it was full of guests."

She was right, of course. We'd only put in the hot tub early this fall, after a successful summer gave us the spare cash. During the slower parts of the fall and early winter, we'd been busy with post-season repairs and redecorating and getting ready for first Thanksgiving and then Christmas, and collapsing in small, exhausted heaps when we weren't up to our eyebrows in some house project. And we'd gotten used to thinking of the tub as the guests' domain, not ours.

Important safety tip: take time for ourselves more often.

"Like it?"

"Oh, yes."

She was purring, but she still sounded much too coherent. I crouched over her, cupping a breast with one hand, pushing two fingers of the other inside her. So hot and tight, gripping against my hand. Slow in and out fucking, pushing against her swollen G-spot, my thumb on her clit and the relentless caress of the jet. She was so hot that I expected the snow to sizzle as it hit her, but it just melted, joining the water that made her body gleam. "Are you going to come for me?" I whispered in her ear, and she convulsed silently.

I didn't let up, though. Lucie, once she got going, could come for a long time. There's nothing I like better than seeing her becoming utterly boneless with lust, and she certainly obliged, bucking and contracting against my fingers in wave after wave of orgasm and cooing softly.

Until suddenly her noises weren't soft any more. She bucked back against me, almost pushing me over, arched, and howled her pleasure to the snowy night, drowning out the carols, drowning out the howling wind. Drowning out everything but the roar of my blood.

The sound echoed through my clit, ringing me like Santa's sleigh bells, only much sweeter. I'd forgotten, after years with Lucie's quiet ways, how hot a screaming woman can be. (Okay, I hadn't forgotten it. I just hadn't let myself spend too much time being wistful over the one thing missing in a great relationship.) These unfamiliar—yet entirely Lucie—noises galvanized me, pushed me toward the edge as fast as a touch might. I ground myself against Lucie's shuddering body and added my own cries to hers.

We slumped down together, limp and sated. Somehow, we

managed to arrange ourselves so we were supported on the seat and not in danger of drowning. I can't speak for Lucie, but I know in my case, brains weren't involved in the process. I pulled her close, cuddled her still shuddering form against me.

"Wow," she choked out, and buried her face against my shoulder. A little while later she repeated it. "Wow."

"I've never heard anything that beautiful, love. What broke the dam?"

She shrugged. "I don't know. The jets. You. The contrast between heat and cold. You. This amazing storm. You. Christmas Eve magic. You."

All around us, the rooftops and holiday decorations of Provincetown were disappearing under snow. Our own deck was getting buried except right around the hot tub, and the lights on the backyard trees were obscured by snow. We'd freeze getting back to the apartment, and cleaning up once the storm was over would be backbreaking, and at some point I'd have to think about all the income we weren't getting from the canceled bookings. But for now, safe inside our private Christmas Eve of steam, hot water, and desire, that didn't matter.

"Hearing you let loose like that was the best Christmas gift you could have possibly given me, love," I whispered to Lucie.

She giggled in a floaty way, still on a post-orgasmic high. "That's good," she said. "I didn't have much time to shop. But I think I can give that present over and over—now that I've found it."

THE USUAL

KI Thompson

I've always wanted to fall in love, but I never really believed it would happen to someone like me. Quite frankly, I've never had the time or the desire to date someone for long. The inane chitchat you have to go through in order to get to the sex bores me. Don't get me wrong. I don't take women for granted or treat them as sex objects; believe me, they're quite satisfied by the time I'm through with them. I'm just not interested in sharing my life, or my living space, with one particular person.

That's why it really threw me for a loop the day I met "the one." She hated me. Well, maybe "hate" is too strong. Let's just say she wasn't exactly enamored by my winning personality. But I loved her from the moment I saw her. I had just moved to New York City and asked the doorman of my building to recommend a good place to get a late-night breakfast.

When I peered into the window of the Greek diner on the corner of 9th Avenue and 23rd Street, she immediately caught my eye. The olive complexion, the jet hair piled atop her head with several wisps falling around her face, the full lips, and ebony eyes were certainly striking. But the quick smile and easy familiarity with her customers at two in the morning on that brisk December night really touched me. Somehow, being there felt right, and good, and I wanted to be a part of the warmth going on inside the diner—her warmth. I wanted to belong, and I wanted to belong to her.

She plunked a heavy cream-colored coffee mug on my table, took one long look at me while she poured, and said, "It's late, I'm beat, and I'm not in the mood. So what'll it be?"

"Was it something I said?" I lowered the menu to give her one of my most endearing smiles.

She sighed and shifted her weight from one foot to the other. Tossing the order pad onto the table, she lazily placed one hand on her hip. "Look, I know your type, and I don't have time for it. I've got one more hour on this shift and then I go home to bed...to sleep...*alone.*"

Personally, I thought the emphasis on *alone* was unnecessary, but sitting in the cozy booth, sharing the friendly atmosphere, my cold hands wrapped snugly around the cup of hot coffee, I felt invincible. Nothing she could say would deter me. Besides, I had just found out she slept alone.

"Well then, what do you recommend?" I gazed intently at the menu, feigning interest in corned beef hash with an over-easy egg.

"What do you like?" Her response sounded automatic. I grinned and winked, but she only rolled her eyes. She picked up the pad and waited.

"How's the hash?"

"Fine, if you like artery-clogging meals." She reached for my menu, but I pulled it back.

"What do *you* like to eat?" I wanted to know so I could choose a restaurant she would enjoy going to.

Instead, she pointed to the left-hand side of the menu. The top item read, "Fresh fruit, yogurt, and granola."

"I'll have the hash." I folded the menu, grinned again, and held it up. She snatched it and whirled off to the kitchen. I love diners.

The food came fast and was surprisingly good. When I reached for the ketchup bottle, she grimaced and stormed to the patrons across from me to refill their cups. She dropped the check off at my table, and I threw down an absurdly high tip, but she seemed unimpressed.

"Thanks." She gathered up my dishes as I rose to leave.

"I'm Jill," I said, but she ignored me. "The food was great and the service even better, although, if I could give you a piece of advice, you might try smiling a little more often. It makes the customers happy."

The look she gave me was not the kind I usually received from women, but then, she didn't know me that well yet.

It didn't take me long to discover she only worked the night shift and attended NYU part-time during the day. So I dropped by the diner every Friday night, about an hour before she got off work. There's something oddly intimate about being in a diner at two in the morning with the same strangers night after night. I looked forward to every Friday; it was fun to share my life experiences with her.

"I came in second place in my elementary-school spelling bee," I bragged.

"How nice for you."

"Ask me to spell something. Go ahead." I waited expectantly.

"Are you always this obnoxious?"

"Obnoxious. O-b-n-o—"

"I guess you are. Here, spell this." She began to hold up her middle finger, but I grabbed her hand.

"Now, now. The customer is always right, remember?" I held onto that soft, smooth hand for as long as I could and let my fingers wrap gently around hers. My heart thudded painfully, and I wanted nothing more than to kiss her right there in the diner. Slowly she retracted her hand and looked away. Mumbling something about returning to work, she strolled back to the kitchen.

The following week she didn't even glance up as she poured my fourth cup of the night and cleared the remnants of the hash. I was delaying my departure, not wanting to step back out into the frosty night air. I was dreaming about her now, and had increased my visits to the diner to three times a week. Her name was Irene, which I found out early on because everyone knew her—and she knew them. I seemed to be the only stranger in the place. Try as I might, I couldn't get her to include me in the convivial circle of her regulars. I was an outsider looking in, and she was content to keep me at arm's length.

"Say, that new foreign film is playing at the Angelika tomorrow night." I took a sip from my mug. "If you aren't busy—"

"I've seen it." She gathered up my dirty dishes and flung my napkin on top.

Now, I'm usually fairly patient when I want something, and I wanted her badly. But after weeks of being spurned, I was frustrated. Perhaps I needed to shift tactics. This time I waited out in the cold until I saw her exit the front door and the manager lock up behind her. She was juggling a book bag, her purse, and a large brown paper grocery sack. I saw my opportunity and hastened to her side.

"Here, let me give you a hand." I snatched the paper bag from her grasp and slipped it easily into the crook of one arm. She hesitated and eyed me warily, but with her load lightened, she slowly resumed walking down 9th Avenue.

After several minutes, the silence was killing me. "Would you like me to hail a cab?"

She shook her head. "I live a few blocks away."

My pulse revved. I was going to find out where she lived. Maybe she'd invite me up for a drink or a friendly cup of coffee. Now I was getting somewhere. A little more patience and soon I'd be removing her clothes. I gazed at her surreptitiously, observing how sexy she looked even with ruddy cheeks and Rudolph nose. Her breath came in soft puffs of white clouds, and her eyes sparkled like fireflies in the glow of the street lamps. She was beautiful and gazed straight ahead, as though we were complete strangers who happened to be walking down the same street in Manhattan at three o'clock in the morning.

I tried again to engage her. "So you go to school during the day. What are you studying?"

I hadn't realized she'd stopped until a few steps later. Turning around, I noticed a frown on her face and a guarded look in her eyes. "Why don't we cut the crap," she said. "I told you, I'm not interested, so why are you doing this?"

I shifted the bag to my left hip, wanting to convey all my stomach-wrenching, mind-blowing feelings in my words and in my expression. I wanted her to not only hear what I said but experience it intensely. I laid bare my heart so she could see who I was inside and how much love I was capable of giving. "Do you believe in love at first sight?"

She blinked. Then a slow grin formed and quickly built into a chuckle. From there it evolved into a guffaw, then into such a cacophony of laughter, cackling, and coughing that for a moment I thought I'd have to perform the Heimlich maneuver. When she finally gasped for air and clung to the wrought-iron railing of the steps in front of a building, I'd had enough.

"I'm so glad you find this amusing."

She held out her hand, signaling for me to wait until she could catch her breath. She'd almost pulled herself together when a giggle burst forth, but she quickly shoved it down.

"I'm sorry," she breathed, "but that's such bullshit."

I tried my best to show how hurt I was, but knew I was only kidding myself. "Okay, you're right. I think you're hot and you have great legs. It's gotta be maybe thirty degrees out, I'm freezing my ass off, and I just want you to ask me inside for a cup of coffee. If you can't stand me after ten minutes, you can toss me out. Okay?"

Once again that wary look crossed her face, like a beaten dog being offered food from an outstretched hand. An agonizingly long heartbeat later, she motioned me up the stairs and withdrew her keys from her purse. Once inside, I followed her to the second-floor landing where she unlocked her apartment door and led me inside.

It was a typical studio apartment—excruciatingly tiny, with only one window. But what made it really stand out was the absence of any furniture, save a full-size bed. No mementos, no pictures—though nails randomly decorated the walls—nothing of personal note or value to speak of. A stack of books on the floor by the bedside and a single, pathetic strand of flashing Christmas tree lights drooping from the window were the only additional items in view.

"So you're into minimalism." I glanced behind me in case I'd missed something.

She stood in the center of the room, following my gaze, as though trying to see what I saw.

"My ex took everything." She sighed heavily and tossed her coat and bags into a closet. "I bought the bed last week."

In the kitchen, I handed over the groceries, and she began to remove the contents.

"Would you like some tea?"

To say I was feeling a little sheepish would have been an understatement. I watched the deliberate way she poured water into the kettle and set it on the stove. The click-click of the gas burner before it roared to life sounded eerily loud in the empty room.

"Sure," I said. Not knowing what else to do with myself, I strolled over to the bed, removed my coat, and sat down. Normally that would have been a precursor to my next move if I were planning on seduction, but now I felt inexplicably sad. I crossed my leg and dangled it nervously while she removed two mugs from a cabinet, dropped a teabag in each, and waited for the whistle to blow. Moments later, she handed me a chipped green mug and sat beside me.

"So, were you together long?"

"Four years," she said, blowing gently on her tea before taking a sip. "I think I was in lust more than anything else, and deluded myself into thinking it was love. Still, it hurt."

She looked so small and fragile, completely unlike the woman I bantered with on my visits to the diner. I suddenly felt like a cad, pressuring her into letting me inside her apartment, ready to pounce at the slightest opportunity.

"Nothing wrong with lust," I said, trying to lighten things up. She peered at me and frowned. I must have exceeded the boundaries of polite conversation and was making it worse. I mentally berated myself—sometimes I'm amazed at how insensitive I can be.

"Is everything a joke to you?" she asked.

"Well, it's better than being depressed."

"I'm not depressed."

"I didn't say you were," I said.

"You thought you could just come up here, have a quick

fuck, and be on your merry way, right? No strings, no emotion, no attachment. Just a good time."

"That's not true."

"Then why are you here?"

"I..." What could I say? She hadn't believed me when I told her it was love at first sight, and a big part of me didn't believe in it either. Yet something was there, something I might not be able to define, but the feeling was so strong that if it could take shape, it would be as solid as a New York City cab.

"I just...I just want to be near you," I blurted. "You seem to be...normal, in a city that doesn't encourage that. I like the way I feel when I watch you take care of your customers. It makes me want to do nice things for people too. And yes, I think you're beautiful, and sexy, and if you'd let me make love to you right now, I'd be deliriously happy. But more than anything else, I don't ever want to see you look as sad and vulnerable as you do right now. It hurts *me* to see that, so I can't even imagine how it must make you feel."

For a long moment she didn't move, but then very slowly, almost imperceptibly, she leaned away from me. Her eyes never left mine, and her look of mistrust was replaced by something I couldn't decipher. I hate it when I can't read what's going on in someone's mind, so I figured I might as well cut my losses. This one had too much baggage that she didn't seem to want to let go of. I needed that like I needed to be caught near the East River alone at two a.m.

"Look, it's late. I'm sure you're tired after working so hard, and all I'm doing is making it worse." I rose from the bed, careful not to spill the now lukewarm chamomile on the quilt. But before I could take a step, her hand rested on my forearm.

"I'd really rather you stayed," she whispered. Her dark eyes were warm and moist, with a hint of melancholy in their bottomless depths. It was the kind of expression I usually ran headlong in the opposite direction from. It was the little-lost-puppy look, the kiss-it-and-make-it-better look, and it scared the hell out of me.

Wordlessly, I took the mug from her and placed both of them on the floor. I kicked off my shoes and then wrapped my arms around her and lay back on the bed. For the longest time I held her, and as far back as I could remember, that was all I wanted to do. I don't know how much time had passed, but very quickly I felt comfortable in that empty little space. For some reason, I no longer felt like an outsider.

Soon my eyelids felt like weighted curtains, and I struggled to keep them open. They had no sooner slid shut when I felt her warm lips and cool breath on my neck. But I thought if I opened my eyes, or moved in any way, this spectacular sensation would end. So I lay still, allowing my skin the delicious pleasure of her attention. When her hand slowly wandered from my thigh up to my belly, I was definitely wide awake.

She rolled on top of me and continued her kisses down my throat and into my open collar, all the while rocking gently against me. Her weight, combined with the rhythm of her movement, created a delicious friction that I let my body revel in. She explored farther down my chest, kissing through the fabric of my shirt, and I could feel the damp areas left behind by her lips. The moisture gave me chills. She fumbled at the buttons on my jeans, and a warm hand slipped inside.

"Oh, yeah."

Those were the first words I had spoken in quite a while, and it sounded as though I had shouted in church. Fortunately my outburst didn't interrupt her musings on my clit, because her fingers spread me open and slipped inside. I was wetter than I realized and sighed at how good it felt to be touched and stroked and how much I wanted her to make me come. The insistent pace of her rocking brought my body into sync with hers, and knowing that had been her intent from the start really turned me on.

Up to this point I had remained completely unmoving, but I finally brought myself out of my inertia and clutched her ass, squeezing her cheeks and pressing her into me. She moaned into my mouth as her hand continued its work. For an exquisitely brief time, we hovered in that moment between heaven and earth when you're not quite sure where you belong. But the rush in your ears and the pounding in your chest quickly remind you of your mortality, and all that matters in that moment is the explosion that rips through your body.

She rode me a while longer, drawing out the last vestiges of her orgasm, and then lay still. I held her tight, needing to ground her to me, needing to make it all real. Her heart beat loudly against mine and I rubbed her back, trying to soothe her. A short while later, she fell asleep on me. A long while later, my legs began to fall asleep as well, so I gently rolled her off and onto the pillow. I tried to be as quiet as possible and extricated myself from her arms. She only murmured briefly while I covered her with the quilt. Then grabbing my coat, I tiptoed to the door and out into the shocking cold of the night.

I stayed away from the diner a few days after that, unsure of my feelings as well as what to expect. But I couldn't stay away long. I needed to know what she thought of me, if I was the cad I believed I was, or if I should hope at all. Bracing myself, not against the cold but against what awaited me, I entered the diner early Friday night and stumbled to my usual table.

"Hey, Jill."

It was the security guard who worked the graveyard shift and sat at the counter. He always ordered pancakes with a side of bacon. I was surprised he remembered me and knew my name. A quick glance over my shoulder to see if he was talking to someone else, and I waved weakly at him.

"How's it goin', Jill?"

The homeless guy who never had anywhere to go and came into the diner to keep warm at night grinned toothlessly at me. Most places would have thrown him out long ago, but she wouldn't hear of it. He always managed to scrounge up enough change to buy himself a cup of coffee, but if he couldn't, she would pour him some anyway, and slip him something extra, too.

I sat at my table, bewildered by the sudden recognition of several other patrons who nodded my way. Maybe I'd walked into the wrong diner.

"Hey." Irene poured me a cup of coffee. "The usual?"

I searched her eyes and found recognition there—and more. I wanted to touch her and make her laugh, make her come, make her feel in an instant everything she ever wanted to feel. I wanted to take away all the pain that anyone had ever inflicted on her. I wanted to buy her furniture.

"Yeah." I smiled. "The usual."

LAST CALL

Karin Kallmaker

Nobody knows why she goes by Nebraska. If asked, she laughs and admits the closest she ever got to Nebraska is Iowa. Nobody at the Shady Times Bar knows—except me.

"You want another one of those?" Nebraska looked down the bar at me with the smile that had claimed my heart more than three years ago.

I tipped my club soda at her and a few moments later caught the filled glass as she slid it down the bar toward me. A noisy group jostled through the big swinging front door and made a beeline for the round table on the far end of the dance floor. It was early and the jukebox was still set for Elvis. I was lonesome tonight, but that was the status quo.

A few minutes later, the waitress murmured the party's order, and I watched Nebraska go into action. Her hands caressed the necks of tequila, rum, gin, and vodka bottles, deftly tossing them hand to hand. Glass flashed in the light, sparkling like miniature rainbows. Blue, green, and red prisms refracted in the mirror, spilling colors over her white-blond hair. Peach juice splashed color into the mix, followed by deft squirts of cola from the tap. I never could take my eyes off her, and tonight was no different. I watched her fingers nimbly twist lime slices and remembered that night, six months ago, when those fingers had been as deft with parts of my body, leaving me as filled—and mixed up—as the contents of the shakers she lined up across the bar.

One by one she tipped, flipped, and poured the shakers' contents into the row of tall glasses, and topped off her signature Nebraska tea with a wedge of orange. I could taste it against my lips, the fruit filling my nostrils as the smooth liquor warmed my mouth before sliding seductively down my throat.

I shook my gaze away from her hands on the next batch of drinks. It had been six months since I'd tasted the magic of her mixology. Six months since I'd tasted her lips, too.

"You're quiet tonight, Rikki." The flurry of activity completed, she leaned against the bar, looking at me with Amaretto eyes. "What's new in the exciting world of insurance?"

"There's nothing new and nothing exciting." I set down my club soda. Tonight was a night it would only make me thirstier. There was no courage in that glass. "Nebraska, I—"

"Two Buds, two Coronas, and a pitcher of premium margaritas," the waitress called.

Nebraska faded back to work, and I stared into the dull bubbles of the club soda. No courage in that glass, but the thousands of glasses that *had* had Dutch courage in them, that I'd consumed sitting on this very barstool over the years I'd loved Nebraska, hadn't helped me tell her how I felt either.

Maybe if I had one drink tonight, then I'd be able to take the chance. Just one drink.

A bowl of peanuts slid down the bar toward me, and I intercepted it. Nebraska winked as she uncapped bottles of beer. I knew if I asked her for one of her Nebraska teas, just one, she'd make it for me. She was nobody's cop. She wasn't my sponsor.

If she made me that drink, I'd be back in the tank, all over again. She'd never go out with me again. I'd be just another alcoholic whose commitment to AA was a revolving door. Of course here I was, sober as church, and she still wasn't going out with me.

I had trouble swallowing the suddenly dry peanut, and I closed my eyes to the ever-present memory of the gentle ruffle of her fingers in my hair. After a couple of years of flirting, laughing, and me downing her Nebraska tea, we'd had that one night, six months ago, when she'd been depressed, she'd said, and I'd still been at the bar at closing. She'd let me take her home and it was all a blur, except she tasted sweet, her body had been my fantasy brought to life, and her vocal appreciation had brought out the laughing explanation of the nickname. That old ex in Iowa had said she could be heard in Nebraska when she was particularly pleased. She'd been pleased that night with me. It was a good name for a bartender, but her real name, Jennifer, suited her better.

At least I thought so. The shapely jeans, sparkling hoops of gold that tangled with her long hair suited a Jennifer very well. I remembered her laughing, in the afterglow, and telling me about her nickname as the upstairs neighbor pounded on the floor about the noise. Alcohol-induced sleep had already been claiming me, and my next memory was close to morning, when she stirred. I felt her sit up but was too woozy to react.

She'd sighed, and then I'd heard her say, low, "What are you doing, Jenny? You promised this wasn't gonna happen. You don't need another drunk."

Her fingers had stirred my hair, gentle and kind. And then she'd left.

When I'd turned up at the bar that night and asked only for club soda, she hadn't commented. Night after night she'd fizzed club soda into a tall glass and added a twist of lime, six months of nights, and never said a word about my change in habits. Club soda and peanuts were all I had these days. But I knew I was still a drunk to her, one of the people who can't say no to it, who have to have it, who'll lie and connive to keep the booze available. Another person who couldn't control her choices, including where she spent hours every night. I was a drunk as long as I sat in this bar, eyeing the shakers and the bottles. How could she know if I was there to watch her or to yearn after the booze when I still wasn't sure myself?

She was mesmerizing, making use of several years as a street juggler while she'd gone to art school. She liked the Shady Times, and the owner certainly liked her ability to draw a crowd. When annoyed, she talked about going to work for one of the downtown hotels where the money was even better, but she never did. Sometimes, after we spent a slow evening picking apart a movie or book, or fixing the world's problems, I thought she stayed because of me. Nothing in her eyes, not since that night six months ago, confirmed that.

I got out my cell phone, my sponsor's speed dial ready to go. I wanted that drink, I wanted that courage to get up off this barstool, walk behind the bar, and kiss her. And say, in a sober voice, with clear eyes and a brain that connected one thought to another, "I want to go to the movies with you. I want to find out what makes you laugh so hard you can't breathe. I want to watch you sleep, and wake you in the night. I want to spend the rest of my life seeing if they can hear you in Nebraska, calling out my name."

I tossed back the rest of the club soda, tired of the taste of peanuts and lime juice. If I called my sponsor, he'd say I should get the hell out of the bar, that I was asking to fall off the wagon. That I'd lose what was left of my self-respect. If he knew about Nebraska, he'd tell me she'd lose all respect for me the moment I asked her for that drink. I was still a drunk every moment I sat on that barstool, regardless of what was in my hand. Some nights I lusted after the alcohol almost as much as her. I wanted to stay, and win her affection. I had to leave to maybe earn her respect. Either way, I lost her. Choices like that only make the booze all the more attractive.

"Another soda?" She was back in front of me, wiping the bar with her rag. "Did you finish that mystery? I've been meaning to ask."

"Yes, and I did finish it. I don't know—I figured out who did it pretty early on. The detective is hot but not all that bright. I kept thinking if I were in trouble, she wouldn't be the first person I called." I slid my phone back into my pocket.

"Oh, I didn't have a problem with that," she said as she returned with another frosty glass of club soda. "I liked her sexy but ditzy. But I got lost when the bad girl changed overnight. Page like one-eighty she's wicked and evil. Page one-eighty-one she's suddenly cooperating with the police. It didn't make sense."

"She changed for love, didn't she?"

"So what if she did?" Nebraska shrugged. "That kind of change doesn't stick. If the woman she loves goes out of her life, she'll go right back to being evil. She never repented the things she'd done. She didn't change to be a better person, just to get the girl. It felt like a costume to me, clothes she put on to attract the other woman. Like when a dru—" She flushed. "Sorry. I guess some of it hit home. You know about my ex."

I nodded. That's right, she'd been talking about what's-her-name, not me. "Like when a drunk stays sober until the first argument, then tells you you're the reason she fell off the wagon."

I tried not to flush, remembering me doing just that to my last girlfriend, who'd left me about the time my nightly hours at the Shady Times had become a new habit.

"Like that. Drunks blame everybody and everything but themselves." She left to prep a second round for the big group in the corner, and the night's trade began in earnest. The swinging door whooshed steadily in the background, making the noise swirl around me in uneven waves. It got so busy that her boss came out of the back to do the simple orders and run the credit cards. There was no mystery about why he was called Shorty.

I watched her fill orders, eyes and hands flashing in the light, putting on a show that brought her great tips. She must have made forty Nebraska teas along with all the other drinks she mixed, and I wanted to taste every one of them. I wanted to tell her that the night we'd spent together had truly changed me. The club soda wasn't a new shirt. I repeated that to myself, trying to believe it.

I got out the phone. I put it away. I caught her watching me, and it felt like she knew that every time I opened my mouth I wanted to order that drink.

By the time she announced last call, my heart was beating like I was carrying a hundred pounds on my back. The craving was so intense my stomach hurt, and I was seeing double. Get out of the bar, my sponsor would say. I knew that's what I had to do.

"One last club soda?" She looked up from stacking dirty glasses in the dishwashing racks under the bar.

"What I really want is a Nebraska tea."

Her hands never paused in their work. "Are you asking me to make you one?"

"Yeah."

She didn't react, but it was only because of the night we'd

spent together that I saw her eyes go from light amber to dull brown. She had picked up a shaker when I managed to say, "No. Don't make it."

She still didn't say anything. I realized she was watching me teeter on the precipice, guarded, too hurt in the past to let herself feel anything about whatever I might choose.

I got unsteadily to my feet, drunk on memories of a thousand cocktails and beers. "I need to settle my tab."

"You can do it tomorrow."

"No. I need to settle it now. The whole thing. I won't be back."

The bar got quiet, at least for me. There were people around, some very drunk and others just loud in their exhaustion. The jukebox faded to nothing, and there was just my voice and hers.

Her eyes still a murky brown, she asked, "Why?"

There was the truth, and there was what I said. "Because if I stay I'll drink, and I don't want to start counting hours and days again."

"I'll get the book."

She was back in just a few moments, showed me the total, and I gave her my credit card. When she came back with the slip, pausing to wipe down one last section of the bar, I signed it and didn't look her in the eye. My heart was still beating miles a minute, and it was all about good-byes.

The big door swung open and closed as people left, letting in cool night air as bar noise and music escaped.

More not-the-truth. "I've stayed this long because this is familiar. But I'd be better off cultivating a seat at the coffee place across the street."

"I understand." Her eyes were light amber again, though they shimmered like Amaretto in a clear glass. She blinked several times before she added, "Good luck. Congratulations."

No courage in the glass, there was no courage in me either. I had always wanted to blame my lack of happiness and the dead-end job on my girlfriends, my boss, my parents—even the demon alcohol that wasn't supposed to make me as drunk as it did. I never told her I loved her because alcohol kept my mouth shut. Here I was, six months sober, and my mouth was still shut.

It wasn't the booze, it was me that was a coward. I'd never reached for anything I wanted but the next drink.

Her smile faded. Nebraska...eyes like Amaretto, hands like a magician. Funny and insightful—if I wanted her in my life after tonight, I had to reach for her. But not like a drink, not like an addict, not like I had to have her and if I didn't I'd die. I had to pull her to me, like a fragile spirit to nurture. A woman I had to be good for, and who had to be good for me.

"Jennifer," I said, softly, so Shorty and the few customers left wouldn't hear.

One slender eyebrow lifted at my choice of name. "What is it, Rikki?"

"If I stay it'll be because I think I love you. I'm leaving because I have to do what's right for myself, finally."

She stood there, her eyes shimmering.

I turned to the door. A customer had left ahead of me, whooshing out into the night. The jukebox was back to Elvis, still lonesome, as I pushed the door open myself. It swung closed as I let go, pivoting back and forth, alternating sound between the music and the silent, cool night.

Elvis wanted to know if she'd wish for him on her doorstep. Then I heard her voice, louder.

"—sorry, Shorty. I won't be back. I have to—"

The door came to a rest, and I knew I would not come back again.

The quiet thrum of distant traffic was all that filled the night air until Elvis, lonesome but wishing he wasn't, sang out into the cool quiet. I was lonesome, too, but it was finally my clear-headed choice.

There were quick steps, hurrying across the parking lot behind me.

"Rikki," was all she said.

"I won't change my mind."

"You don't have to." She was standing right next to where I was rooted, unable to make my legs move. "I just quit."

I said the first thing that came into my head. "But you love your job."

"Yeah. I might love you. I can't have both, though. You're taking a chance. I can too."

"What are you going to do?" My heart went back to beating like it had inside, so quick and harsh that I thought if she was just teasing me I'd die from the pain.

"Tomorrow, I'll find me one of those fancy hotel bars down-town that won't let my girlfriend sit around all hours. I should have done it before this. Where I don't bring my work home with me so she and I can talk about books over dinner."

I think I was smiling. My face hurt at least, and my brain kept playing back what she'd said, trying to commit it to memory. "Why didn't you say?"

"I was waiting for you to know."

She pushed all that silky blond hair behind one ear, and I was all at once aware of the stale taste of club soda and peanuts in my mouth. I had no idea what the next step was, but I figured we would work that out. "Would you like to come back to my place and talk?"

"It's been six months." Her smile flashed in the night. "Even-tually we'll talk."

I touched her face and shivered, realizing that the next time

I kissed her I wouldn't forget by morning. That if I kissed her right now, by morning I would remember forever the crease of her thigh alongside her hip, the muscles of her stomach against mine, and I'd know for sure if they could hear her in Nebraska.

So I kissed her. Later, we talked.

FINDING MY FEET

Shanna Germain

They say that the thing you want is right in front of you, if only you know where to look. But there's the rub: How do you know where to look when you don't know what you want? Or worse, when you know what you want but can't have it? Where do you look then?

I thought I couldn't have what I wanted, but what did I know—I was looking at the wrong thing. I was looking at my own face in the mirror, lining my blue eyes, putting on coral lipstick, brushing my light brown hair back off my face. I was looking at Sun's dark eyes beneath her darker brows and the way her teeth showed, small and white as Chiclets, when she smiled. I was looking at her curves beneath her wrap-around skirt while she poured our chai. I was looking at the tapestries on Sun's walls, the fabrics she'd brought back from Singapore.

I moved around her dining room, touching a red and orange fabric, a green and gold. A blue one that matched my eyes. I dared to imagine her there in the bazaar, touching the blue and buying it, thinking of me.

"The place looks amazing, Sun," I said. "I can't believe you've only been back two weeks."

She pushed the hair away from her face. "Oh, thanks," she said. "There's still a lot more to do."

Sun would tell you she's goal-less, she would lament over her inability to find her type-A gene, but then she'd spend a year in Singapore doing relief work before coming home to repaint and redecorate her house. I could almost hate her for it if I wasn't convinced I was in love with her. Her year away hadn't changed that, despite my...hope was the wrong word...half-wish that it would.

I sat back down at the table across from Sun, put my hands on my warm mug. I had to keep my fingers moving—without something in their grasp, they threatened to get away from me, to reach across the table and wrap themselves in Sun's dark straight hair, to close her dark eyes. Sun didn't know how I felt—we'd been friends since college, when we played together on a beach volleyball team. And we'd stayed friends through all of her boyfriends, through all of my boyfriends and girlfriends.

Most times, it was enough to know that I could be here, across the table from her, with my eyes on her face. Now that she was here, though, after so long away...I looked down and counted the dark specks of spices that floated in my chai.

From the ceramic bowl in the middle of the table, Sun picked up a piece of candied ginger. She dropped it into my chai.

"Sweet and spicy," she said. "That hasn't changed, has it?"

I swirled my mug, letting the ginger sink. Then I took a sip: sugar-sweet, with that lingering spice in the back of my throat.

"No," I said. "That hasn't changed."

"Good," she said. "Some days, I feel like I've been gone forever."

I kept my eyes on my chai, the way the spices met and swirled at the top.

"So, I have a surprise for you," Sun said. "I brought it back from Singapore."

Her at the bazaar, choosing something just for me. It was better than the blue tapestry. I pressed my palms tighter to the mug. Stay still.

"You didn't need to do that," I said.

Sun laughed, husky and rich.

"Maybe you don't want it then?"

But she didn't wait for me to answer. Just stood and lifted something from a side table—a silver tray holding a squeeze bottle, some cotton balls, a clear glass bowl of liquid. Sun set the tray on the table between us.

I picked up the squeeze bottle. The dark liquid inside smelled like cloves and ginger.

"What is it?" I asked.

Sun's smile reminded me of Mona Lisa. Half smile, just her lips, sly.

"Henna," she said.

"Like body paint?"

"It's more like a stain. More permanent."

Sun flipped her hand over—on her palm, right in the center, a cluster of small flowers in reddish-brown. Tiny, intricate. I wanted to feel them. I squeezed the bottle so hard that a bit of henna came out the top. Stay still.

Sun leaned forward and put her fingers over my fingers around the bottle. "I want to henna you."

I was distracted by her warm fingers. Maybe I could feel her fingerprints pressing into the back of my hands. Maybe I could feel the henna design scratching lightly. I couldn't be sure.

"What? I mean, you do?"

Sun took the henna bottle from me. She turned the bottle over and over in her palm, watching it spin.

"Yes," she said, "but only if you don't mind. I saw this woman in Singapore, and she had her whole body done for a wedding. Hands, face…her feet."

I dipped one fingertip into the clear bowl on the tray. The liquid smelled like lemonade.

"Sugar lemon water," Sun said. "It helps the henna set."

I put the fingers wet against my chai mug, let the heat seep in. I didn't dare move—I didn't want to distract her from her story. It was selfish, but I wanted to hear her tell how she'd thought about me in Singapore.

Sun turned the bottle over, pressed in the sides, and some henna came out of the metal tip onto a napkin. It was even darker against the white napkin, the color of clay mud.

I stayed quiet, waiting.

"Her feet…" Sun said. "They were so beautiful, and they… they made me think of you. When we used to play beach volleyball. Remember?"

Sun looked up then, her dark eyes on my face.

"I remember," I said.

"I always watched you when we played, your feet," she said. "You had such beautiful feet."

Something started in my belly, worked its way into a giggle.

"My feet?"

Sun poked the metal tip of the bottle against the napkin. Made three small dots in a row.

"Don't laugh," she said.

I had to take her hand then, put my fingers over her fingers on the bottle. Hold her still.

"I'm not laughing," I said. "Well, okay, maybe a little. But my feet, Sun? I've been..."

I stopped. How to tell her I'd been lusting after her for all these years, her eyes, those small hands, her laugh, when she'd been...she'd been watching my feet?

Sun pulled her hands out from under mine, leaving only cold air. She put the bottle back on the silver tray.

"You're right," she said as she lifted the tray from the table. "I'm sorry, that was stupid. Let's just have our chai. You can tell me about the teaching, how that's going."

"Sun, wait." I reached for her hand, for her arm, but only caught the corner of the tray. Liquid splashed onto the silver, sending up the sweet scent of lemon and sugar between us.

Keeping my hand on that tray, just on the corner, feeling the carved designs, feeling Sun pulling away from me, I thought it was the hardest thing. And then I realized that I had to say something. That was so much harder.

"Sun," I said. "Yes, I'd love to have you paint my feet."

"You'll be cold," Sun had said. She was right. Now I was on her living room floor, leaning against the front of her couch, my jeans rolled up to the knees and a blanket wrapped around my shoulders. A thick towel was folded beneath my feet.

Sun was on the floor, cross-legged in front of me. She lifted my foot, held it with her palms under my heel. Her touch sent shivers up my leg.

"Okay?" she asked.

I nodded, but didn't trust myself to speak. Her hands on my feet, her gaze there too, I had never imagined. I'd always thought my feet were ugly—tiny and short, the way they curved out near my big toe. But Sun's hands told another story, her fingers around my toes, sliding up over the ball of my foot.

"You have to stop shivering so I can start," she said.

I tried. Held my teeth together tight, but it just made the rest of my body shake harder.

Sun snugged my foot against the inside of her thigh, right up against the thin fabric of her skirt, and held it until it didn't shake anymore. My foot was still, but the inside of my body was all shakes. Sun picked up her squeeze bottle, moved it in circles over the top of my foot without touching the tip to my skin.

"I'm just working out the design," she said. "Some people use books, but I liked the way the women did it, just stared at the skin until they found the pattern there."

I must have looked skeptical because she said, "Close your eyes, relax. Have faith."

I did as she said. At least the close-my-eyes part. I wasn't sure the ability to relax was an option for me. But I willed myself to breathe slow, in and out.

Soon the cool point of the bottle touched the side of my foot, near the instep. The metal tip traced my skin in a pattern I couldn't distinguish. After a few twists and turns of the tip, the still warm henna pulsed into my skin. It *was* like a massage but with lines of henna instead of fingers. Warm and tingling with spices, the henna patterns made my foot feel alive.

I realized I didn't pay attention to my feet, not ever. They got me from one place to another, they sometimes wore cute shoes. That was about it. But with Sun's attention—the way she tilted my foot to get better access or the way she pressed her thumb to my instep to hold me still—I wondered. What was it about feet that made her want to do this? Was it just a friendship thing? Or was it something more? I wanted to ask, but I was afraid. And so I just stayed still with my eyes closed and my feet in Sun's hands.

When she finished with the henna, Sun dipped cotton balls in the lemon-sugar water and patted it all over my feet. The gentle way she applied the cool, sticky liquid made me feel once again like I was being pampered. When she stopped, the skin on my feet felt like it was hardening, like if I moved, it might crack and slough off like an old shell that I'd outgrown.

"All done," Sun said.

I opened my eyes. I'd been in that half-dozing state that comes with massages and daydreams. My feet were covered with intricate brownish patterns. Flowers and twirls and other things that I didn't have names for.

"They're beautiful," I said. I thought I meant her designs, but maybe I meant my feet too. The patterns and the sticky sheen of the lemon juice seemed to bring out the curves of my feet and toes. Seemed to make them sensual. Not mine, but someone else's.

"I told you," Sun said. Her throaty laugh. "So, you can't really move for a while. You want a book or something?"

She had her hand still on my leg, between my ankle and the bottom of my rolled jeans.

"We could just…talk," I said. It sounded like something out of a bad movie. I wanted to take the words back as soon as they were words. My face burned hot, even as my feet were freezing.

Sun didn't seem to notice. She scooted next to me on the couch, her shoulder pressed into mine. Her feet sneaked under the blanket that covered my legs. She leaned her head on my shoulder so that her long hair fell against my neck.

That's the thing they never tell you about being a girl who likes girls. You get to have another girl pressed up against you, have a friend who hugs you to her, or who dreams about painting your feet in a faraway market—and it might mean everything. Or it might mean nothing. Just friends.

"Sun," I said. My eyes focused on my new feet. Sometimes you changed one thing and the whole world looked different.

"Hmm?" she said.

"Have you ever, you know, liked a girl?" I wanted to stop talking as soon as I started, but—words, you can never take them back. Before, I'd had to force the words out, how I'd been okay with her painting my feet. Now I couldn't shut up.

Sun was smarter than I was. I'd known that for a long time. She didn't say anything. She turned her head toward me until her breath was warm against my neck. Her lips pressed warm against my skin. First kiss. It wasn't even on the lips, just against the pulse that beat fast in my neck. Yet my skin tingled just like it had beneath the henna.

She shifted her weight until she faced me, and then brought one leg over mine to straddle me. Her skirt covered my legs and hers.

How often had I dreamed of this moment and not this moment over the years? In my dreams, I was always the perfect lover, could tell by Sun's body how to touch her. But this wasn't a dream, this was Sun, rising above me. Real as day.

I didn't know what to do. My hands were so still at my sides that it was like they were the thing painted, the part of me that should be immobile. Sun settled herself against me, her body warm where it met mine. She picked up my hands and put them beneath her skirt. With the flat of her palms, she pressed my hands to her thighs. Her skin was smooth and muscled. When she was convinced my hands would stay there, she let go of them and leaned over and kissed me. This time on the lips. This time pushing her tongue between my lips into the corners of my mouth.

My mouth filled with the tang and spice of her tongue. Ginger and cloves. Her fingers on the edges of my lips as she kissed me added the flavor of sweet lemon. Beneath it all, there was the taste of Sun. It was a flavor I'd smelled for years—alderwood soap and lilac lotion.

She pushed her thigh hard against my hand. I took it as the hint that it was, and let my fingers explore the skin there. I brought one hand into her vee, expecting panties. Her lips, clean-shaven and silky, met my fingers.

We both moaned as I touched her there, my finger sinking into the shallow groove between her lips. She was wet already, and when I ran my finger up and down, she grew wetter still, covering the end of my finger.

As we kissed, Sun's fingers traveled down from my lips and across my shoulders to find their way to my nipples. She feathered them with her thumbs, touching me so lightly I thought I might be imagining the movement of her fingers. But my nipples knew better, hardening and pressing toward her soft touch.

I entered Sun with two fingers, and she broke the kiss and sat up straight, sighing. I wanted to see her—all these years of dreaming of what she looked like, and I didn't know if I'd get another chance. I untied her skirt and pushed the fabric back until I could see her lower half. In her belly button, a small red stone. Her hips spread over my legs. The bare, shiny cleft of her pussy, the same dark brown as the rest of her.

I dipped two fingers inside her to watch them go in. Just the tips. With her hands on my shoulders, Sun lowered herself slowly over my fingers. I could feel her skin sliding over them, stretching around them. It seemed she was going to make it last forever, but then she was down on my hands, my fingers all the way inside her. She stayed that way for a second, then rose and lowered herself again.

"Don't move...your feet," she said, as though I was the one moving and not her. I wiggled my fingers inside her, just to show that I had the power to move something. I loved that the movement made it hard for her to get the rest of her words out. "You'll ruin...all...all my hard work."

"Okay," I said. Which sounded stupid. I would have done anything she'd asked. Not moving? That was a cinch.

She pressed her fingers to my lips, and I opened my mouth. My tongue on her fingers was lemon pucker and soft skin. Pulling her fingers from my mouth, Sun leaned back a little, opening her center to me. I could see her pussy lips and the hardening pink nub of her clit. She put her wet fingers there, back and forth. I worked my fingers harder inside her so she didn't have to move so much, and she let herself go slack a little.

"Don't stop," she said. "Don't..."

Her eyes were closed and I watched her. Watched the way her thighs tightened as she rocked back and forth. The way she lowered herself over my fingers, sucking them inside her. The way her clit glistened and peeked beneath her fingers. And when she came, the way everything quivered and flowed, skin and arousal and breath.

After a few minutes, Sun rolled to the side of me. Her breath still moved in and out of her in fast little gulps. She pulled her wrap-around skirt around her lower half like a blanket and rested her head on my belly. My T-shirt had ridden up, and her cheek on my belly was warm and damp, like she had a fever.

My insides felt all twisted up, trying to take everything in: my arousal, my disbelief that this had actually happened, my fear of the future. I didn't know what to do with my hands, still damp from Sun.

"Sun, why now, after all this time?" She was quiet for so long that I wished I hadn't asked. Why couldn't I just shush and let things happen? What if this was a one-time thing? Now all I would remember about the ending of it was how I'd pushed.

Sun's head stirred on my belly, but she didn't look up.

"I just…" When she exhaled, her breath tickled my skin. "I thought about you a lot in Singapore, and I realized I was just afraid. So I made up this plan: I'd offer to do your feet, and if you laughed or freaked, then I'd be able to say it was just an idea. And we could just stay friends."

Another small silence. This time I was able to keep my mouth closed. I stayed still and waited while she kissed the skin above my belly button.

"But you didn't laugh. Well, okay you laughed a little, but you were willing. You didn't make me feel stupid."

She scooted up and put her head back on my shoulder. We both looked down at my feet, white beneath the hardening henna. They say that the thing you want is right in front of you, if only you know where to look. But sometimes it takes the thing you want to show you where to look, so that you're both looking at the same thing.

I wiggled my toes, careful not to crack the drying henna. "How long will they last?" I asked.

"Depends on how well you take care of them."

"And if I didn't? How soon would you have to do them again? Like, what if I took my jeans off right now, messed them all up?"

I couldn't see Sun's smile, but I could feel her cheek as it pushed out against my shoulder. She didn't answer my question. She just sat up and reached for the button of my jeans with both hands.

IN FLIGHT

Andrea Dale

I met Pam at the hawk rehabilitation center. She was a member of the staff; I was volunteering in the gift shop to help pay off a rash of parking tickets that weren't really mine but had been racked up by my now very ex-girlfriend, Jennifer, on my car.

I was still dealing with a lot of anger toward Jennifer. It wasn't always conscious but it was constant; at any moment, I could stop and feel the acidic burn in my chest. She'd fucked me over good, in just about every way imaginable. She'd stiffed me on the rent, made off with the widescreen TV and DVD player we'd bought together, and left me without enough money to pay the damn parking tickets. She'd buggered off before I'd found out about the tickets, and I'd had no way to prove they weren't mine.

The only time I wasn't seething was when I was with the birds.

I'd been learning about each one—the golden eagle, the Harris hawk, the peregrine falcon, the kestrel. There were the various owls, too, snowy and barn and screech. I'd been given the preliminary tour, which involved tidbits of information like "don't open the cages *ever*" and "don't stick your fingers near the birds" and "for the love of all that's holy, don't feed them." In my spare time, I'd been snatching a read of a few pages of books in the gift shop. I knew how delicate the birds' digestive balance was in captivity; just a few ounces in either direction would mess them up.

All the birds were here permanently; they'd never be released into the wild. They'd been injured beyond repair, or had been bred in captivity and never known the free skies.

And yet they were all so serene, so peaceful. So in control, in a way I couldn't imagine ever feeling again. Even caged they were alert and proud, their eyes glittering with a strange intelligence. They saw everything, even if they didn't react with more than a flick of their heads or a rustle of their wings.

Pam's dark eyes also seemed to never miss a thing, and she moved with a similar slow grace. But she had a quick, friendly smile and a soft laugh. She was lean and rugged, and smelled of the sunscreen she faithfully coated herself with several times a day. She kept her brown hair pulled back in a ponytail, and I couldn't quite tell if the streaks of gold were from the sun or an expensive salon. I suspected the former. Her hands were long-fingered, her nails short because she worked with birds and ropes and thick leather gloves.

I suppose I went out there after my shift that Saturday as much to see her as to stroll among the cages and admire the birds.

When she asked me to help out because one of the handlers had come down with the flu and she was short-staffed, I suppose I agreed for the same reasons.

Despite Jennifer's betrayal, I was also glad for the excuse to spend some quality time with Pam. The thought of a relationship made my stomach hurt, but I could still enjoy Pam's sleek legs encased in worn, fitted jeans or khaki shorts, her firm breasts high and round beneath her green tank top and long-sleeved, unbuttoned cotton shirt.

She showed me how to tie a knot using one hand to loop the rope around, because with your other hand, you were always holding the end of the rope near where it was attached to the bird's ankle by a ring.

I deftly mimicked her movements.

"Wow!" she said, and I could hear the admiration in her voice. "I've never seen anyone pick that up so fast. Well done!"

I'd been practicing at home with a length of twine. I didn't tell her that, though. I wanted her praise, any way I could get it.

The tasks were simple, repetitive. Get hold of the bird. Move the bird to an empty cage. Rake out the bird's cage, clean the water dish and refill it, and then move the bird back. Pam took the cages on one side; I handled the ones across from her.

Rudy, a red-tailed hawk, put up a fuss when I picked him up, spreading his four-foot wingspan, the bells on his jesses jingling like an ice cream truck gone mad. I set him on the thick leather glove that covered my left hand and arm to my elbow, and he calmed down a little. Not completely, though: he continued to ruffle his wing feathers and glance around sharply, readjusting the way his sharp talons dug into the scarred leather.

"Keep your elbow a little lower than your wrist." Pam had moved up next to me so quietly I hadn't heard her hiking boots crunch on the gravel walkway. "They want to be on the highest spot possible, and if you drop your wrist, he'll try to climb up your arm."

Her soft laugh fluttered the hair along my neck. "I once had a golden eagle try to sit on my head," she said. "I learned fast after that."

She made a low, crooning noise at Rudy. He looked at her, contemplated whatever she'd apparently said, and settled down a bit more.

"He likes you," I said.

"He doesn't like anybody," she said. "It's not in their nature. For them it's all about respect. Ever read those fantasy novels about the kids who had magical kestrel familiars?"

I admitted that I had, only willing to do so because she obviously knew about them, too.

"We get slews of kids come through, wanting to make friends with the birds, and they're so disappointed." Pam shook her head. "As much as we often want them to, they're never going to *like* us. They're not like cats or dogs or even horses; there's no devotion. The best you can do—and believe me, it's not a minor thing—is be someone they can respect. There's a level of trust they'll give you, but only if you earn it."

Respect. I looked at the hawk on my wrist. He looked back at me, dark eyes expressionless. Jennifer hadn't shown me any respect, and I didn't know if I was worthy of it. I'd been taken in by her lies, blinded by her sweet talk. She'd probably mocked me, laughing, as she'd walked out the door with the shattered remains of my life.

"I'm not very good with trust," I said.

Pam cocked her head, the action reminiscent of Hecate, the horned owl. "You and Rudy seem to be finding a comfortable balance, though."

"I trust him not to eat my eyeballs out of my head," I admitted, and was rewarded with one of her delicious gentle laughs.

"Well, that's a start, then," she said. "C'mon, let's get this finished up, and then we'll go grab a beer."

I hadn't been around long enough to know Pam's sexual proclivities, and despite my enjoyment of watching her (okay, and smelling her, even if that makes me sound like a creepy stalker) I assumed she was straight. I wasn't looking for a relationship anyway, and why get my hopes dashed even if I was?

We went to a local bar that night, a quiet one that had more in common with an English pub than a sports bar or redneck dive. My pale ale was frosty cold and fizzed a little when I worked the slice of lime down the narrow neck into the beer.

"I know you're doing community service hours for us," Pam said. She looked down and then back up at me. "You don't have to tell me why, but if you're okay with it, I have to admit I'm curious."

"The short answer is unpaid parking tickets," I said. "The longer answer involves an ex, her unrequested use of my car, and her flagrant disregard for slips of paper tucked under the wiper."

Pam rolled her eyes. "And I thought not replacing the toilet paper was bad. I'm sorry you got screwed. You didn't deserve it."

I lifted one shoulder in a shrug. "Dunno. Maybe I did."

She paused in the act of taking a swig, revealing the long, slender line of her throat. "What do you mean?"

"I shouldn't have trusted her. I did, and she took advantage of that."

"You can't blame yourself for what she did."

For a moment I couldn't figure out how to respond, because Pam had put her hand over mine. "Maybe I'm a bad judge of character," I said finally.

"And maybe your ex was a manipulative shithead."

I blinked, startled by her bluntness, and also by the realization that she hadn't really reacted to the fact that my ex was a woman. "She was, but I didn't see it, and that's my fault."

Pam's hand, warm on mine, squeezed just a little. "There are people who'll take advantage of us, yes. But that can't stop us from loving again." Before I could say anything, she forged on. "Take Rudy, for example. We rescued him from a house where he'd been ignored, underfed, and crammed in a tiny cage. But he's okay now. He's learned to trust again."

I wanted to say, "But he's a *bird*," but instead, I said, "Food for thought," and changed the subject to the song that was playing.

She accepted that I'd closed off, and I appreciated that. Still, I felt a painful twinge at the end of the evening when we parted, and she said, "By the way, I'll make sure the time you helped me out today gets logged into your total hours."

I hadn't worked overtime to pay off my debts, but I didn't have the courage to tell her the real reasons.

I did, however, make it clear that I was interested in learning more about the raptors, and when the gift shop didn't need me behind the register, I was outside. Pam encouraged my interest; she loved to share her own enthusiasm.

When my community service hours ended, I simply started volunteering at the center.

"That's fantastic!" Pam said when I told her, and hugged me. "I wasn't looking forward to losing you."

I told myself she meant as an extra pair of hands to help out. I enjoyed the hug all the same, relishing the feeling of her breasts pressed against mine, her strong arms encircling me, her hands on my back.

Despite my best efforts, I was interested in Pam. I just wasn't willing to take the chance of another disappointment, another heartbreak. She might not like girls. She might not like me in that way.

I was happy being her friend—happy but frustrated. I savored the time we spent together, even as I sighed with longing or had to catch myself out of a fantasy of nuzzling her neck, smelling the sunscreen and sweat, or licking my way down to her glorious breasts.

It didn't help—or maybe it helped too much—that the closer we grew, the more apparent it became that Pam was a touchy-feely type of girl. A hug, a pat on the shoulder, a touch on the arm.

I would just enjoy it, I told myself.

That worked for several weeks, in fact. Until the day Pam said, "Rudy and Falco need some air time. Want to learn how to fly the birds?"

I'd sort of already learned. I'd trailed along on two of the daylong Falconry Experience Courses when the trainers took the class out in the field. But I knew what Pam was offering here—the opportunity for me to be officially in charge of one of the birds.

Honored and thrilled, I agreed.

We drove to the nearby hills in a truck with specially designed cages in the back for raptor transport.

It was a gorgeous late-summer day. The leaves were still dark green, not yet starting to turn to autumn's flaming palette. It had rained a few days before, and the ground was lush with grass, clover, and tiny white chamomile flowers. The afternoon sun was warm, and we stripped off our outer shirts before we'd gotten out of the truck. Pam slathered sunscreen on her arms and offered me the bottle.

I dutifully smoothed it over my own arms, the smell turning my brain to mush because it reminded me so strongly of Pam. I was definitely going to have some solo fun tonight with this scent permeating my sheets.

"You missed some. Here." Pam squeezed some lotion onto her hands and, before I fully realized what she was going to do, ran them over the back of my neck.

My hair was pixie-short—Jennifer had liked it long, so in defiance I had chopped it all off after she left—and thus Pam had easy access to my skin.

Specifically, the very sensitive skin at the nape of my neck, the place that a former lover (not Jennifer, thankfully) had referred to as my sexual bull's-eye.

I shivered. I could feel the gentle massage of her hands against my skin all the way down to my clit. My nipples clamored for attention, pressing against my bra and T-shirt. I never wanted her to stop touching me.

Unfortunately, we don't always get what we want. She capped the bottle and tucked it into the truck.

The birds were excited, sensing the chance to soar. They rustled their features and shifted their feet on our wrists as we hiked out into a sloping meadow surrounded by tall pines. We let Rudy and Falco fly, tempting them back to us with bits of raw meat. Then we allowed them to swoop up into the trees, where they perched high and surveyed their surroundings like kings.

Pam pulled a thermos of coffee and two metal cups out of her backpack, along with little packets of sugar. She offered milk, but I shook my head. We sprawled on the soft grass and sipped, chatting idly about the weather, the falconry center, all light-hearted topics.

Then Pam fell silent, and I sensed her shift beside me. Not just physically—her mood shifted, too. I couldn't quite read it, but something about it made me shiver deep inside.

"I wanted to say…" She trailed off, glancing at me and then away, as if unsure if she should continue.

"What?" I said. "Go ahead, spill."

"It's just...I'm really glad that you're enjoying the birds so much," she said. "Not because the center needs volunteers, but because...I like spending time with you."

My breath caught in my throat. As much as I'd been trying to deny my feelings for her, I really, really wanted her to say more.

"I like spending time with you, too," I said, knowing how lame it sounded.

Suddenly she laughed, the sound spilling from her throat like golden sunlight. "What a pair we are! Okay, I'm going to put myself on the line: I'm attracted to you. I know you had a bad relationship, and I don't want to scare you off, but I can't keep suppressing it. If you want me to back off, I will, but—"

Yeah, Jennifer had messed me up, but a girl has needs, and I liked Pam as much as I lusted after her. So I gave in to what my body wanted, put my hand on her cheek, and cut off her words with a kiss.

Gentle at first, exploring, seeing how we fit and moved together. In fact, we eased down on the carpet of grass in the late-summer meadow and just kissed, tasting each other. She liked it when I nipped at her bottom lip, and when she responded in kind, I moaned into her mouth. Her laugh was breathy, and hitched when I ran my tongue behind her ear, tasting salt and something that was uniquely *her*.

I could've stayed there until the sun sank behind the hills, just kissing her like that, but thankfully she had the sense to pull back and say, "We need to get the birds back."

I felt bereft when we stopped touching, but I didn't take it personally. I slipped on my glove and whistled for Rudy.

The falcon dropped down from the tree; if it hadn't been for the bells, he would've been completely silent. He landed on my wrist, and I fed him a piece of meat.

"Look at that," Pam said. "He comes right back to you. He trusts you."

I wanted to say that I didn't know why, but I didn't want to break the moment.

"Hey," Pam said, and I looked at her, at the tiny beads of sweat dotting the bridge of her nose. "The important thing is, no matter what anyone else does, *you* don't break a trust. Your girl-friend screwed you over, but that didn't change the way you deal with people—or with the birds. Rudy trusts you, and I know you'd never give him any reason not to."

I understood what she was saying: that she trusted me, too.

And if this was going to work, if this was going to go any farther, I had to trust her, too.

The only thing I didn't trust right then was my ability to speak. I just nodded. Pam smiled, gave me another kiss that sent a fresh wave of moisture to my panties, and called Falco to her arm.

We put the birds in for the night and closed up the center. We didn't stop at the bar for a drink. Instead, I just followed her home.

Her apartment was like her—simple, clean, bold lines and colors, no pretense or artifice. I didn't get a good look at most of it because I was looking at her, and then we were in the bedroom, and I could see only the wide bed with its wine-colored spread and imagine her spread out across it, wanting me.

We kept kissing, lips sliding over lips, whispering little sweet-nesses, as we tugged at each other's clothes, breaking apart only when a shirt had to be pulled off overhead or a fastening proved particularly stubborn.

"So pretty," she whispered, bending her head to capture my aching nipple in her mouth. Hands and fingers, lips and teeth, and I'd been wanting her for so long that it took only a few moments before my legs were weakening and I needed to feel her *more*.

She knew, somehow, and she pushed me back on the bed and trailed her tongue down between my breasts, along my belly, to a spot just above where I really needed her to touch me.

She looked up at me then, and threaded the fingers of her left hand through the fingers of my right. "Trust me?" she whispered.

I nodded.

Her touch wasn't gentle anymore. We were far past careful and tentative and exploring. "So wet, so sweet," I heard her murmur before her tongue began a dance on my clit, swooping and diving and circling like a hawk intent on its prey, and I had no escape.

Her fingers slipped inside of me, and I soared.

I flew, because I knew I could come back to her.

KRISPIN

Rakelle Valencia

Krispin rode down from the hills as each spring dawned. The early morning sun sparkled off of the dew in her wake as she passed through pastureland of hibernating forage. Breath from her horse's nostrils preceded her with fog so that she rode through a constant ethereal mist in her approach back to the main ranch holdings from one of the winter line shacks.

About ten winters' endings now, since being orphaned at seventeen, she had made this ride, usually atop her rawboned, strawberry roan gelding still retaining its shaggy winter coat and the heavy feathers on its lower legs, toting a brawny mule behind with a now empty pack saddle.

And the last six of those ten years, I hovered around the corrals gripping tightly to a thermos of hot coffee, black and strong, waiting to exchange the reviving liquid for the cold leather reins and solid cotton lead of both animals.

Five years my senior, Krispin had never really seemed to notice me, even though we had been acquainted through primary schooling in town and the sweat of summer ranch work. She was somewhat of an enigma, a loner, hardened, and a woman of few words.

But a woman she was. And knowing my own preferences since before puberty, I held Krispin up against all others, and none had compared. Perhaps it was only a girlish lust borne of my unconsummated fantasies that had made Krispin grow in my heart to a love I felt would burst, or that could be read easily on my blushing face whenever I was in her presence.

Regardless, the exchange for coffee and leads to the animals was made silently again this year as Krispin shouldered her laden saddlebags and twitched her rifle from its scabbard, and I quickly took the beasts in the barn for untacking, rubbing down, and a hearty meal of grain mixed into the leftover second-cut hay from the long winter. She followed at a slow mosey, wrestling the rifle into her arms like a squabbling babe while trying, with chilled fingers, to wrest the screw-cap off the thermos, dangling its plastic mug by a looped pinky finger through the small handle.

The big mule, in his two-inch wide leather comfort halter, stood statue-still with patience as I hefted the saddle from the roan and loosed the bridle before directing the horse to the feed bunks to await currying. Krispin's mule wore an old-fashioned sawbuck that she had carved specifically to nestle into the back of this animal. I ran my hand over the worn wood, admiring its warm lines and detail to fit before releasing the double cinches, breast strap, and brichen to extricate the rigging.

Without prompting, the mule went to the side of Krispin's gelding, sharing in their bountiful breakfast. I toted saddle then sawbuck one at a time to the tack room, returning with brushes, curry, and hoof pick. Krispin leaned against the open barn door-frame, eyes closed, breathing in the scent of her coffee.

I watched her for a moment. Her head tilted over the mug as

she inhaled deeply. The ten-X beaver felt hat hid her shoulder-length hair that usually escaped in unkempt straggles. She was wearing her familiar thick wool overcoat of red-and-black plaid with a sheepskin liner and collar. Her collar was pulled up around her ears as if early springtime had not deigned to touch her yet. Her chinks (short chaps) had new overlays of rugged leather crafted to look as if they belonged there. But even the overlays bore the marks of rope work that had chewed through the original layer of leather. The bottoms of her Wranglers were stacked atop serious Wellington work boots that showed no fancy stitching, except what surrounded the saddle that had been added as a buffer to her spur straps. And her spurs were simple, muddied, and quiet, with small, blunted rowels. She had shed her work gloves in favor of the warmth emanating from her plastic mug. My heart leapt at the simple joy she seemed to be taking from the cup of thick coffee.

Krispin could make my stomach jump into my throat and my heart drop to shaking knees with her presence alone. My hands trembled as a flutter moved swiftly throughout my body to end in the juncture of my legs where spring long johns and denim jeans began to feel wet and clammy. Blushing embarrassment took me back to the job at hand. I squeezed between the two solid stock animals and began to work the circulation back through their tight muscles.

Krispin, shed of rifle and thermos, moved in behind me, effectively blocking my escape. "I brought you something." She reached into one side of her bloated saddlebags tugging a string-wrapped, large square package free.

Dropping the grooming tools into the feed bunk, I tentatively took the offering while staring too blatantly into eyes that were ice blue, framed by sun-creases at the outer edges.

When I hadn't moved, Krispin pulled the latigo string holding the bundle together. "Mountain cat." The supple hide spilled over my arms and reached for the barn floor on either side. "It was harassing the brood cows near to a week before I got a real good sight on it."

The golden fur was thick and full, luxurious. I ran my fingers through it and brought the pelt to my cheek, squeezing my eyes shut as the succulent sensation ran through more than just my face. *Krispin. She smelled of horses and wood smoke with the fading crispness of winter struggling against springtime. And she was, to me, as rare a beauty as the tanned hide that she had gifted me with.*

My eyelids flew open at the shock of wayward thoughts. I dropped the fur from my cheek to hold it tightly against my chest. Krispin reached out to stroke that same cheek with the back of her cold hand before turning to retrieve her rifle and coffee.

Then she was gone.

I thought I felt her fingers lingering along my cheek. I replayed her touch in my mind over and over as I settled her stock in the barn. My mind drifted into that warm daydreaming state. Parts and pieces in pictures real or imagined flooded my senses. *I reached out, brushing hair from her eyes, and taking the moment to run my fingers through the even lengths that hung to frame her weather-worn face. I cupped her ear and she leaned into my touch, closing her eyes with a look of wanton need coupled with seeking the comfort of another human, another body in all of its sensuality and compassion.* My mind had taken away her hardened silence and gave me visions of her needing me as much as I felt I needed her. But was that still Krispin?

Taking the exquisite hide to the smaller room of two in the bunkhouse, I brushed my hand along Krispin's bunk that had been empty and cold for far too long, as I made my way over to my own. There were no other women in residence in the bunkhouse room this early in the season. I had actually just arrived to help my uncle during spring break from the university and after an all too short stay, would not see this room again until summer began.

Spreading the fur over my bed, I knew what I wanted to do. I stoked the wood stove to glowing and then stripped off all of my clothes. Like a child I dove to land the length of the pelt and then rolled myself into it. The sensation was both intoxicating and relaxing, drawing me quickly into a fitful sleep plagued with visions of Krispin.

Her calloused hands slid over my buttocks, squeezing playfully before they moved up my sides to my small rounded breasts. Krispin thumbed each nipple until they turned dark red and stood stiff. We were laughing. She clasped under my jaw, moved in to brush a kiss across my lips, then turned my head to the side as she suckled one of my breasts into her warm mouth.

I woke to the sound of the shower running. It was my turn to lean against the doorframe, luxuriating in the warm steam emanating from the hot streams of water that brushed several scents of soaps to fill the humid air.

The shower room had three standing showers with hazy glass doors, three toilet stalls, and a tub in an enclosed area at the far end. Sinks and a long countertop lined the opposite wall, with a large length of mirror that made the room appear to be doubled. Krispin was in the first shower stall that could be seen fully through the open doorway. She had always taken the first stall, leaving the further stalls for those shyer.

Her confidence in her own body and strength of character could come off as snotty. But I had known Krispin far too long to let negative ideas invade that knowledge, or fall prey to false perceptions she would allow others to believe. Krispin was her own person, with no explanations and no apologies. And the few who could understand that had mostly come to jealously despise her for her inner strength.

To me, that alone made all the difference. She knew what she wanted and would take it. I often wished she would take me in the same manner—no questions, no explanations, just a raw coupling of our bodies and our beings.

She leaned back to rinse her hair before taking up a razor and lifting a leg in cramped quarters. Then she bent to her work. Krispin remained in the shower longer than usual, emitting audible sighs and standing for periods to allow the hot water to rush over her face or shoulders. It was the little things in life most of us passed by without any particular notice that Krispin took in as if each touched her very soul.

My pulse pounded throughout my body. I could hear and feel it in my ears. The hard thumping in my chest reached to my belly. And a rhythmic throbbing tortured my nether lips, which felt like they were swelling.

The water abruptly stopped. I could see Krispin's hazy form leaning against the side wall while she wrung her hair behind her head in both hands, staying a minute in a position of leisurely stretching. She was like the cat I wrapped around my naked body—lithe, sleek, strong, and dangerous, an animal to be avoided in most situations.

I should have moved back into the bunkroom. I shouldn't have stayed there leering. The textured glass door popped open, and out walked Krispin in all of her naked glory, toweling her hair and squeegeeing water from her ears. She knew I was standing there. She knew I was staring. She had probably known the second I arrived to lean against the doorframe.

Krispin roughly rubbed the short towel over her wet, glowing skin, ignoring me for the moment. She dumped the sodden cloth on the countertop and then turned to look me straight in the eyes. I froze until her minty breath woke my senses. "You look good in that." And she tugged the hide up a little, rolling a lapel of sorts at either side of my neck.

"Thanks. You look good too." Which I regretted saying as soon as it escaped my lips. I felt like a starstruck schoolgirl floundering in front of a world idol.

She laughed, a deep-throated sound that echoed off the walls. "I mean—"

A rough pointer finger pressed across my lips, stifling any other ridiculous quips I might have come out with.

She was beautiful, more beautiful than I had ever imagined. In her nakedness she wasn't vulnerable like most would look or feel, but more real, maybe surreal. In that moment, I was ashamed of wanting her, or not ashamed, more like afraid. Fear flushed through me quickly, and my knees turned weak in response. My brain interrupted to tell me that maybe I had come too far, that this might be more than I could handle.

I remembered the day that we sat across from each other at a table in the mess hall, near a window, sunshine flooding in. Her hat was set on the chair beside her, and a rogue lock of hair fell forward as her head tilted downward, reading a slip of paper my uncle had handed to her. Her eyes were intense with seriousness. And right then and there I had wanted to reach over just to tuck that wild lock of brunette hair behind her ear. Just to touch her.

My body had shivered, stirring to a greater passion than I had ever experienced. It went from my head to my toes, and I felt in that moment that there would be nothing as powerful, or fulfilling, or as enrapturing, than the passion that overtook me for those few seconds. And if there ever was…I might not survive it.

She must have surmised the fleeting fear in my eyes because she didn't kiss me. She had never kissed me, even though one kiss might have satisfied my carnal hunger and my newfound passion for probably the rest of my life.

Krispin passed me in the doorway, picking clean, almost new clothes from her bunk and slowly donning them. She plucked her wool coat from the wrought iron hooks on the wall near the door, adjusted her Stetson atop her head, and left.

My heart grew too heavy in my chest. *Krispin. Perhaps one day.*

Krispin.

EYES

Maggie Kinsella

C laire," she says. She asks if she can touch my face, and I let her. Her fingers map my face with cobweb brush. Cheeks, eyelids, mouth, hair. "The name suits you. It sounds like 'clear.'" Her fingers drop away. "Are you blond?"

"Yes. You're good."

She smiles. Her milky eyes are like pebbles washed by a river. "And you're beautiful."

"No," I say.

"Can I take you to dinner?" she asks, and I let her.

She takes me to one of the restaurants overlooking the harbor, an overpriced, understated place where the waiters are barely polite. They have to let her dog in too, although you can see that they're not happy about it.

The waiter leads us to a small table near the back of the room. It's sandwiched between the spare cutlery and a trailing ivy on a plinth. The only view is of the door to the restroom.

"We'd like a table with a view please," says Lydia, and her

voice holds just the right touch of authority.

The waiter's mouth tightens, but he leads us to a table by the window. Baltimore Harbor shines beneath us like the Milky Way.

Her dog sits under the table, rests his nose on his paws, and sighs to himself.

Her cloudy eyes are fixed on me, and, suddenly self-conscious, I try to chew quietly.

She touches my hand. "Be yourself," she says, and smiles.

It's as if the sun has slanted into the room and touched her face.

We leave, replete, and walk around the harbor where the water taxis flutter past on the glassy water.

"It's beautiful," I say.

"You're the beautiful one," she says.

She kisses away the denial on my lips, and I let her.

Summer glides along, and we're a threesome. Her. Me. Her dog.

"What happened to your face?" she asks one day, as her fingers slide over my cheek. They linger on the scars.

"Flammable nightgown, open bar heater," I say. "I was eight."

Her sigh whispers over my skin like her fingers. When the sun sets, she takes me to her bed, and I let her.

We spend our days together. We walk around the harbor, and I describe for her how the seagulls wheel and soar. She smiles when I buy ice cream and give half of mine to her dog. I drive her to Virginia, farther than she's ever been, and she runs her fingers over the bark of tall trees and feels the sounds they make in the wind.

The woman in the gay-friendly B&B gives us a downstairs room. "It will be easier for your wife if she doesn't have to navigate the stairs, and easier for you to let the dog out in the night," she says, and I don't correct her assumption.

"Wife," Lydia says, complacently, and kisses the taut, shiny skin where the scar pulls my eye permanently open.

"Will you move in with me?" she asks, as we lie together, wrapped in fine cotton sheets. Her fingers strum patterns on my breast.

I'm too breathless with the moment to answer her immediately. *Me,* I think, my fingers stealing up to rub my scar. *She wants me.* Instead of answering, I let my fingers walk in silent pathways over her body. I stroke her cheekbones and her eyelids, and she hums in response. I dare to think of a future.

Back home, she has a letter. There's an experimental research foundation in Los Angeles. Money is available: for the operation, for medical care, for travel. She will travel to L.A. and have the operation. Maybe then she will be able to see.

"I'll have to go without you," she says, and I let her.

I stay in her house and look after her dog, who is pining. We pine together. I've moved in without giving her an answer, but it feels right. The dog and I sleep in her bed and console each other. We both lose weight, and my scar pulls tighter.

Lydia calls. The operation was a success. She can see; a little now, more each day. One day she tells me how she can see the outline of the palm trees along Santa Monica Boulevard; the next day she describes their fronds. She tells me about a woman she saw; a woman with a face of calm, serene perfection.

"But not as beautiful as you," she says. She believes that, and I let her.

The dog and I wait for her calls, which come every day at the same time.

"I'm coming home in a week," she says. "I can't wait to see you."

The dog and I meet her at the airport. She walks alone with no attendant to assist, slowly, cautiously, stopping to study each sign, her mouth moving as she spells out the letters. My hands grip the metal railing in the arrivals hall. The dog pants by my side.

I don't know if she recognizes me or her dog from the old pictures in her head, but she walks straight up to us. She studies my face, runs her fingers over the scar as she used to do, mapping the reality with new eyes. I tuck my hand over her arm out of habit, and she lets me. She sees the hastily averted glances of the curious, she sees me, and she sees her dog.

"My dog is beautiful," she says.

When winter comes, and the snow hides the ugliness of Baltimore, my scar pulls tight with the cold, and her dog dies.

"There goes my old life," she says, and she cries.

She has a job now, and she stays out some evenings, drinking pints in B.J.'s Sports Bar with her colleagues. She talks about work, about friends, about independence and freedom, and I let her. Sometimes she's late home, stealing into our bed with red ale on her breath. I pretend to be asleep, and she lets me hold the lie.

"Where shall we go on vacation?" she asks. "Europe? Hawaii? Somewhere warm and cheap like Mexico?"

I remember how we walked together, my hand tucked over her arm. Lydia needs me less and less now; she knows which shirt to wear to match her eyes, the spice rack is no longer arranged alphabetically, she knows if someone tries to shortchange her without my steely-eyed gaze to guilt them into honesty.

I am waiting for her wings to unfurl to the heavens. I am waiting for her to leave me, and I will let her.

Lydia comes home with vacation brochures. She spreads them in a glossy multicolored fan on the coffee table. They are all for the same place: Toronto.

I arch an eyebrow in question. "I thought you wanted some-place in the sun?" I say. "Toronto in March will be no different from here."

She sits on the couch, drawing me down beside her. Her hands encompass my own, sliding over them in soothing rhythm.

"One big difference. We can get married." She searches my face. "Will you, Claire? Will you marry me?"

And I let her.

HIDE

Alison Tyler

Leather. I have always loved the smell, the feel of it on my skin. There is something insanely sexual about the texture, the way, after years of wear, it molds to the owner's body. Perhaps it's the Neanderthal left in me, the cave girl clad in a mountain lion's hide, but wearing skins makes me feel more alive.

For myself, I choose sleek leather pants and riding boots, a leather vest worn open over a white T-shirt. On a lover, I like to see a black leather jacket cut close to the body, thigh-high leather boots pulled over opaque black stockings, and nothing, or very little, in between. I like to stroke a woman's skin through the skin, her hide through the hide, testing the dangerous "give" in the texture, the supple caress. Breathing in the sinful scent, the medley of near-intoxicating odors.

My love for leather has lasted close to twenty years, since I bought my first motorcycle and its accompanying biker jacket. And, despite a Harvard education and an inclination toward writing poetry, my fixation has become my means of employment: I own a leather goods store in the hip part of L.A., on Melrose Avenue.

At thirty-seven, I'm older than the kids who walk down the strip in racer-back tank tops and baggy jeans, younger than the matrons who glare as they drive by in their Jaguars and Saabs. About the same age as the woman who walked into my place in the middle of a slow day, a Wednesday afternoon.

She was stunning, just my type: long legs, red hair falling in loose curls past her shoulders, golden-green eyes that flashed at me in the late afternoon light. She strode into my store like a lioness on the prowl, the smell of her prey teasing her, making her fine nostrils flare as she moved up and down the aisles. I watched her from my perch behind the counter, watched as she touched the skimpy, pounded-leather dresses, ran her fingers along the smooth jackets, the shiny slacks.

I watched her, but I didn't say anything.

There are some customers who come in looking to buy clothes that will make them look cool. I recognize the posers, the Hollywood Rocker set, who belong to the young L.A. crowd. They're happening only because they're young and in L.A. These jokers snag the vinyl jeans, the butt-hugging suede, the thigh-high micro minis. Others, my raunchy sex-fiends, buy shiny black chaps, cutaway dresses, unbelievably short shorts, bras and bikinis studded with silver. They spare no expense to buy what it takes to make them come, and I cull most of my money from them.

But I wait for, and wish for, and fantasize about the she-tigers, the lady lions, the ones, like this redhead, who need the feel of the hide on their naked skin. Need the scent of it caressing their lovely bodies. These customers are the ones I opened Hide for in the first place, and they are the beauties I wait for.

And watch.

She had on a mint-green halter top that made her eyes glow the same color, and cutoff jeans that showed me a bit of her panties when she bent to look at the boots lined on the wall. Her ass made me dizzy, the way it filled out those shorts, the way the faded denim hugged her sweet tail. She was a beauty, a thoroughbred. A prize.

"Do you have this in a sex?" she asked softly, startling me from my daydreams of what she'd look like in a black leather jacket, fishnets, and black motorcycle boots. Startling me from a picture of her tied down to my bed with all leather gear in place and a pair of stiff scissors in my hand.

"A *six*?" she repeated, moving closer to the counter. I saw that look in her eyes, the look of the huntress, the look of the goddess, and I nodded quickly and motioned for her to follow me to the back.

She did, high-heeled sandals clicking on the wood floor, and I opened the door and ushered her in, spreading my arms to show her my private collection.

"Ohh." A sigh. She had found Nirvana.

"Your size," I said huskily, "Everything. All of it. Try on any piece you want." She went quickly to the first rack, her long red nails stroking the sides of the lace-up pants, her palms caressing the velvety-soft insides of the jackets. Butter-soft leather, black as midnight, some pieces shiny, others worn with age and love.

"Where?" she asked, looking around the room. There are mirrors on the walls but no private dressing room in the back.

"You can use the rooms out front," I told her. "Or change right here."

She shot me a look, one that made me melt. "Here's fine."

In a second, her green top was on the floor, her shorts next, and panties last—no bra, she didn't need one—and she was into the first outfit before I could fully register the concept of her body.

The skin, the hide, sliding against her pale, naked body, turned me on more than anything I can possibly imagine, more than simply staring at her nude form could have done. She'd chosen one of my favorites, right from the beginning, a pair of tight black riding pants and a matching vest, worn over nothing but her pale, creamy skin. She slid into her sandals and then swung her hair out of the way to catch her reflection in the mirror.

"That was made for you," I mumbled.

She nodded, more to her mirror image than to my statement, and stared at herself in the critical way that I've noticed even very pretty women do. That look never appears on my own face. I'm secure in my body, in the strength of it, the lines of it, but that may be because of my years or because my father treated his daughters and sons alike. We were given no special treatment, no coddling. When I look in the mirror, I don't see a painted picture, a gilded reflection. I see straight to my soul.

She wasn't sure, wasn't totally satisfied, and she kicked off the shoes, peeled down the slacks, and went rifling through the racks, clad only in the leather top, showing me all of her charms, her golden-furred pussy when she turned my way, her pink pussy lips when she bent over.

"Do you like that?" I asked as she reached for a dress, one with laces at the sides and back. It was a dress made for a motor-cycle lady, made as specifically for this woman as if she had been the designer's muse.

She slipped off the vest for an answer, sliding the dress over her head and then stalking toward me and turning, wanting me to fasten the laces in back. I did it with shaking hands, moving her long hair out of the way so I could do it right. She was tall, at least 5'10" in bare feet, and the dress fit her like a leather glove. She moved away as soon as I was done with the laces, sidling up to the mirror and then pirouetting in front of it.

She liked this one better. I could tell. The way she pursed her lips at her image, the way she moved a few feet back and looked down, her chin tilted at an angle, taking in her entire reflected twin.

"You could try it with fringe boots," I suggested, unsure of how much input she wanted. She seemed to be on a mission, and if she were buying to please a lover, I'd have to watch my step.

"Yeah," she looked at me expectantly. "What do you have?"

I rushed to get the highest pair from the rack out front and grabbed my favorite motorcycle boots as well. While I was nearby, I shut and locked the front door, turning the *Out to Lunch* sign face forward.

When I returned, she was still standing in front of the mirror, but now she had on a pair of fishnet hose, snagged from one of the inventory boxes. "Hope it's okay," she said, giving me a different kind of look with those lake-green eyes.

"Sure." Anything you want, unsaid but implied. I handed over the boots, and she slid them on. Again, a perfect fit. She walked a few steps forward and a few steps back, almost doing a dance. Then she turned to face me.

"What do you think?"

Did she want a salesperson's opinion, or that of a lust-filled admirer?

"You're stunning," I said, my husky baritone going down another octave. But I was quick to correct myself, my mind working instantly, "I mean, it looks stunning on you." I've never been one to stutter. As I said, I have always felt confident in my dark looks, confident in the lean, sturdy weight of my body. But this woman made me shake.

"Yes," she turned to regard the mirror again. "I like this one best."

I pulled together my nerve. "Is it for a special occasion?"

"No. Just for myself. I needed a lift. And leather always makes me feel...sexy. Something about the scent, the smell of it."

I nodded.

"You understand," she asked, "Don't you?"

"It's why I have the store," I told her, wanting to touch her, restraining myself from taking her in my arms and stroking her through the soft leather, feeling the place, the wondrous place where her skin ended and the hide began. The leather and the skin, the hide on the hide. Circling it, sniffing it, getting down on the floor and pressing my face to her body, wrapping my arms around her waist and smelling her animal scent through the musky odor of the hide.

"What's your name?" she asked then, breaking me from my daydreams.

"Patrice." My voice sounded so deep to my own ears. Deep and filled with longing. I wanted to own her.

"I'm Diana."

Of course she was. Diana, goddess of the moon. The queen and the huntress.

She walked a step closer, clicking in those fringed boots. "Why do you keep all of the best back here?"

The honest reason is that I don't want it to appear on just anyone. You need to love leather to wear it right. I've only found a few people I considered worthy of owning the best. This lady was definitely one of them.

"I don't like to waste it."

Now she was the one to nod. Another step closer. "Patrice?"

"Yeah."

"Do you want to feel?"

Another step.

I bowed my head. Was she teasing me? "Yeah."

She moved quickly then, into my arms, and I rested my head on her shoulder and breathed in the smell of her body, right at the underside of her neck, that secret, haunting she-woman smell. Then, with her scent still tickling my nose, I went down to my knees and pressed my lips to her sex, kissing her there, smelling her there, getting wave upon wave of the mingling perfumes, the leather and the lady, the sweet smell of the old leather, the fresh scent of the woman.

I stroked her body through the skin, dragging my palms firmly along the sleek lines of her hips, over her thighs. She moved away from me, dancing away, sliding free from the dress and returning to the rack, completely nude, choosing another pair of pants and a tight jacket with zippered sleeves. She never took her eyes off me as she pulled on the pants, wriggled into the jacket. She zipped into the second pair of boots, the cycle ones. Then she came back, wanting me to feel her again.

I grabbed her lower this time, moving my hands down her calves to her ankles. Holding her tightly here, through two layers of leather, the slacks and the boots. Gripping into her body firmly enough so that she could feel my strength. My desire. In my mind, I could hear a poem (hundreds of years old) that could have been written for her specifically. A poem for a huntress:

Lay thy bow of pearl apart.
And thy crystal-shining quiver;
Give unto the flying hart
Space to breathe, how short soever
Thou that mak'st a day of night,
Goddess excellently bright.

I suddenly knew what it would be like to have her riding behind me on my Harley, her arms tight around my waist. Knew what it would be like to reach our destination at the top of the Hollywood hills in a secret grove of Eucalyptus trees, where we'd be alone except for the moon and the wind. I'd turn her around, bend her over the seat, and slide those leather jeans over her hips and down.

"Down," she said, again pulling me out of my fantasies. "Lie down."

I followed her order immediately, going quickly from my knees to my back on the wooden floor, watching wide-eyed as she straddled my legs and slid down my thighs until she was sitting sex-to-sex on top of me.

She could tell that I was packing, I was sure of it, the synthetic cock pressing at her through two pairs of leather jeans. She could feel the ache of it, wanting her, and she smiled as she reached out and stroked it, stroked me through the hide, caressing me. I could tell from her look of ecstasy that I had met my match. Finally, after many years of searching, many more laying in wait, I had found my leather lady.

She didn't touch the button fly, didn't make a move to undo my pants. She only stroked, and teased, and played with me through the worn leather.

But she denied me.

Her hands continued to work, her fingers to dance their intricate steps up and down the crotch of the jeans. Then, without saying a word, she began moving her body forward, taking over from her fingers with her sweet little pussy, rubbing in circles, endless circles of her hips against mine. Around and around. I helped her, grabbing onto her waist and finding that fast, pounding beat. Moving her up and down, then a quick circle, up and down the rigid shaft of the molded cock. Wanting nothing more than to rip open the buttons, tear off her slacks, and slam it into her. But then, wanting nothing less than losing the feel of the leather, the softness of it, the slender caress of it tight on us both.

"What do you want?" I managed to whisper, the image of her on my cycle still burning in my head, the feel of her skin where it showed, at her wrists, at the neck of her jacket, at her throat, the bits that I saw inflaming me. The leather of her body, the hide and the hide, engulfing me.

"What do you want?"

If she needed me inside her, I would. I would take down her slacks, unbutton my own, and plunge the phallus into the wet heat of her pussy. I could smell that wet heat, knew what it would feel like as it dripped down the plastic dildo and matted against my fur. But if she wanted to come in the leather, come through the leather, I'd do that too.

She surprised me.

"Shh, Patrice. Don't say anything. Let me."

In a flash, she was up and grabbing the motorcycle gloves from the edge of my desk. Then she motioned for me to stand and undo my fly. I did it, my fingers slipping only once in their hurry to loose the buttons.

Her gloved hand reached in, took over, freeing the flesh-colored cock and bringing it to her lips. The leather-covered fingertips reached lower, probing, trying to find my cunt beneath the harness. I didn't need her to touch me there, simply watching her mouth around the head of the cock drove me crazy. She worked me hard, worked me well, sliding the cool leather across the feverish skin of my flat belly, bringing me to a boiling point with the inferno of her mouth as she deep-throated the cock and pressed her lips all the way to my body. She knew...she knew everything. The two sensations, skin on skin. The slickness of her glossy lips, then the smooth leather caress, the heat of her tongue trailing lower to tickle my thighs, then the heavy weight of her gloved hand going back between my legs to tickle my asshole.

I stroked her fiery curls while she worked, faster and faster, the glove and her tongue, the leather sliding on the wetness of the cock, the oiled-up feeling as her hand moved piston-fast on the shaft. But then suddenly she settled back on her heels and looked up at me with a mixed expression of lust...and anticipation. I did not let her down.

I drew her to her feet, lifted her into my arms, and brought her to my heavy wooden desk. Quickly I peeled the gloves from her hands and slid them on my own, delighting in the warmth left by her body heat. Then, just as quickly, I unzipped her leather slacks and pulled them down, only to her thighs, giving me the perfect access to her pussy and asshole. Lovely. Perfect. I parted her ginger-furred kitty lips with two fingers and found her clit, teasing it with my gloved hand. Brushing my fingertips against it until she cried out from the intensity.

Then I went to work with my mouth, treating her as she had treated me. My fingers and my tongue. The leather and the love. I could not get enough, tickling her with my thumb and forefinger until her juices ran down the sweet silken slit between her thighs. Then I lapped every drop, breathing in deeply to catch the most haunting woman-smell, musky and sublime, mixed with the scent of the leather, warm, dark. Living.

The combination of it: the smell of her, the taste of her, the mingling scents together had my pussy dripping sweet juices down my thighs. Before she could come, I stood, grabbed her around the waist, and impaled her with the cock, slamming into her, pressing my body hard against hers. Poetry in motion, this time written by yours truly.

Sinful. Dangerous. Wild. Alive.

The skin on the skin. The hide on the hide.

UNBUTTONING

Kay Jaybee

Laura looked at her reflection in the mirror. The short summer dress highlighted her newly slimmed-down waist and flattered her hips. The open-collared neckline suggested a hint of cleavage, and the plain cornflower blue fabric was lifted by the presence of thirty tiny white buttons that ran down its entire length.

"Do you like it?" Jenny sat on the edge of the bed and looked at her partner. "It's a 'Congratulations on getting back down to a size twelve present.' "

Staring at herself, Laura nodded silently. It had taken twelve months' hard work to get this new figure, and without Jenny's support she'd never have done it. She ran her hands through her freshly highlighted chestnut hair, causing it to sway around her shoulders. "I love it. Thank you."

"Thank goodness for that." Jenny leapt up and came to stand behind Laura. "I was afraid you'd hate it."

"Why?" Laura looked at her lover's face, noting the slightly creased furrow of her brow that always indicated she was worried about something. "I didn't want you to think that I only love you because you're a size twelve now. I loved you at sixteen, and fourteen as well, you do know that don't you?"

"Of course I know that," Laura turned and embraced her girl, placing a tiny kiss on the end of Jenny's nose. "Now, why don't you go downstairs and put the kettle on; I'm gasping for a drink."

Having reassured Jenny, and successfully made sure she was out of the way, Laura hurriedly jumped into action, for it wasn't only Jenny who'd been to town. Dragging two small bags from under the bed, she hid the contents of one in her bedside drawer and emptied the other onto the floor. Glancing again at the reflection of the dress's white buttons, she grinned wickedly and formulated a plan.

Jenny hollered up the stairs, "Coffee's ready."

"Thanks, babe," Laura called back at her, making sure her dress was back in position. "Actually, can you help me a moment?"

Jenny headed back to the bedroom. Recognizing the unmistakable glow of desire on Laura's face, she stopped dead in the doorway and automatically ran a correcting hand through her curling ginger hair.

"I went shopping, too." Laura held her arms out to Jenny.

"Really?"

"Yes. I have presents for you, well, for us."

Jenny didn't say anything, but her heartbeat stepped up a notch as she approached her partner.

Laura ran her small hands down the length of Jenny's green floral mini dress, feeling her nipples spring to life beneath the satin bra that kept them captive.

Breaking away, Jenny reached out to pull Laura's new dress open, but Laura put out a restraining hand. "I can't remember who it was that said *unbuttoning* was the sexiest word in the English language, but I think he was right." Laura trailed a single violet fingernail across Jenny's cheek. "So how about I open these buttons one at a time, as a reward?"

"A reward for what?"

"You'll see." Laura teasingly dipped her head to one side and kissed Jenny's breasts through her dress. "So, will you play my game?"

"How could I refuse?" Jenny felt her body stir with the tension of excited uncertainty. It had been a long time since Laura had wanted to play the dominant partner, and the mere idea made her pulse quicken as she listened carefully to the rules of the game.

"No moving, no speaking. If you manage two minutes without reacting to whatever I do to you, I'll undo two dress buttons. If you last more than two minutes, I'll undo four buttons. If you fail, move or talk, you will be punished." Laura regarded Jenny sternly. "Yes?"

Jenny opened her mouth to reply, but Laura put a finger up to her lips to indicate that the game had already begun, and she should remain silent.

"Each session will be timed by the wall clock." Laura turned Jenny around so that they could both clearly see the clock face before yanking the flimsy green dress over her lover's head.

Using only her palms to press against Jenny's turquoise satin bra, Laura rotated them slowly, feeling the hidden nipples grow harder against the pressure. As the tension built in her, Jenny's eyes fixed themselves on the clock's red second hand. The continuing agitation of her nipples was making her mouth go dry, and she struggled not to make a sound, while the remainder of her breasts tightened with neglect. The instant the hand of the clock indicated that two minutes were up, Jenny exhaled in relief.

Laura dropped her hands, took a step backwards, and with unbearably slow fingers undid the first two buttons. Jenny stared at the tiny area that had been revealed, which was little more than the top of Laura's cleavage, but already she was desperate for the next buttons to be opened. Licking her lips, she waited for Laura's next move.

Ignoring Jenny's chest this time, Laura knelt and began to slowly lap her tongue around the neat belly button. Over and over again she licked and nipped at the pale toned flesh, concentrating on just that one square inch of skin. The clock hands seemed to be ticking by even slower than before, and Jenny barely made it to the 120th stroke before biting back a whimper and pulling away from Laura's intense attention.

The undoing of the next two buttons made Laura's chest more clearly visible, and Jenny longed to be able to reach out and stroke the pink flesh. She gave an involuntary step forward, causing Laura to look triumphantly angry.

"You moved! You are obviously not to be trusted. I will have to restrain you." Staring into her eyes, silently challenging Jenny to complain, Laura went to the drawer where she'd hidden her purchases, and produced a pair of shiny blue handcuffs. Deftly she snapped them around one of a surprised Jenny's wrists, before pulling both her arms behind her back and fastening them together.

"No more disobedience or I shall have to punish you further, understand?"

Jenny nodded her head, her excitement growing. They'd often talked about buying restraints for each other, but until now neither had been brave enough to do it.

Keeping one eye on the clock, Laura lay on the floor and began to lick at Jenny's toes. One by one, sensuously lingering damp caresses that made Jenny's whole body want to shiver. She clenched her teeth; willing herself to keep her feet firmly planted against the floor and not lift them higher as her instinct was screaming at her to do. Again Jenny watched the clock, concentrating on dispelling the amazing sensations that were shooting up her legs by mentally marking every click around its face, until finally she let out a shuddering sigh and won the right to have another couple of buttons opened.

Without giving her time to inspect the contents of the now flapping dress, Laura began to work faster, concentrating on the side of Jenny's neck.

Closing her eyes tightly, Jenny was thankful that her neck wasn't as sensitive as Laura's was, and again managed to count the seconds away in her mind, holding out against the nips and kisses for three whole minutes before a shiver of frustration ran up her spine and forced a mewl from her lips.

Laura congratulated Jenny's stamina with a brief peck on the lips, before rewarding her with the sight of more underwear-free flesh, making Jenny's stomach buzz with anticipation as her mind leapt ahead to the final reward that would surely come at the end of the game, as long as she could hold her nerve until then.

Aware of her own rising desire, Laura knelt again before her girl, and easing Jenny's legs open wider, began to rub a single finger hard against the satin knickers that covered her sticky pussy. Laura hardly had time to get into her stride before Jenny's legs buckled above her, and she let out a moan of lustful defeat.

Immediately drawing back, Laura stood up and pointed to the wooden chair in the corner of their bedroom, ordering Jenny to bend over its seat. Jenny hesitated, but a look at Laura's lust-creased face forced her to move forward. Awkwardly, without the use of her hands, Jenny positioned herself across the chair and braced herself for what was to follow.

Taking a leather paddle from her recent purchases, Laura flashed it briefly in front of Jenny's face before bringing it down hard on her left buttock. Jenny barely had time to squeal in pain from the first stroke when it landed on her right side, sending sparks of hot pain through her prone rump. Tears sparked in Jenny's eyes as she took her punishment, biting back the cries of agony welling up in her throat.

After sixty seconds of being smacked, Jenny felt the wonderfully cooling breath of her lover blowing her inflamed ass and, uncaring as to whether she was allowed or not, let out a sigh of longing, amazed at how much the unexpected spanking had turned her on.

Laura pulled Jenny up and gave her an evilly playful smirk. "You withstood that well, my bitch. One button only though, I think, as you made a sound."

Jenny's damp eyes watched in angry frustration as only half of the flesh she thought she'd won appeared before her. She could almost taste how good Laura's skin would be beneath her lips, and swallowed hard in an attempt to control herself.

Sensing Jenny's struggle made Laura's own arousal more urgent. She quickly repositioned her lover before the ticking clock, and bending down behind her, ran her sharp fingernails over Jenny's fast-bruising buttocks. Trailing the outline of the paddle impressions and dancing a single digit up and down Jenny's buttcrack, Laura listened carefully for any signs of disobedience. Yet Jenny was biting her lips and concentrating with every atom of her being on not responding, on not acknowledging how utterly delicious this situation was, on refusing to admit that the presence of Laura's fingers against her battered behind was pure heaven.

Two and a half minutes later Jenny let out a shudder, taking a step away from Laura's intensely stimulating attentions.

"You're getting better at this." Laura slapped both buttcheeks hard with the palm of her hands before moving away to undo four more buttons.

Jenny stared at the now half-open dress. She'd seen Laura's body so many times over the past three years, but somehow this prolonged revelation of her silky flesh made it feel like the first time, and excitement pounded in her chest.

Still smarting from the assault to her buttocks, Jenny stood statuelike as Laura moved behind her, rubbing her completely exposed chest against Jenny's smooth back. The image of what was happening behind her grew rapidly in Jenny's mind. She tried to shake it off and glared at the digits on the clock face as she took some deep calming breaths. How could only fifteen seconds have passed? She squeezed her eyes closed, but Laura's nipples were being pushed up and down her spine, and she badly wanted to touch them. Her hands wriggled in frustration within the constraints of the handcuffs, and with only a minute passed Jenny's resolve cracked in an explosion of frustration. "Bloody hell! Will you just do it, *please*! Fuck me *please*!"

Laura broke off her attention immediately and forced a cross expression onto her flushed face. She'd been longing for the moment when her lover might beg her for more. Her blue eyes flashed, but Laura said nothing as she reached into the hidden bag, producing a small rubber ball gag.

Jenny's eyes widened. This really was new territory, and for the first time since they started the game, Jenny felt a wave of uncertainty, but Laura didn't give her the chance to voice her fears. She forced the rubber gag on top of Jenny's tongue, fastening the elastic strap so that it trapped the ends of Jenny's hair tight against her neck.

"You look fantastic." Laura stood back to admire the view. Jenny stood meekly, unsure, semi-bound, gagged, and gorgeously vulnerable. Laura had longed to do this to Jenny ever since they'd been together, but had lacked the nerve. Somehow, in losing her excess weight, Laura felt surged with a new sexy confidence, and as she stared at Jenny, she knew all her sacrifices and the boring exercise regime had been more than worthwhile.

Little flecks of saliva began to gather at the corner of the gag, as Jenny failed to control the dribble forming in her mouth. Laura smiled tenderly and whispered into her ear, "Watch the clock, babe," before holding Jenny close and licking the moisture away from around the gag. Covering her face with butterfly kisses, she licked her lover's eyelids and nipped at her ears.

Jenny thought she'd go mad. She longed to touch Laura, to kiss her back, but both actions were now physically impossible. As Laura stood closer still, her chest rubbed slightly against Jenny's bra, causing waves of friction that felt like little electric shocks. If it hadn't been for the gag, Jenny knew she would have been howling with desperation. Her clit throbbed beneath her knickers, which had glued themselves to her skin with her wasted liquid. Yet somehow she managed to keep still for an entire two minutes, only stepping back with relief the moment her time was up, as fresh tears of frustration threatened to form.

Laura's dress was almost fully open now; only the section around her hips remained secure as another two buttons were undone.

Her game almost at an end, Laura began to hurry, her own need for satisfaction beginning to parallel Jenny's. "Only one minute for two buttons now." Her voice became husky as she violently stripped away Jenny's bra and pants, causing a stifled whine to escape from around the black rubber ball. Laura ignored the noise and began to nibble at Jenny's right tit.

The sixty seconds seemed more like ten minutes as Jenny struggled not to push her breast harder into Laura's mouth, wishing as she planted her feet hard against the floor that they had been secured as well so she physically couldn't move them, rather than having to rely on her fast-fading willpower.

Breaking away, Laura panted deeply, proud that Jenny had withstood so much, and hastily opened two buttons from the bottom of her dress.

Jenny knew it had been coming, but as Laura's mouth attached itself to her left nipple, she couldn't keep still. Her body began to shake, and the desire that had been running through her began to drive her further toward an orgasm, whether she was allowed to or not.

Laura broke away, but as Jenny braced herself for further punishment, Laura shook her head, "No, honey, this time, you win." She couldn't wait any more. Just the thought of all Jenny had endured for her was enough to tip her over the edge, and her own neglected body was screaming to be touched. Ripping open her blue dress's last few buttons, Laura stood victorious before Jenny.

She was wearing a thin leather belt that fit exactly over her clit. Without taking her eyes off her lover, Laura pulled the final item from her shopping bag, and screwed a strap-on dildo into its place on the belt.

Jenny's body trembled uncontrollably as she watched Laura approach her. Pulling off the gag, Laura planted her mouth over Jenny's while ramming the tool into her dripping pussy, pumping hard until Jenny's body jerked against her with a moan of pent-up ecstasy.

With a low growl Laura withdrew and, undoing Jenny's hands, steered her still quaking body toward the bed, where she deftly fingered her to a second climax.

"I love that dress," Jenny murmured into Laura's ear as her cuffs were finally unclipped, "and I love the handcuffs, gag, and dildo—but mostly, I love you."

Laura's eyes twinkled mischievously. "I love you too, babe, but I'll love you even more in a minute, when you've used all our new toys on me…"

SAND CASTLE QUEEN

Rachel Kramer Bussel

I think I fell in love with Margaret the first time I saw her buried under the sand. We were neighbors on a little stretch of beach in Puerto Rico, off the beaten path of tourists with loud clothes and louder voices, an oasis from everything but sun and sea, both of us there to escape the monotony and humidity of summer in the city. I'd also come away to lick my wounds, to finally get over Jill, who'd left right before New Year's and six months down the road still haunted my every move in the not-so-big Apple. It was like her perfume, that cheap one she bought at the drugstore whose name I could never remember but whose scent was unmistakable, was everywhere, and even though we'd made a no-contact pact, I would find myself standing in front of some random store like Banana Republic crying as I remembered that one shirt she'd bought from there, the white button-down I'd torn off of her in our kitchen, sending buttons flying and her crying out.

I'd needed a vacation from everything—my ex, my job, my

life—but hadn't been able to get away from my punishing law firm gig until now. And when I go on vacation, I go all out. I stocked up on cheesy, trashy beach books, worked out so I knew I'd fill out my brand-new bikinis in a tangle of colors, everything from tie-dye to day-glo to blinding white and juicy red, and didn't bring my laptop or my BlackBerry. That first day, I didn't know what to do with myself, and took many long, long walks along the hot, perfect sand, letting the warmth of the sun bake my skin like a toasty marshmallow over a flame. But like the gooey dessert, I was still raw and tender inside, pale and prickly even as my shell turned dark. I met Margaret at lunchtime, sitting around a communal table filled with salad and beans and rice, the smell of meat wafting toward us. She was a perky young thing probably fresh out of college, likely ten years my junior, sporting deep, tanned cleavage, dirty blonde ringlets, a deep smile, cheeks peppered with freckles. She was more dressed up than most of us in a low-cut, clingy white top, wrap-around flowery pink and red skirt, and red flip-flops adorned with flowers. Her hair was done in twin braids, and for the first time since Jill, I felt some of those stirrings down below.

Then I looked away, afraid my face would betray me. But she was the one who came and sat next to me. "So, come here often?" She had a soft, sensual drawl that oozed from her lips like honey, a Southern slant to her words that made my shoulders drop ever so slightly, letting one more bit of New York stiffness evaporate. Then she let out a loud laugh, followed by a snort. Score one for individuality. "I'm sorry," she said, continuing to giggle and then holding out her hand. "I'm Margaret. Or Maggie. Or Magpie. Take your pick." She stopped talking and looked up at me through extra-long lashes and intense hazel eyes. I've never really gotten hazel as an eye color; it seems wishy-washy, flecked, only halfway done. I prefer the intensity of a brilliant sky blue

staring back at me, and have fallen for girls simply because their
eyes bewitched me so. Or a silky coffee brown, usually with hair
to match, one that made me think of the perfect cup of coffee,
warm and welcoming. But hazel, until Margaret, seemed iffy,
noncommittal, and just what I was trying to avoid.

"I like Margaret, actually. I'm Stacy," I said, still thinking
about those eyes. I let her chatter on while I took her in, already
wondering if she could be "the one." Then I heard the magic
word. "I live in Charlotte, North Carolina, but I'm originally
from Memphis. And I'm working on getting my certification so
I can open up my own yoga studio/child care center for children.
I love teaching kids; they're so pure of heart, and they make
me melt with their little hands and big questions. They're much
better suited to the kinds of yoga I like to do, and their bodies are
so resilient. They're always thinking, too, always so far ahead of
us. I want to have my own brood of them someday." She again
stopped talking, as if invisibly clamping a hand over her mouth.
"Sorry again. They just make me so excited. I'm like a big kid."
I smiled again.

"It's okay, really, I like it." Maybe she was what I needed, I
thought. A hot woman who also liked kids. Sure, I didn't live
anywhere near her, but I wasn't thinking beyond that moment.
I was on vacation from overthinking as well. We were at a
dyke-owned resort, so I figured she had to be into women, or
at least, open to the idea. Not everyone there was queer; some
were straight (or mostly straight) women who just wanted to
relax and not worry about being hit on, to feel free to sunbathe
topless and walk around wearing just skimpy bikini bottoms
or, for the more daring, nothing at all on the resort's grounds.
Most of the women around us were with families, cherubic little
faces running up to pairs of mommies, or older, retired women
with white hair holding hands, the occasional nuclear family

interspersed. Margaret seemed to be alone, but as much as she talked, wouldn't divulge anything personal. I followed suit, simply saying I'd come to get away from the pressures of city life. But as the days passed, I became smitten, picturing us here celebrating our anniversary, taking our kids. That's always been my downfall, getting too ahead of myself, yet I can't help where my mind goes when I'm not looking. Most of the women around us were couples, and I didn't want it to seem like I was just hitting on her 'cause we were both single, the way straight people try to set me up all the time with their lone lesbian friend.

Every day for a week we shared meals, and it was the first time a woman had made me wait that long, not even so much as tipping her hand. Margaret was driving me mad, and after lunch, I'd race back to my room, lock my door, slide between the crisp white sheets, and plunge my hand between my legs. I'd think of her curls tickling my face as she leaned down to kiss me, think of her teasing me with her body, slithering up and down mine, naked, her pussy near yet out of reach, her hovering over my lips, letting her scent waft into my nose but not taste her. I wanted more from her than just sex, I knew that from the start, but it began with her body, with being naked next to her, with seeing and feeling and tasting her inside and out. My fantasies got so intense I almost couldn't look at her when we shared meals and took to wearing sunglasses, hoping I wasn't blushing as she regaled me with tales of her life in Charlotte. New York and North Carolina don't seem to have much in common, but I didn't care. Sometimes love, and even lust, are utterly irrational.

To stave off the thoughts that were becoming increasingly hard to handle, I took to long walks on the beach, walking so far I almost got lost, seeking oblivion as the waves crashed in my ear, kids splashing, Spanish and English and languages I couldn't identify swirling in the air. I found an outdoor bar and sat, a chilly banana dacquiri blasting onto my tongue. I knew I was getting burned, my marshmallow skin going from tender brown to crispy burned black, darker than it should be, but I didn't mind. I went for a run even though my lone blue one-piece wasn't really made for that.

Then I waded into the water, out just enough so I could raise myself on my toes. I shut my eyes, raised my face to the sun, and offered it what I can only call a prayer. My fingers wound their way between my legs, between my lips, stroking fast and furious, pinching my clit, and then plunging deep inside, the water cool against my hot flesh. I thought of Margaret, pictured her pretty face poised in climax, pictured her opening to me, giving herself to me fully, completely, and I in turn doing the same. Since the first time in longer than I cared to admit, I was ready to let another woman all the way inside.

I walked back just as the sun was starting to descend, and for a moment, all the hotels started to look alike. I wondered what I'd do were I to get lost, with only a handful of crumpled bills, my room key, and my broken Spanish to guide me. And then I saw that crazy spill of dirty-blonde curls, heard that miraculous laugh, as if calling to me. I jogged toward her, my chest heaving in the ill-armed suit. "Hey," I called, as if I hadn't just been conjuring her.

I could only see Margaret's face, and the light was dim, but I swear her eyes lit up. She was covered in sand everywhere save for her head and arms, her body buried and transformed into a curvaceous mermaid, complete with an elaborately curved tail, her hair spread out on the sand, her breasts molded into extra-large mounds, my very own sand castle queen. A squealing child ran up to her and patted her tail, gazing adoringly at Margaret. "Thank you, sweetheart," she said, the words dripping off her tongue like honey.

"Wow," I said, sitting down on a nearby towel and simply observing her. Somehow, it was okay to blatantly ogle her when she was herself but not. I placed one hand on her sand-covered breast and said, "May I?"

I felt a little silly asking if I could cop a feel of what was pretty much just sand and water, but it felt so intimate, there in front of whoever might walk by, with her unable to move more than her head. "Please do," she said, her eyes twinkling as I caught my breath. As I placed my palm over the round curve, massaging it instinctively, pressing the flat of my hand where her nipple would be, I wondered what she was feeling down below, whether she wished she could escape her sandy bondage and snake her fingers between her legs. "How's that?" I asked, my voice husky, the passersby skittering away as if sensing our need for privacy.

"Considering the circumstances, it's fabulous," she said, laughing as I dipped my hand between her artificial breasts. I was playing, yet I wasn't, emboldened by her sand-encrusted outside.

I leaned closer to speak directly into her ear. "What about those circumstances? Is there something else you'd like me to do if you weren't buried under layers of sand?"

"Stacy, I..." she trailed off as my hand moved up to caress her cheek, actual skin on skin, hers soft and delicate. I moved my fingertips toward her lips, and she parted them, allowing me room to trace her pink lips, her hair whipping around in the sudden breeze. "Yes, there is, but it's complicated. There's someone back home and it's over, but it's not official yet. And I keep lying in bed at night and thinking about you. And not in a platonic way. I don't know what to do about these feelings I have for you. We're so far from home and you're so tempting..."

"It's okay, whatever you want to do I'll abide by, but don't push me away. I don't want to pressure you, I just want to be close to you," I said, realizing it was true. For once in my life, I wasn't letting my raging libido make my decisions for me. Seeing her trapped like that, vulnerable yet proud, standing her ground, I fell for her hard.

"May I?" I asked, indicating the indentation between her curves, which suddenly seemed perfect for my head.

"Please do," she said, and I rested my head between her breasts, almost thinking I could hear the phantom beat of her heart. Surely that was my imagination, yet I smiled to myself.

I must have dozed briefly because when I heard her say "Kiss me," I was startled, groggy, unsure if I was awake or dreaming.

"Here? Are you sure?" I looked around to see who might be spying on us. We were staying at a queer resort, but this was the public beach, and I didn't want to cause a commotion. But no one was around, the families having found some other, sunnier spot to park their towels. It was a sign, perhaps. I brought my lips to hers, tasting the salty flavor of their softness, the warmth right underneath as she raised her head to meet mine. We kissed like that for what felt like hours, until I needed to touch her for real. "Can we go in? To your room? I know what you said earlier, but Maggie…" My voice caught on her nickname, my eyes beseeching her, letting her know I wanted more than this momentary passion, much more.

She looked at me, as if trying to read my mind through my eyes. "Yes, we can, but I want to be in charge," she said. "I like you too much to be reckless." I nodded, even though by that point I wanted nothing more than to be reckless.

I helped her scoop away the layers of sand, delicately unearthing her body. As she revealed herself to me, I found her more beautiful than I had before, and while part of me wanted to treat this as merely a summer romance, inside I knew it was about much more. We silently got her out of the sand, and then I found myself too shy to keep talking, my heart pounding as I followed her, both of us barefoot, to her room. "I need to shower..." she said, her words trailing off. I followed her inside and silently undressed her, then myself.

I stepped forward, turning the knob so the hot blast hit me, before lifting her inside. I reached for the soap but was distracted by a bottle of body wash, and opened it to find it smelled of cotton candy, which could've been sickeningly sweet but somehow wasn't. "Let me," I said, when she reached for it. I poured some onto my palm and as the hot water beat down on her breasts, I massaged her back, admiring its smooth length, the muscles simmering below. Margaret was no helpless Southern belle, but she had a charm that I didn't see in New York all that often either. She had sassy flirtation down to a T, but I sensed there was more. My hands moved to cup her breasts, pinching her hard, wet nipples, letting the shower wash away the smell of sugar. "I want you, Margaret," I said, my voice husky. "Here, now, and after, too."

"Mmm..." she moaned, arching her ass against me, giving me permission to touch her there. I toyed with her nubs, resting my face against her back as she kept on moaning, the sounds getting deeper the more I twisted. Her nipples were the perfect size, and she responded to each twist and tug. But soon I needed more.

"Turn around," I ordered, and when she did, I wasn't quite prepared for the look of pure desire etched across her face. Whatever had been holding her back before, whoever she'd given her heart to before today, had slipped away. In that moment, she was all mine, body and soul, and I took full advantage, sinking to my knees to taste her sex. Margaret spread her legs wider, giving me access to her sleek, shaved lips. She ground down against me, the water continuing its pounding as I got lost inside her, my tongue diving deep. My hands moved to her ass, squeezing those firm buttcheeks as my lips met hers, before pulling back to suckle at her clit. I looked up at her, the length of her body a gift, as Margaret came against me, shuddering and holding onto my head for balance.

I wanted to say, "I love you," but I knew it was too soon, too cliché. Instead I stood up and kissed her, the now cool water in our eyes. We turned off the flow, wrapped ourselves in fluffy towels, and got into bed. Under the covers we stayed, all night into the morning. I didn't know then that we'd make that resort our annual vacation spot, now bringing kids of our own, or that we'd make a ritual of burying one or both of us in the sand. I didn't know anything beyond her skin, her smile, and I didn't need to. I trusted Margaret to lead me wherever I was supposed to be, and sure enough, that's exactly what she's done.

CUTS

Shannon Dargue

CLONK! That was the sound it made. It wasn't the *rip* or *snick* or *zing* I had come to expect. Nope. As the big, toothy blade took a bite out of my left thumb, I clearly heard a *clonk,* and felt surprisingly little.

Without looking at my injury, I clamped the other hand around my thumb and used my knee to turn the table saw off. Leaving a trail of blood droplets the size of Loonies, I made my way to May's office where she (thankfully) had the door propped open. "How bad?" I croaked. Thrusting both hands in front of my supervisor's face, I uncurled the fingers of my right hand and averted my eyes. "Is it gone?" Before answering, May grabbed my wrist and yanked my latest mishap high in the air. Although she had a chokehold on my hand, big crimson drops began to rain all over my crunchy overalls.

"You're bleeding pretty bad, but it's still there, I think—most of it anyway."

What the hell did that mean? I sat in May's chair while she stood and applied first aid.

"This may not feel too bad now," she advised, "but it's gonna hurt like hell tomorrow. You'll be home awhile. Don't worry, though—comp should cover ya." She seemed so calm, like she'd seen this a hundred times before. Maybe she had. May's been a carpenter almost twenty years now. "Sam, you okay?"

"Yeah, yeah...But can we go to Saint Monica's? Does it have to be General?" I pleaded. My hand was beginning to really hurt, but at least the gauze contained the bleeding. "I mean, what difference will it make?"

May spoke slowly, as if maybe my brain had leaked out of my thumb and landed on the floor with the rest of the mess. "The difference is, John will chew me a new one if I take you across town when we're six minutes away from Calgary General Hospital. Now—can you walk? Are you okay to get to my truck?"

Sitting in the passenger seat, my mind started to wander. *I wonder if Kellie's on today.* May took every corner a little too fast, causing my head to bounce off the window. Each tap on the glass pushed out the last thought and brought in a new one. *Maybe I won't see her.* Bonk. *God, I miss her.* Bonk. *It's been a long time.* Bonk. *Does she miss me?*

"Hey, you okay, kid?"

"Yeah, I'm fine," I lied. I felt like I was going to be sick. If Kellie was on the evening shift, I couldn't possibly avoid her.

It had been six weeks since I last laid eyes on my best friend. Six weeks since I ruined everything with my drunken confession. I was a living, breathing, lesbian cliché. I had fallen madly in love with my lifelong, *straight* best friend, spilled the beans, and split before the one I loved had a chance to say something awful like "I'm flattered." As Kellie staggered to her bed that night mumbling about needing to "sleep on it," I called a cab and left her a note:

Kellie, I need to clear my head. I'll call when I can, Sam.

The next morning, a below par sounding Kellie called and had a chat with my answering machine. " Sam...Sam, are you there? No? Okay. Uh, I sorta think I remember you mentioning you were in love with me. Umm...We need to talk. Call me, okay?" I almost picked up. My hand hovered over phone as I mustered the courage to say it all again sober. But when I heard the "we need to talk" part, I reeled back as if the phone was suddenly spitting deadly venom. Nothing good *ever* follows those four words. I never did call Kellie back. And she's not one to play chase—not even with me.

So there I was, forty-four days later in the emergency room of the hospital where Kellie was a nurse. *Shit.* I knew I'd have to face her eventually, but that really wasn't the day I felt like doing it.

After getting bounced through triage and into the patient waiting area, I urged May to go home. I wanted to be alone while I wallowed in self-pity. I also wanted to snoop. Around the next corner and down the hall a bit was the nurses' station. On the wall behind the counter, they had a big whiteboard with the nurses' schedules.

Peeking James Bond-like around the corner, I didn't see her. But I couldn't see the board either. I scuttled as quickly as I could down the corridor, flashed a fake smile at the bearded lady behind the desk, and saw it—*K. Mercer.* She was there. Realizing I was no longer smiling, but rather just showing my teeth to that poor woman, I hightailed it back to the waiting room.

"Is there a Samantha Weatherby?" an irritated nurse barked. "Weatherby?"

"That's me. Here. I'm Sam." I showed him May's now bloody

handiwork with a gruesome thumbs-up gesture. We went for a walk.

An hour after my arrival, I had some answers. While I hadn't cut through the bone, I had managed to lose a substantial portion of the soft tissue of the pad of my thumb and a good bit of the nail. In a nutshell, I was brought to a room and given some jammies. They couldn't just stitch me up and send me home. I had to wait for the on-call plastic surgeon. He wouldn't be long, they assured me, and when he arrived, I would go straight to surgery. When that was over, I would return to my room with three beds and wait eight hours before I could go home (hopefully, with a functional thumb). Oh, well, at least I had some painkillers in me.

With the pain in check, the knot in my gut loosened and I became more aware of my surroundings. I realized the other beds were unoccupied. *Cool.* I also noticed the empty chair to the left of my tiny bed. *Not cool.* I was completely alone. I wanted Kellie there. *My* Kellie. I wanted my peach-smelling Kellie beside me to tell me I would be okay. I wanted so badly to take back what I said, to be able to look my best friend in the eye again and not feel like I had betrayed a sacred trust. I could have loved her forever and just kept my big mouth shut. But I blew it. We would never be able to erase that night. Five whispered words had changed everything...

I had just gotten dumped and Kellie was at my door, armed with a six-pack. "Jesus, Sam. It's nine o'clock on a Saturday night, and you're in your pajamas! It's time for an intervention. Get dressed."

I tried to talk her into staying in and watching *The Terminator*. No good. Tossing a beer in my direction, she threatened to put me out of my misery if I didn't start showing signs of improvement. I shuffled to my room and pulled on my cleanest jeans and shrugged into a big black hoodie. I was warming to the thought of going out. Booze, crappy techno, half-naked gay boys, and Kellie definitely sounded therapeutic.

We always ended up at gay bars because Kellie liked the atmosphere. She said she could "dance without getting pawed by horny hetero guys." We found a table near the dance floor while we waited for the place to pick up. Putting another beer in front of me, she sat back, furrowed her brow, and asked, "So what happened? I thought you and Casey were good."

I drained half my beer and released the mother of all burps before answering. "Me too, but apparently I'm 'emotionally unavailable and distant.' She said we weren't growing as a couple." I dismissively waved my hand as if to clear the air. "Same old, same old. Really I'm fine. It's picking up in here; let's dance."

We weaved our way to a corner away from the smoke machines. As we separately moved in time with the music, I wondered why I had yet again failed in the relationship department. I never seemed to click with any of the women I had dated. It wasn't that I didn't enjoy their company, or that I wasn't attracted to them, I just never felt that *something* people always went on about. I wondered why it didn't really bother me at all.

As Kellie swayed and gyrated to the throbbing beat, I watched her. I was glad she dragged me out; being around her always lifted my spirits. The sight of her, or even just the sound of her voice on the phone, never failed to smooth away all the rough edges in my head. Kellie meant the world to me, and as I stood there watching her, I felt something shift. A sort of tingly feeling started in the pit of my stomach, fluttered its way through my chest, and fizzled between my ears. *Uh oh.* Moving my eyes from

Kellie's wiggling midsection to her lips, I felt an intense pull. *No way...* Someone's beer exploded near my shoe.

"Sam! Hey! Where'd you go?" Kellie's hands were on my shoulders. Apparently, it was *my* beer.

"Can we go home?" I didn't feel so good. There were no singing angels, cooing doves, or any of the other crap I read about. The room *was,* however, spinning, and I thought I might puke. Realizing I was in love with Kellie wasn't exactly magical.

As Kellie's place was only a few blocks away, we didn't bother with finding a cab to get back to my apartment. Holding my arm as we walked, Kellie blathered on and on. "Maybe you should get one of those *Dr. Phil* books...Maybe you could find, like, *Loveless Lezzies* or somethin.' "

"I am not loveless—I love lots, and you're drunk, so shut up." I fished keys out of her purse and let us into the three-story walk-up.

Slumping on Kellie's couch, I tried to calm my frayed nerves. I failed, however, as soon as Kellie plopped down beside me and wrapped her arms around my neck. "You'll find her, Sammy. And you'll love her completely. You'll see—you just haven't met her yet." She kissed the top of my bowed head.

"I have," I said to my lap.

"Oh, my god! Really?" Her arms slipped from my shoulders. She excitedly gripped my thighs. "Tell me, tell me. What's her name?"

Oh, shit, here it comes. "It's Kellie."

"Weird! That's my na—" I watched as realization hit her like a ton of bricks. Her grip loosened, and although it looked like she was trying to form words, no sound escaped her lips.

Almost inaudibly, I whispered, "It's always been you, Kellie."

Pulled from the past by the sound of a man clearing his throat,

I turned my head and looked up at the porter. He was reading my clipboard. "Good evening, Samantha. Let's go get that thumb fixed up." He wheeled me and my bed off to surgery.

I woke around eleven in my now dark room to someone squeezing my foot. I was thirsty and in a considerable amount of pain. I jerked my foot away and tried to say something, but all that came out was a little barking sound.

"I brought you some water." It was Kellie. Tears glimmered on her lashes but didn't drop. "I saw your chart earlier, but I didn't know if you wanted me here with you." Clearing her throat to stop her voice from betraying her, she gave me the news. "They saved your thumb. You lost a little length because they had to reshape it, but for the most part, you got lucky."

At that point I really didn't care all that much about my cut. Kellie was there, and that was all that mattered. I suddenly felt like a tremendous asshole for shutting her out the way I did. "I'm so sorry," I sobbed. "I never meant for it to be like this. I can go back, Kellie, I can go back to how it was before. Please, I need my Kellie back." I was beginning to hyperventilate.

She rushed to my side and hugged my head. "I'm here. Sam, I'm here. Just breathe, honey, breathe with me."

As I matched my breathing to hers, I fell asleep with my head still wrapped in her arms. I slept until the doctor came in at five to talk with me. Kellie was there beside my bed, still in her lavender scrubs, sleeping in the chair.

"Kellie, psst...I'm allowed to leave." I touched her cheek gently to wake her. "Let's go." I went into the washroom and freshened up as well as I could. I found some Listerine. *Score.*

I sat on the edge of the hospital bed and gathered my things. Kellie settled beside me. "You know, Sam, you turned my life upside down. You turned my life upside down, and I didn't have my best friend around to help me make sense of it."

Ouch. Here comes that talk. "I panicked," I said. "But I'll fix it. We'll be back to normal soon. It'll be like that night never happened."

For a long moment, she just looked at me. And then she did it. Kellie slowly leaned forward and touched her lips to mine. I sat there unmoving, unsure of what was really happening until she pinched my leg. "I love you too, Sammy. Now kiss me already." I softened my mouth and felt her melt against me.

Kellie came home with me that day two years ago, on the premise of helping out for a while. She's still here...

ABSINTHE

Jennifer Fulton

I n the walled garden, night jasmine bloomed. Vines had long ago claimed the marble bench on which Eloise sat, their lithe, entwined suckers furnishing a latticework cushion. Lilies grew in fleshy clumps throughout the garden, waxen blooms pale in the moonlight. Eloise considered these, as she did on this day each year, alone beneath the apple tree, attuned to the sound of a key in the latch and the wet crunch of footsteps on fallen fruit.

Come dawn, she would gather her cloak about her and tread the damp grass back out into the world. Why wait, Eloise asked herself, when she could leave early, in possession of her dignity? Perhaps promises made to strangers on trains did not count. Perhaps some wickedness had befallen the woman who owned this garden, precluding their rendezvous.

There were rules for chance encounters, and Eloise feared she had broken every one of them: do not entertain romantic fantasies, do not believe promises of future meetings. People would say almost anything to avoid an awkward goodbye after intimacy. Her pigheadedness had only made the situation worse, compelling her futile return to the designated spot, year after year, just in case Madame had been unaccountably detained.

And here she was once more, alone in the ruins of Eden, feeling as Eve might had the Serpent passed her by.

The warm July evening that set this folly in motion had its beginnings at Victoria Station in London. The year was 1939 and the Night Ferry to Paris left, as usual, just before 10 p.m. The journey took place on a train named Contentment that swayed and rattled down to the Dover docks where it was loaded aboard a ferry with rails and disgorged some nine hours later across the channel at Dunkirk. Back on terra firma, it sped into Paris by nine in the morning, just in time for warm croissants and café au lait in the garden at the Ritz.

In the dining car, Eloise ordered Coquilles St. Jacques Meuniere and champagne, determined to take her mind off the notion of heavy train carriages sinking to the bottom of the Atlantic. At the next table, another lone diner read a French newspaper. At first Eloise mistook her for a gentleman. She wore a pinstriped suit, and her short black hair was combed smoothly back from her forehead.

Catching Eloise's eye, she lowered her newspaper and said, "Good evening." Her voice was husky and quite deep but distinctly female.

As Eloise murmured a somewhat startled hello, the maître d'hôtel arrived at the woman's table, and they conversed in rapid French. He bowed and called her Madame, and then approached Eloise and said, "*Excuse moi*, Mademoiselle. I took the liberty of explaining your predicament, and Madame invites you to join her for dinner."

"My predicament?" Eloise blinked, whereupon the man lost

his crisp command of English and ushered her from her chair.

"Charles prefers to circumvent the embarrassing spectacle of two women dining alone in his car," Madame explained dryly.

"Your husband is not traveling with you?" Eloise at once felt gauchely American for asking a question that was none of her business.

Madame did not appear to take offense. "Henry would not be so inconsiderate. Besides, he loathes the French."

Eloise wondered how Henry felt about his wife's choice of attire. She couldn't help but stare a moment longer than she should. Even the shoes were masculine, black and highly polished. It struck her that Madame was almost certainly the kind of woman her parents had warned her about before she left Baltimore—a bohemian intellectual who flouted the rules of society and pursued a dissipated lifestyle in the company of avant-garde artists, political nonconformists, and other hotheads. According to Aunt Constance, with whom Eloise would be traveling in Europe, the cafés of Paris overflowed with such women, recklessly smoking cigarettes and even sampling the illicit Green Fairy. In this day and age.

"Is this your first trip to France?" Madame asked.

"Yes. I am to join my widowed aunt. She has been taking the cure in Dax. We're planning to tour the Continent."

Madame had eyes almost as black as her hair. She regarded Eloise with warm indulgence. "You are not concerned by the political situation?"

"My aunt says we shall avoid Czechoslovakia."

"The invasion being an inconvenience, to say the least?"

Eloise nodded. Something in Madame's tone made her feel slightly defensive. "My aunt says General Mussolini is making Italy more efficient, and Mr. Hitler is doing the same for Germany."

"Efficiency charms a certain type of person, it seems."

Eloise could not help but smile. "Aunt Constance married a man who counted every penny."

"And she outlived him," Madame noted. "Efficiency, indeed."

Eloise laughed and her body relaxed all of a sudden. It was such a relief to talk to someone willing to say exactly what she thought.

"Where are you from?" Madame asked.

"Baltimore."

"I was just reading about one of your countrywomen. Clara Adams. The first woman passenger to fly around the world."

Eloise shuddered. "She must be very brave. I would never dare do such a thing."

"You may surprise yourself one day. I've found we never know what we are truly capable of until we are tested."

"Have you been tested?" Eloise asked, emboldened by the champagne.

Madame's expression altered momentarily as though a shadow had passed across her thoughts. "Not as I shall be," she said. Then her eyes were bright once more, and she offered a small platter of appetizers. "Do try a truffle pastry. They're always good."

As Eloise politely nibbled a nasty-tasting morsel, Madame introduced herself and they exchanged the usual courtesies, making innocuous conversation over fine food until they were the last passengers in the dining car. Madame then summoned Charles and requested her usual, which was how Eloise came to be acquainted with absinthe.

"It's illegal in Britain and France, now," Madame said. "However, we are soon to leave Dover, and we will not arrive in Dunkirk until the morning. At sea, we shall be in no-man's-land, as it were. Free to ignore the laws of both nations. Imagine."

There was something wicked in the dark glitter of her eyes and the white flash of her teeth. She observed Eloise with disquieting concentration, the way people study artworks they want to own. Eloise recognized that covetous appreciation from auctions she attended with her mother, who crammed the walls of their home with peculiar paintings by foreigners.

They were obliged to continue their refreshments in Madame's compartment, for the train would soon be loaded aboard a ferry, carriages squeezed one alongside the next, for the sea journey to France. By a stroke of luck, their compartments were side by side in the same carriage. Madame said it was not luck. Railway officials sought, for the sake of propriety, to locate unaccompanied females in one carriage and lone males in another.

A waiter followed them bearing a pitcher of iced water, a bowl of sugar lumps, and two Madeira glasses. He placed these on a small table between facing couchettes, bowed, and left.

"Pray sit down." Madame indicated one of the modest seats, and not for the first time, Eloise observed that she was remarkably civil for a person on the fringes of society.

She wondered at the wisdom of retreating to Madame's compartment. For all she knew, her elegant companion might pursue all manner of vices. Eloise had no doubt that Mother and Father would consider the Englishwoman an unsuitable acquaintance, even decadent. Common sense dictated that Eloise remain in her company no longer. She had, after all, promised to conduct herself prudently on her travels.

Guiltily, she blurted, "Perhaps I should bid you good evening, Madame. You've been so kind, but I simply cannot impose any further upon your hospitality."

Madame smiled and drew a step closer. She was taller than Eloise, a fact made more pronounced by the immediacy of the small compartment. Up close, her eyes were not black after all. They were the color of mountains at dusk, a serene purple gray, and etched with fine long lashes.

"Consider this an adventure," she coaxed softly. "You are far from home and free to do as you please. Do you really wish to leave?"

Eloise knew the answer her parents would expect of her, but her throat closed over the obligatory words. Unable to endure Madame's teasing stare, she lowered her head and sank onto the couchette.

Madame remained standing before her, and Eloise was overwhelmed by a strange urge to touch the fine weave of her jacket. The hairs on the back of her neck prickled, and an oily sensation settled in her stomach. She hadn't noticed Madame's fragrance in the dining car, but an elusive medley of scents troubled her senses now: freshly laundered cotton sullied with traces of smoke. Violets languishing in a shadowed forest. A tease of vanilla and some other subtle spices.

An inexplicable panic rose in her, constricting her breathing. Eloise decided champagne and travel were a perilous combination, one that had obviously gone straight to her head. Fortunately, nobody was here to witness her lapse in judgment. She was in Europe, far from the censure of her family.

Recklessly, she allowed her gaze to meander up the starched white shirt front before her to the collar Madame had loosened, the hollow of her throat, and the strength of her chin, and finally the shadow beneath her lower lip.

Madame was no longer smiling, and as Eloise stared at her mouth, it parted slightly as if compelled by a sharp release of breath. "I'll walk you to your compartment if it is truly your wish," she said, taking a step back.

Eloise met her eyes and found them shuttered, the warm

indulgence supplanted by a more distant expression. "No," she said, embarrassed to have betrayed her indecision. "I would prefer to stay."

Madame gave her a long, assessing look, took the seat opposite, and drew a bottle from her luggage. After rearranging the items on the small table between them, she poured a measure of Pernod Fils from the bottle and then placed a slotted silver device over each glass, forming a bridge from rim to rim. On this she set a lump of sugar for herself and two for Eloise.

Holding the pitcher high above Eloise's glass, she let a thin stream of water slowly descend onto the sugar lumps. These immediately began to dissolve and drip through the slots. Transfixed, Eloise watched a milky mist rise up through the amber green liquid in her glass. An herbal fragrance floated from the liqueur.

After Madame had repeated this ritual for her own aperitif, she removed the silver spoons and toasted, "To your education, my dear."

Eloise took a cautious sip and quickly covered her mouth. The liquid was cool, yet her throat burned. The taste was both bitter and sweet. It seemed she had consumed a licorice-tainted flower bud. With each breath it opened farther, teasing her tongue and cloying her nostrils with the scent of wild meadow.

"It's a taste one acquires," Madame said. "Take some more. You'll find it improves."

Obligingly, Eloise took another sip and then another. "I have heard many are addicted to this beverage," she remarked.

"It can cast a spell," Madame conceded. "But you're in no danger from a glass or two."

Her hands were pale and fine like those of the marble statues Eloise had seen at the British Museum. Impulsively, she touched one and was almost surprised to find it warm instead of cold.

"Forgive me," she said, hastily withdrawing. How could she explain herself?

Madame seemed unconcerned. "Will it bother you if I remove my jacket?"

"Not at all." Eloise wanted to shed her own shoes and stockings but suppressed this wayward urge.

Beneath her jacket, Madame wore a plain white shirt tucked into pants that fit quite loosely. These were supported by suspenders, or, as the British termed them, braces. She rolled up her sleeves and opened the window of their compartment, producing a thin cigar. "Do you mind?" she asked. "I would offer you one, but I don't care to see a beautiful woman smoke."

Eloise found this sentiment surprising on several counts, most notably that Madame had paid her a compliment. This was rare; Eloise's looks generally failed to excite attention. She was unfashionably narrow of shoulder and small breasted, and tonight, in a long-sleeved, deep green dress that buttoned at the front, she felt about as dull as she could be. Her mother said the fabric flattered her pale complexion and copper brown hair, but Eloise thought it made her look insipid and showed up the cinnamon freckles sprayed across her nose and cheeks. She had tried to cover these with powder, but she knew they peeped through.

As Madame lit her cigar, Eloise said, like a chatterbox, "I've never smoked. Some of my friends from college do, but my father won't permit it. He says only fast women smoke."

"He has a point." Madame's perfectly etched mouth tugged a little at the edges. "If I may ask, how old are you?"

"I'll be twenty-four in September. On the first of the month."

"There's a decade between us. And an ocean." Madame looked pensive. "Will you be back in London after your travels?"

"Only briefly, alas. I've already spent six weeks there, seeing the sights."

Madame sent a slow drift of smoke out the window. "I shall be in Berlin later this month. Are you including Germany in your tour?"

"Why, yes. My aunt is quite desperate to see one of those vast parades they're showing on the newsreels. She thinks the German uniforms are very glamorous."

Her companion fell silent for so long that Eloise wondered if she'd said something tactless. Finally, after imbibing some of her own green liqueur, Madame remarked, "Your aunt sounds like a very silly woman."

"I fear so." Even as she giggled her reply, Eloise found Madame's comment increasingly hilarious. It was all she could do not to roll with laughter.

Aunt Constance was her mother's older sister, a strident big-bodied widow who had inherited a vast fortune from her husband and had no children on whom to lavish it. This meant she'd always spoiled Eloise with extravagant toys and clothing Father considered absurd.

The sable coat Eloise now carried with her had been consigned to cold storage when Aunt Constance sent it for her sixteenth birthday. Her father had only allowed her to retrieve it on her graduation from Vassar. Eloise ran her hand across the fine soft fur and could almost imagine herself wearing it in Russia, standing on the timeless steppes described with such calm passion by Countess Alexandra Tolstoy in one of her visits to the college.

"Are you cold?" Madame asked, studying the fingers Eloise had buried.

"A little," Eloise admitted. Indeed, she was shivering. She felt hot inside, but chills kept crawling across her skin.

Madame extinguished her cigar and closed the window, drawing the curtains so the compartment seemed warmer. She cleared the table and folded it away, and then sat down just inches from Eloise. Slouching back against the corner where the seat met the wall, she stretched her legs out before her, crossing them at the ankles.

"Is that better?" she asked, tilting her head to face Eloise.

She was so beautiful Eloise had trouble finding a sensible reply. Her skin was the color of a honey-dipped pearl. It beckoned Eloise's fingers. Oddly compelled, she slid along the seat until their thighs almost touched. It was as if she were in a dream, trying to find her way out, needing an anchor to keep her from drifting. She lifted her hand, and when her fingertips connected with skin, she gasped and quickly shrank back.

But Madame caught her by the wrist and placed the imprisoned hand on her cheek, sandwiching it gently beneath her own. "You can touch me, Eloise. I'm not offended, and we are at sea. Rules don't matter here."

"I feel...intoxicated," Eloise confessed.

"Then I recommend you make the most of it. I can't imagine you'll have the opportunity once you are traveling with your aunt."

Madame regarded her with an expression Eloise had never seen before, a look so frank and knowing she felt her every thought and feeling must be transparent.

To her shock, Madame's lips brushed her palm. Blood rushed up Eloise's neck to her face. Her heart pummeled against her ribcage and beat a rapid tattoo in her ears. Her limbs were heavy and languorous, yet her mind seemed brilliantly alert. She tried to make sense of the impulses she could barely repress. She wanted to reach for Madame. She wanted to kiss her. What was happening to her? Was this the legendary effect of absinthe? Did Madame also feel this way from consuming it? Eloise immediately knew she should leave, but she remained exactly where she was, an accomplice to her own undoing.

Her dress felt too tight at the throat, so she reached for her buttons, fumbling to unfasten the top few.

"Allow me," Madame said, as one of the buttons snapped off and flew onto the floor.

Eloise lowered her hand and tilted her chin up in defeat. The brush of Madame's fingers against her skin as the other woman deftly unfastened one button after the next made her mouth go dry. She wanted more. More than the incidental collision of skin.

"Let's loosen this a little." Madame slid a finger beneath the bodice's neckline and slowly worked her way along.

Eloise heard a sound and knew she had whimpered. Mortified, she averted her eyes.

Madame's hand stilled at her nape. "Would you like me to kiss you?" she asked, her breath damp on Eloise's cheek.

Eloise could only nod, aware of a hot, flooding sensation between her legs and a clamoring need to act on all she was feeling. She moved closer, bringing their bodies into contact. Madame's lips brushed hers with unbearable delicacy. It was not enough.

Eloise kissed her in return but more firmly, communicating what she wanted. Madame's fingers moved from her nape through her hair, cradling her head. Their next kiss was completely different. Madame parted Eloise's mouth with her own and deliciously explored her, sending goose bumps marauding over the hidden parts of her body. Her breasts, her thighs, her spine. Madame's tongue teased its way deeper, and her hands finally delivered the caresses Eloise craved. A shock of desire made her freeze for a split second when Madame found a nipple and slowly teased it through the fabric of her dress.

Somewhere in the recesses of her mind it occurred to Eloise

that she should not be doing this with a woman, but she cut the thought loose. Almost immediately another took its place, and this time she broke contact, just barely.

"What about your husband?" she whispered against Madame's lips.

"Henry and I have in common...separate interests." The hands did not pause in their work for a moment, one of them sliding beneath Eloise's bodice as the other fully unbuttoned her. "Our marriage is a convenience, for both of us."

Eloise's teeth chattered as her dress was drawn from her shoulders, and Madame's lips abandoned hers to heat the skin she was baring. Helplessly sagging against the back of her seat, Eloise surrendered to sensations she had never known. Madame's touch was the complete opposite of the nervous grabbing and aggressive intrusion she had experienced while dating in college. With every stroke and bite and kiss her flesh blossomed, and the moist ache at her core became a throb, as though a tiny separate heart beat there.

"Madame," she gasped, as her brassiere was discarded. She felt dizzy and overwhelmed.

Dark, glittering eyes lifted to hers. "You want me to stop?"

"No." She caught a handful of Madame's shirt.

"My name is Sylvia," Madame said, pulling Eloise to her feet. "Let's make the most of what Spartan comfort British Rail affords us."

She tugged at a lever and the narrow couchette folded out to a fully made-up bed. Eloise thought her face was probably scarlet at the sight of the pale sheets and the feel of her dress sliding past her hips as Madame helped her out of it. She felt exposed and self-conscious, excruciatingly aware of her imperfections. The freckles on her chest, her small breasts and thin hips. Madame must have felt her stiffen, for she reached past her to the lamp cord, dimming the lights. Then she took Eloise in her arms.

Tenderly kissing her cheek, she said, "You are enchanting and I want to make love to you."

"I don't know...much," Eloise mumbled. "I mean, I haven't—"

"There's nothing to worry about. You're perfect." Madame drew back the bedding and lowered her onto the cool sheets. "We can stop anytime. Do you understand?"

Eloise stared up at her and had the strangest feeling that she had been waiting all her life for this moment, for this woman. "I don't want to stop."

She watched with dry-mouthed longing as Madame dropped her suspenders and unbuttoned her shirt. When she unfastened her pants, Eloise shamelessly reached out for her, begging, "Hurry. Please."

Laughing, Madame said, "An impatient virgin. How very tempting."

Divested of her clothing a few seconds later, she seemed to Eloise to be the perfect woman, an Aphrodite—high breasts, gentle curves, strong but feminine. Leaning down, her breasts grazing Eloise's, she tucked one finger into the elastic of her bloomers and said, "You won't be needing these."

Once naked, Eloise shyly moved over to make room in the narrow bed, and Madame joined her. For a moment, they lay on their sides, facing one another; then Madame slipped an arm beneath Eloise's shoulders and drew her so close they seemed to glide against each other with every breath.

"Promise me something," she said.

"Anything." Eloise planted a small kiss in the hollow at the base of her throat.

"Afterwards. Later. Always remember this exactly as it truly was."

"What do you mean?"

Madame caressed her cheek. "Don't allow anyone to make it ugly."

"That would be impossible," Eloise said, wallowing in her fragrance and the sensual dialogue of their bodies. She felt Madame sigh.

"You know very little of the world."

Angling her head so she could look into her eyes, Eloise said, "The only world I want to be in is this one. Right here, with you."

"Then kiss me," came the reply.

And in the silken haven of Madame's flesh, Eloise discovered herself.

The next morning, Madame handed her a folded slip of paper and a heavy key. "If you wish to see me again, come to this address a year from now. Let yourself in through the gate in the wall, and wait for me in the garden."

"A year? Why can we not see each other sooner?"

"Because the world is about to change, and we cannot make plans. The best we can do is try to keep a promise."

"I'll come on my birthday," Eloise said, imagining how special and perfect that would make the day. She looked down at the address: Le Chambon-sur-Lignon. Across the top of the card, a name was printed in plain black letters: Lady Sylvia Devon.

"It's a villa I have in the mountains," Madame explained as Eloise confounded herself, trying to accept that she had not only been relieved of her virginity on a floating train by a woman wearing men's clothing, but that the woman was also a British aristocrat. Such thrilling misadventure was the type of thing that could only happen abroad.

"Of course you are welcome to visit any other time," Madame continued, "but I may not be there. I shall see to it that the servants know who you are." A film of tears spiked her lashes and made her eyes even more eloquent in their beauty.

"What's wrong?" Eloise asked.

"I believe I'm afraid. Most unlike me."

"What are you afraid of?"

"Honestly?" Madame seemed momentarily bemused. "That I'll never see you again."

"Oh, but you will. I promise. I'll be there on the first of September next year." Eloise hoped her sincerity showed in her eyes, but she sensed a quiet, inexplicable sorrow in her companion.

They held one another, and Madame placed her lips to Eloise's forehead. "Whatever happens, be careful, my beautiful girl. Go back to America soon."

The last time Eloise saw her, she was striding through a sea of people, across the cavernous, arched hall of the Gard du Nord, followed by a stringy little man dragging her luggage on a cart. She looked back once, blew Eloise a kiss, and walked out of her life.

In the five years that followed, the world indeed changed, and so did Eloise. When the Nazis marched into Paris, Aunt Constance rushed back to Chicago. Eloise was supposed to go with her, but instead she fled to the Auvergne to find Madame's villa. She wrote to her parents telling them not to worry; Germany was not at war with America. Predictably, they sent money. Lots of it. Each time urging her to come home.

In the end, she left her departure too late. Pearl Harbor was bombed, and it was no longer safe to live in the little cottage she'd been renting, so she went to Sylvia's villa on the outskirts of the Le Chambon-sur-Lignon, and Monsieur and Madame Raynaud, the couple who maintained the villa, took her in.

There, in the relative tranquility of the mountains, Eloise put to good use the money she'd saved from her parents, doing what she'd been doing since 1940—forging documents for the Résistance, delivering packages, and escorting rescued British and American pilots from one safe house in the area to another, she and her Allied charge riding their bicycles past groups of German soldiers like any rural couple.

Her Résistance connections gave her the identity papers of a dead girl from Marseille who was killed on a mission, and even now, she carried Bernadette Touchet's documents out of habit.

Paris had been liberated, Allied tanks were rolling through the Auvergne, and it seemed everyone had a special bottle of wine saved for the celebrations. Eloise wanted to get drunk and have food with salt on it, but instead she saw some men drag a collaborator from his home and hang him, and she could not stop crying. She'd pedaled back to the villa as fast as she could that day and had remained there ever since, too numb to think.

Surely Madame had to come now. The war was over, at least in France. If she didn't come, it could only mean one thing, and Eloise would go home. She couldn't stay here forever. The Raynauds had contacted Lord Devon, and he said Her Ladyship had left for a trip to Switzerland one day and had not returned. That was in 1943. He thought she may be dead.

Eloise refused to believe it. She faced her wristwatch to the moon. The hands pointed north. Midnight. With a ragged little sigh, she opened her knapsack and took from it the bottle of Pernod Fils she'd been saving since she first came to the garden in 1940. On each of her birthdays she'd brought it with her and left with it unopened. But not tonight.

She walked through the garden to the mausoleum beyond the apple trees. On a marble slab that confined several of Madame's ancestors, she set down the bottle, two glasses, precious sugar, and a pitcher. Into this she poured some water from the hip flask she always carried.

Draped in the dark sheet of night, her table seemed to belong in a dream and she in a ghost world. She wondered where the girl on the Night Ferry had gone. Sometimes she mourned her, for it seemed Eloise had died, and in her stead, evicting every trace of her softness and naiveté, was Bernadette, who did her thinking in French and did not trust a soul, her own included. She had witnessed too much.

Where could she take refuge within the occupied territory of her mind? Where was peace to be found but in memory? Eloise closed her eyes and conjured the feeling of a narrow bed, a low ceiling, the rock and sway of the boat train, the magic of Madame's hands on her bare skin, the taste of her mouth, the heat of their passion.

With a certainty she'd too long scorned in herself, she whispered, "I met the love of my life, and there will never be another."

Eloise could not explain why she was convinced of that. She supposed some of life's most important events masqueraded as chance and were only later proven to have been destiny. Meeting Madame had changed everything, and the truth was, even if she could go back in time and make different choices, she wouldn't. She regretted nothing. Only the loss of what might have been.

Tears rolled down her face as she placed a single sugar cube on the silver spoon over one glass and two cubes on the other. She lifted the pitcher high and slowly released a shimmering trickle of water into each glass.

"Goodbye, Madame," she said, and felt the air stir behind her as if her words had summoned a ghost.

Shivering at the thought, she looked over her shoulder to the wall of granite and the statues of angels that decorated the mauso-leum. Deep in shadow, still and silent, the angels stared back at her, and for a split second she thought one of them moved.

Laughing at herself for this fancy, she wiped away her tears and loudly declared, "I hope no German soldier is stupid enough to think he can hide from the Americans, here in this garden." On the off chance, she added, "Deutsche? Lassen Sie Ihre Waffe fallen! Kommen Sie hier."

She didn't even bother to reach for the gun she always carried with her. Most of the German soldiers still hiding in the country-side were not trying to return to their units. They simply wanted to surrender to the Americans so they could sit out the rest of the war in a prison camp instead of fighting the Russians.

As she'd expected, there was no answer to her command about dropping weapons. Instead, a soft click made her breath freeze in her chest. A tiny flame pierced the darkness and spread a halo just far enough to illuminate part of a face. A cigar tip glowed as its owner took a puff.

"You had me terrified there for a minute," said a husky voice.

Eloise lurched to her feet. She tried to walk, but her legs were shaking so violently she had to clutch the marble coffin so she would not fall.

"You're here?" she gasped, and Madame stepped out from behind a statue, set her cigar down on the pedestal, and closed the distance between them.

It had to be a dream. But the hands that caught hold of hers were warm, and the body she felt was flesh and blood. The lips that trailed across her face were those she had longed for night and day. Frantically, she slid her fingers into Sylvia's hair and kissed her so hard and so long, they both had to stop and catch their breath. Their faces were wet. Eloise had no idea whose tears were smeared over her cheeks.

"I thought you were dead," she croaked.

"I know." Sylvia cradled her close. "I'm so sorry, my darling girl."

"I can't believe it." Eloise ran a hand over Sylvia's face, allowing her fingertips to verify the planes and hollows imprinted so long ago. The bones were more prominent now, and a thin track of flesh was knotted from her right temple to her jaw. Horrified, she said, "You've been hurt."

"Haven't we all?"

"Where have you been?"

"We'll have plenty of time to talk about that." Sylvia drew back a little and put her arm around Eloise's waist. "I have something to show you."

She walked Eloise to the granite wall, collected her cigar, and moved a small urn at the angel's feet. The door to the mausoleum opened, and they entered the lamp-lit interior. In the center of the room a stairway led down. Eloise stared in astonishment as they followed it through a crypt to a concealed storage bunker packed with supplies, and then along a narrow corridor lined with stretcher beds.

"What is this?" she asked.

"A safe place."

Stunned, Eloise sank down on one of the beds. "You were here all along?"

"No." Sylvia sat down next to her. "I was away almost all the time, collecting the people I brought here."

Hurt consumed Eloise. "Why didn't you tell me?"

"It would have been dangerous for you to know."

"I don't understand. If you were here, why didn't you meet me? I came every year."

"I know. I wanted to. So very badly." Sylvia gazed at Eloise as if devouring her. "At first, I thought if I didn't come, you would go back to America and you'd be safe. I wanted that. Later, I just had to protect you as best I could."

"But I knew what was happening in the village," Eloise protested. "Every time the Vichy patrols came through, I knew all the Jews hid in the forests."

"And many hid down here," Sylvia said, "including the ones we took across the border to Switzerland. I didn't tell you because I couldn't. The Vichy did not suspect me or the Raynauds, but if you'd been caught on any of your Résistance missions—"

"You think I'd have told the Gestapo under torture?"

"Anyone would."

Eloise didn't know whether to be angry or touched, but she understood Sylvia's choices. She lowered her gaze to the hands holding hers and realized several of Sylvia's fingers were missing. Everywhere she looked, there were scars. Along the forearms exposed by her rolled-up khaki sleeves. At the base of her throat. Even her beautiful mouth was slightly twisted in one corner.

"I'm not as I was," Sylvia conceded dryly. A pained uncertainty entered her expression. "If you find me unattractive—"

"Stop." Eloise placed two fingers across her lips. "You could not be more perfect. I fell in love with you the moment I first saw you, and nothing has changed."

"Then I am Fortune's pet." A smile of pure joy lifted Sylvia's face, erasing the pain so evident. "I think I fell in love with you the moment you took that first sip of absinthe. I felt like I had corrupted the most innocent creature alive. From that moment on, all I could think about was completing your education."

Before Eloise could reply, she was in Sylvia's arms, where she needed to be. And Sylvia's kiss told her everything she needed to know. The world had gone mad, and yet there was hope.

Love could survive anything. For them it had.

IN YOUR POCKET

Evan Mora

Every day I love her.

Every day I wake up beside her and know I am where I am meant to be.

She's always asleep when I wake up (definitely *not* a morning person), so I have a chance to see her in this quiet, vulnerable space—to see the dark fan of her lashes against her cheeks, to hear the gentle even fall of her breathing, to see her snuggled into the warmth and softness of the countless blankets she's piled atop us in the night. When she heads out the door in the morning, she's a force to be reckoned with—on top of her game and hard as nails, making the world a better place. But in these moments, she is mine alone, and I am happy.

Every day I love her, but today I fell in love with her again.

With a burst of early spring cleaning energy (hey—it's March, I can dream) I tackled the closets, intent on purging all the out-of-style, wrong size, tattered, and old relics I could find. She's a notorious hoarder, and her end of the closet is filled with an abundance of "nostalgia" that I was determined would grace the Goodwill donation box by end of day. I'd nearly finished—had worked my way to the very end—when I came across her old leather jacket. I mean, *really* old. It had looked beaten and weathered the day I met her, way back when...and now? Now it couldn't even charitably be called vintage. But I had to admit that even I had a soft spot for it, remembering how sexy she'd looked in it standing on my doorstep the night of our first date.

I ran my fingers over the stitching, leaned in close and breathed in the faded smell of leather and her cologne. That's when I noticed that the pockets were full. Intrigued, because she hadn't worn the jacket in ages, I reached in and pulled out what looked like a handful of receipts and ticket stubs and dog-eared scraps of paper. I thumbed through them with dawning wonder and then sat down in the middle of the floor, awash with memories of days gone by.

Here were our boarding passes for our first vacation together, a year or so into our relationship. I chuckled to myself—we'd wanted that trip to be so perfect, and in the end, about the only good thing we could say about it was that it was over. A pampered week in the Caribbean sun had turned out to be an overcrowded, overrated bust. The food was lousy, the snorkeling mediocre at best, and the weather—I'm sure it rained almost every day we were there. There was one day in particular where the clouds rolled in thick and heavy and the rain thundered down for hours on end.

But you know? That was the best day of all. We stayed in our little shoebox room and listened to the rain and lay naked on top of the sheets. The air conditioner was broken, and the fan did little to move the hot humid air around the room, but it was perfect. Lying there with her, it felt as though we were somehow removed from time. Like there was no one else in the world but us, and there was nothing beyond those walls, beyond that bed, beyond her fingertips gently tracing the contours of my body. It was like she was discovering me anew, every curve and hollow, from the back of my knee to the swell of my hips. Can you ever really know all the little nuances of another person?

"Did you have this freckle yesterday?" she asked with a furrowed brow.

I giggled at the utter seriousness of her expression.

"I'm sure I did," I replied.

"And this one over here?"

"Yes, baby, that one too. I'm pretty sure they're all exactly where they were yesterday. And the day before," I deadpanned.

"I'm not so sure...I think I need to take a count," she said, fingers tracing over my ribcage, then grazing the underside of my breast.

"That might take a while," I replied. "Redheads are notoriously freckly, you know."

"I've got my whole life," she said.

She was right.

I reached out and framed her face with my hands, brushed her hair back off her forehead, ran my thumb along the beautiful square line of her jaw and over her sensuous mouth. She kissed the pad of my thumb gently and then reached up to capture my hand in her own. I looked at our fingers laced together, at the warmth and love shining in her dark eyes, and knew without question that this was the best trip I'd ever been on.

I sighed wistfully, remembering the hours we'd spent loving each other that day. How we'd stayed in that bed until the rain stopped and our stomachs rumbled threateningly and drove us out into the soggy Caribbean night in search of food. With our flushed cheeks and tousled hair and shy knowing smiles we must have looked like a couple of crazy kids in love, which, I suppose, we were.

Here was something else—a receipt from the Church St. Diner, faded with age and bearing a date I'd never forget. We'd been seeing each other for a little over a month and were completely caught up in the whirlwind intensity that accompanies all such new things. We'd meet in the evening—almost every evening—for dinner or drinks or coffee, and spend hours talking and touching, telling our stories, and getting lost in the minutiae of one another. We'd debate the profound and the absurd, and then spend quiet hours trembling with the force of the passion that burned between us. But no matter how late the hour or how spent we were, invariably one of us would be shuffling out the door at four or five in the morning heading for home. Looking at it now, I had no idea how we'd lived through that crazy time, subsisting on a couple of hours of sleep each night and generous quantities of coffee.

The thing of it was, despite everything we'd shared, we'd never given voice to the emotion that we both knew was there, shimmering between us. We'd speak in generalities about what a great connection we felt toward each other and about the amazing chemistry that we shared. But of love? Not a word. In the quiet of my heart I knew. But we'd both been burned in the past and had entered into this casually, not looking for anything other than a little lighthearted fun. To admit to love could be wondrous, sure, but it was also to chance hurt and pain.

So there we were, brunching on omelettes and sausages and toast and jam, the early spring sun shining crisply in the windows and a fire in the grate behind us. But the light, though bright, held no warmth, and the fire did nothing to dispel the slight chill that lingered in the air. Our cheerful banter sounded forced, and her smile did little to hide the sadness I could see in her eyes.

"What's wrong?" I asked.

She shrugged and looked down, pushing a bit of sausage absently across her plate. "Just tired, I guess..."

"Come on..." I coaxed.

"Generally speaking? Nothing's wrong..."

"And what if we weren't speaking in generalities? What would you tell me then?" I said, heart beating in my throat.

She paused, looking at me with such a wealth of emotion in her beautiful dark eyes that it made me catch my breath.

"I am so in love with you."

The corner of her mouth rose a little then and I smiled in return, feeling as though she'd just gifted my soul with wings. I opened my mouth to tell her how I loved her—to tell her all the things I'd already told her a hundred times over in my mind—when raucous laughter erupted from a table of boys a few feet away, breaking the spell of the moment. We laughed a little then too, giddy in our discovery and with the relief of having braved those words that had gone unspoken for so long. We finished our coffees and paid the bill, eager to be anywhere alone where we could cradle this nascent love between us.

As we settled into the car, I looked at her strong profile and reached over to gently stroke my fingers through her short dark hair. She looked at me then, and for one brief moment a shadow flickered in her eyes. My heart ached with the magnitude of what I felt for her. I reached over and wrapped her in my embrace.

"You must know how much I love you..." I murmured into her ear, "you must."

I knew that day that what I felt for her was without equal. I knew that the only way for me to live my life was with her by my side. I knew it with a certainty that had no credible explanation but that I trusted implicitly. We hardly knew each other, and I knew that such a declaration would be viewed with skepticism from those who knew us until time proved otherwise. As it has.

I ran my finger across the faded surface of the old receipt and set it aside with a smile, thinking of all the wonderful times we'd shared since that day, of the life we'd built together. I continued to thumb through the pile: here was the card that I'd attached to the first flowers I'd ever sent her—pale yellow orchids—with a message telling her I'd never forget that day in the diner. Here were the directions to a cottage we'd rented one year when the heat and noise of the city had driven us in search of cool waters and northern skies. We'd drifted across the tiny lake in a rudderless paddleboat idly fishing by day, and gone skinny-dipping in the silvery light of the moon at night.

And here—here was card the realtor had left in the gift basket by the front door the day we got the keys to our house. I smiled, remembering our excitement that day. I don't think two people had ever wanted something more than we wanted to be in that house—our home, together. The closing had been five torturously long months. We'd watched spring turn to summer, and summer to fall while we waited. We'd drive by, wistfully wondering what was in bloom in the gardens and making plans for all the things we couldn't wait to do in our perfect, perfect home.

We picked up the keys at six o'clock in the evening and tumbled from room to room with giddy abandon, delighting in tiny forgotten details or remembered favorites. The movers wouldn't arrive until the day after next, but it was unthinkable that we wouldn't spend the night. The previous owners had left us with an old green sofa bed in the basement (we'd later learn their generosity was fueled by the knowledge that there was absolutely no way for it to come out, barring destruction of either said sofa bed or the doorframe—both of which we learned the hard way). So we dragged the worn-out mattress up three flights of stairs until we had it proudly lying in middle of the floor in our bedroom, draped in blankets and a sleeping bag we'd had the foresight to bring.

We sat cross-legged on our makeshift bed, eating Chinese

take-out in cardboard cartons, dreaming fantastic dreams, and toasting our spectacular fortune with a bottle of champagne. As dusk turned to night, she produced a quantity of candles and set them about the floor, so that we were bathed in the warm glow of their light, and our bedroom, though meagerly furnished, seemed the most beautiful place in the world.

She kissed me then, a gentle kiss filled with love and tenderness and the promise of a lifetime of tomorrows. She pressed her forehead against mine and said, "You are the best thing that's ever happened to me."

"Likewise," I smiled, and kissed her in return, my pulse quickening at the warm slide of her tongue against mine, the attraction between us undiminished by the passing of time. I could spend hours like that: kissing her, exploring her mouth, getting lost in the taste of her, the sensuous feel of her tongue rhythmically stroking into my mouth, the heady sensation of her body tight against mine.

We moved together, mouths and limbs entwined, so that I was on my back on the mattress and she was beside me, braced on one elbow, one hard thigh between my own, her free hand caressing my breast, teasing my nipple through the fabric of my shirt.

"I want to see you," she said, her dark eyes glittering like obsidian in the reflected light of the candles. She slid her hand beneath the hem of my shirt, drawing it up over my belly, skimming lightly over my ribcage, and coming to rest against the underside of my breast. I arched my back for her and grasped the edges of my shirt where she'd left it, deftly removing it and tossing it aside.

For a moment, cool air teased my nipples, only to be replaced by the heat of her breath and the warm stroke of her tongue. I moaned my pleasure as she suckled my breast, drawing it into the hot moisture of her mouth. My hands were restless, curling in the hair at the nape of her neck, exploring the expanse of her shoulders and back through the cotton of her T-shirt as she continued to lavish attention on first one, then the other breast. It felt like heaven, having her mouth on me like that; but more, it felt like every stroke of her tongue and nip of her teeth was directly connected to my clit. The more I felt the pull of her mouth on my breast, the more aroused I became, feeling my body open and swell, my hips rising off the mattress to grind sinuously against her thigh.

I bit back a whimper of protest when she moved her leg from between mine, and purred my contentment when I felt her nimble fingers open the front of my jeans and slide inside. She found the hard swell of my clit with practiced ease, circling it with a teasingly light touch, then trailing lower to dip into the wet heat she'd created, coating her fingers with my moisture. She retraced her path then, making my clit a slick hard surface beneath her fingertips. She felt so good like that—with her mouth and hand working me—my mind was reduced to a singular thought:

"More..." I moaned, my hips undulating, frustrated that I couldn't feel her skin against mine, frustrated with the layers of clothes that still separated me from the contact I craved. "I need..."

She kissed me again, but this time her kiss was filled with the heavy sensuality that vibrated between us. Her tongue filled my mouth, stroking deeply and fully against my own, its rhythm wreaking havoc with my senses—reminding me of nothing so much as the rhythm I wanted to feel her hand driving out inside my body.

She drew back slowly, nipping my lower lip and sucking it into her mouth, then healing the tiny hurt with her tongue.

"Tell me what you need," she said.

"I need to feel you—please..."

She slid her hands across my belly, then lower to delve beneath the waistband of my jeans and panties, leaning over to press a tiny kiss in my navel. "Here?" she said.

"Yes—no...more—I need to feel more of you..." I pleaded, trying in vain to capture her face in my hands, to draw her to me, to bring her closer. She evaded my seeking hands, moving lower, sliding my clothes down the length of my legs and off, leaving a trail of kisses along the inside of my thighs, down my calves to the tips of my toes.

"Like this?" she asked, her face a mask of innocence as she continued to torment me.

"What I want," I said, holding her eyes with the heat in my own, "is your tongue in my mouth, my hands in your hair, your teeth on my neck, my fingernails scoring your back. I want your skin against mine, your clit hard and pulsing, your wetness against my thigh, and your fingers inside me."

I saw desire flare, strong and fast in her eyes—heard her swift intake of breath. She rose without a word and quickly removed her clothes, her eyes never leaving mine. I gloried in the sight of her, drinking in her high firm breasts, her tight stomach, her gently curving hips. She sank into my arms with a groan, fusing her mouth to mine in a kiss that embodied deep passion and intense yearning, rising desire, and overflowing love. I reveled in the feel of her breasts against my own, her nipples hard with arousal. I ran my hands down the length of her back and over her hips as our kiss intensified, our legs intertwined, and our bodies rocking together gently.

"Please, baby..." I whispered, breaking the kiss and feathering her cheek with loving kisses, "I need you inside me..."

She shifted her weight, sliding her hand between our bodies and groaning helplessly with desire, her forehead against my chest, as her fingers found my swollen core. She stroked my wetness with an almost reverent awe, looking up to meet my eyes in unspoken question.

"Now...please," I moaned, our eyes locked together as she entered me with agonizing slowness, my back arching off the bed as every nerve ending fired with pleasure, a pleasure that only intensified as she curled her fingers back, hitting me in the place she knew made me tremble. Her thumb found my clit, moving in slow circles in time with her thrusts until a sheen of perspiration covered my skin and my stomach muscles tightened; my heart beat out its rhythm like a trip-hammer in my chest, and I felt that delicious tension coil deep in my belly.

I loved when she was inside me like this—for all the endless ways she loved me; I never felt closer to her than when we moved together like this, her flesh in mine, connected in these moments as closely in body as we were in our hearts and our spirits.

"Come for me, baby..." she whispered, her eyes filled with love and desire. She increased the pressure of her thumb and the speed of her thrusts, rocking me with an irresistible rhythm until I cried out my release and pleasure exploded through my body like a starburst, leaving me spent and trembling in its wake.

It was always like that with her. Overwhelming and all-encompassing and shaking me to my very core. I had never been as deeply connected to anyone as I was to her, and I knew that if I spent the next fifty years loving her, I'd still feel as though it wasn't enough. I loved her then—telling her with my hands and mouth all the things for which I had no words until the candles burned low and the sky grew bright with the approaching dawn. We fell asleep in each other's arms; which really was home no matter where we were.

A car door slammed shut somewhere in the distance, breaking my reverie and bringing me back to the present. I looked at the

wealth of cards and receipts and scraps of paper in my hand—
anniversaries and milestones and memories spanning more than
a decade—appreciating in that moment the richness of the life
we shared and the depth of the love we'd been blessed with.
I thumbed through them quietly, each carrying a memory of
happiness, of some remembered moment she'd preserved.

At the bottom of the pile, on a page torn from her
day planner, was the address of my old place, scribbled next to
my name and phone number. It was dated the day of our first
date. I was so nervous that night; I felt such an attraction to her
and such a connection with her, and I wanted so much for her to
feel the same. I worried over my clothes, my hair, chiding myself
for being so girly, and looking at the clock every other minute.
And then she was there, standing on my doorstep in her faded
leather jacket, with a slow seductive smile and looking too sexy
for words.

"Hi..." she said.

She took my breath away.

I heard the door open downstairs and looked at the bedside
clock, amazed at how the hours had passed as I'd sat there on
the floor immersed in memories of our past. I heard her footsteps on the stairs and quickly grabbed a pen from the night
table, adding today's date to the page from her day planner, and
my own words below her distinctive scrawl. I tucked everything
back in her jacket, and carefully replaced it in the closet, stroking
the soft leather fondly, and thinking with a smile of the surprise
she'd experience the next time she leafed through her pockets.

*You had me in your pocket right then and there—I've been
there ever since.*

PURPLE THUMB

Catherine Lundoff

Lisa looked around at the riot of flowers that cascaded over the fences and up the trellis that leaned against the house wall. From there, they flowed in little rivers around the yard. Nearly ripe vegetables grew in neat rows and cages, their tidy order in sharp contrast to the flowers. To add to the whole idyllic picture, the early evening summer air was scented and a few bees still ambled from flower to flower.

She snorted and took another gulp of her beer. How much time did it take to do all this anyway? Sure it was pretty, but what was the point? Even if her condo had a yard, she couldn't imagine wasting her sparse free time doing something like this.

The smell of barbecue wafted its way to her nose, and she turned away from the garden and headed back to the patio to join the crowd of women around the grill. She caught an appreciative glance or two headed her way and gave the assembled group her best flirtatious smile. "Lovely flowers," she trilled, hoping her tone would pass for sincerity.

"Yeah, Marlene does a great job with her yard. Quite the green thumb," a tall brunette drawled. Her dark eyes gave Lisa the once-over and her grin broadened a little. The woman at her side followed her look and stiffened.

Lisa spotted her expression and grimaced. *Dyke drama.* Well, she should have expected it; all three lesbian groups in this town seemed to be much the same. This was what she got for moving from a real city to the Midwest. She thought about Mia back in New York and sighed. It was her own fault: she'd walked away from the perfect woman for the perfect job, and now the perfect woman had found someone else.

That was the moment Marlene swept out of the house, a couple of overflowing bowls in her large hands. Several other women trailed after her carrying utensils and plates and even more food. Lisa looked at it all and wondered what the carb count was on a gallon of potato salad. Not to mention barbecue with corn and all the fixings. She'd better plan on racquetball three times this week instead of two if she ate more than a mouthful.

That thought died away when she joined the line for food and met Marlene's eyes. They were a deep brown, so dark she felt like she was falling into them. She pulled herself back out somehow and gave their hostess the first real smile she'd given anyone since she'd shown up. Marlene grinned back. "Having fun, Lisa? I'm so glad you were able to join us today."

"Definitely. And I love your garden! So many gorgeous flowers!" Lisa gushed, almost meaning it. There was something about this woman that made her wish she loved flowers and gardening and...Lisa forced her imagination a step back. Granted, Marlene was striking, though a tad more ripe than what Lisa usually went for: rounded curves, beautiful eyes, hair that cried out to have Lisa's hands in it—silver streak and all. But that didn't mean she had to get stupid over an almost complete stranger.

Marlene's expression turned sad as she looked around. "By the time I get back to it, most of it will have died off. Gotta enjoy it while it lasts."

Lisa nodded sympathetically. "Work tends to take over."

Marlene's full lips quirked upward in something that wasn't quite a smile. "I wish it was work. Unfortunately, there will be other obstacles to my gardening for a while. But don't let me keep you from enjoying the gathering. We can chat later."

Lisa let the line carry her forward while she tried to figure out what Marlene was talking about. She found herself at a picnic table with the woman who'd been checking her out earlier and her girlfriend. Biting back a groan, she held out her hand to the girlfriend. "Hi, I don't think we've met yet. I'm Lisa. I just moved here a couple of months ago."

The other woman hesitated a second and then took her hand. She immediately launched into a barrage of questions, calculated, Lisa guessed, to keep her from talking much to her partner. Finally, she got them both talking about things to do around town, and the tension eased.

During a lull in the conversation, Lisa spotted Marlene standing by herself on the other side of the patio. Her expression was tired and wistful, and something in it made Lisa get up and walk over to her. "Are you okay?"

"Just feeling a little off. I think a lot of it is having to leave this at the best time for gardening." Marlene's gesture took in the beds.

"Are you going out of town or something?" Lisa ventured. Personal questions were always tricky in this part of the world.

Marlene glanced back at her. "That's right, you don't know. I've got cancer. They're sure they caught it in time, which is great. But it'll be a couple of months of recovery time between the operation and everything else. I won't be able to do much with this place for awhile. Probably get back to it just in time to pack it in for winter."

Lisa cringed before she realized she was doing it. Good thing she'd found out before she decided this woman was attractive enough to pursue. Then she felt a flicker of disgust at her own reaction. It was clear that Marlene had seen what she was thinking from the set of her shoulders and the way she looked away. Lisa realized her cheeks were growing hot at her own rudeness.

For a few desperate seconds, she hunted for something polite to say and failed. Instead, she settled for trying to see the yard with a gardener's eyes. She couldn't manage it until she compared it to her own work. It would be nearly impossible to walk away from any project she'd put this much work into. And it was kind of pretty. As the thought struck home, the next words out of her mouth surprised even her. "When are you going in? Is there anything you need?"

Marlene gave her a long, considered look, and for just an instant, Lisa felt butterflies in her stomach. It was as if the other woman was measuring her, seeing whether she was worth trusting. "It's wonderful of you to offer," she said at last, "but my mom and my ex and her partner are all coming into town to help out when I go in next Thursday. I think I'll be okay." She patted Lisa's arm as if to take the sting from her words.

Guess I didn't pass the test. The realization bothered her more than it seemed like it should have. It wasn't like she was up for playing nursemaid anyway. A card and some flowers would be just fine, enough to show friendly concern but not too much interest.

A group of women converged on them then, all talking at once, and the connection, whatever it was, was broken. Lisa hung around a bit longer and helped clear the tables and wash up. It wasn't something she normally did at these things, but this time it seemed necessary, important even.

By the time she left, she'd been invited to two movie nights and an investment club meeting. She'd even given Marlene her phone number and told her to call if she needed anything. She knew it wasn't too likely, but it was the thing to do, and she was determined to accomplish that much.

Then she went home and thought about Marlene until she had to call her friends back home for a sanity check. She had a mild crush on a sick gardener, for God's sake! Someone who did some kind of warm, fuzzy social service type job on top of that. She went for driven Type A corporate types like herself, always had. Anything else led to whiny fights about how she was never home, never had time. Someone from outside that environment never got it. She decided some overtime and a few hours of working out would soon put this Marlene thing, whatever it was, out of her head.

And it might have, if that had been the last she'd seen of the other woman for a few months. But a few days later, her boss stopped by her desk looking worn and frazzled. "Lisa, I know this is last minute, but my kids and my wife all came down with the flu at the same time, and I've got to get home. Is there any chance you'd be willing to fill in for me at the Well of Hope benefit tonight?"

Lisa's eyebrows twitched upward despite her efforts to control them. The Well of Hope was the biggest benefit of the year for most of the city's nonprofits, and her corporation was one of the sponsors. Getting selected to represent them was a big deal even if it was a completely black-tie event and she was wearing work drag. She looked down in horror at her inadequate navy suit and white blouse.

"And of course you can take off now to go get ready. I know how inconvenient this will be."

It was as if he could read her mind. Lisa grinned up at him and nodded, "I'd be happy to, Frank. I'll finish this up tomorrow and go wrestle my wardrobe into submission now. Hope the family feels better soon." A few moments of enthusiastic thanks and instructions, and the big glossy invitation was all hers. She practically skipped out the door on her way to her favorite high-end department store.

By the time she had finished acquiring a new dress and shoes and having her makeup done, it felt like her credit card was smoking around the edges. *But it'll be worth it,* she told herself fiercely. If nothing else, it would get her noticed, and it couldn't hurt to have Frank owe her a favor. Still, she couldn't help thinking that it would have been nice to have a date to go with her. Mia would have been perfect, she thought with a sharp pang of regret. Or Marlene.

She forced the image from her mind. Besides, out here in the hinterlands, who knew how anyone would react if she showed up with a woman on her arm? Better to go stag and be all mysterious about it. She smiled at her compact mirror before she started up her car and headed over to the benefit.

As it turned out, the Well of Hope was held in the former Masonic temple just outside downtown. Lisa handed her keys to the valet, straightened her wrap, and headed up the acres of white steps, an elaborately hewn marble sphinx on either side. When she finally got to the top, she found herself panting a little and stopped to admire the view.

That was when she heard someone calling her name. Marlene stepped out of the lobby doors and walked toward her with a welcoming smile. The butterflies reappeared in Lisa's stomach and did a slow tango, despite anything she could do to stop them. She kept the nerves from her voice, though, or at least she hoped she did. "Hi! What are you doing here? I'm a last minute sub for my boss, here representing Rapid Tech." *Sure, you don't sound nervous at all*, she mocked herself.

Marlene looked amused, as if women always got gushy around her. Still, her eyes were warm, and she seemed pleased to see Lisa, at least as far as she could tell. "And I'm here representing WomenServe. I don't know if you know about us yet, but we're one of the largest local nonprofits working with women to provide job training, transitional housing, and other assistance. Your company is one of our biggest donors."

"Wow! That's terrific!" Lisa nearly slapped her palm to her forehead. At this rate, she'd be lapsing into LOLspeak. *I can haz hot nonprofit babe? Get a grip!* "And what do you do there?"

They were moving inside now. "I'm the acting exec, at least for another couple of weeks. Then I step down and the new director will take over." Marlene's face went very still, as if this was a speech she had practiced in order to get through it.

Lisa reached out without thinking and squeezed Marlene's arm lightly. It was a gesture that a friend would make, but even so it sent a shiver through her. And perhaps the other woman as well. Marlene met her eyes and her lips parted. For a moment, it felt like they were the only two people in the huge lobby.

At least until the reminder came in the form of a lithe and tigerish dark-haired woman who walked up and claimed Marlene's free arm like she had the right to it. "Hello," teeth flashed in Lisa's general direction. "We'll need to go sit up front, Marlene. You ready?" Her tone suggested that it was more of a command than a request.

Lisa yanked her hand away as if she'd been burned, but the feeling of Marlene's skin beneath her fingers, the look in her eyes when they touched, lingered as she followed them into the hall. Marlene paused to let her catch up, deliberately slowing her impatient companion down. "This is Ana Martinez, the new executive director of WomenServe," She inclined her head slightly at the dark-haired woman. "And this," her smile growing warmer, "is Lisa Allen from Rapid Tech."

Lisa watched herself go from rival to donor in Ana's mind in the blink of an eye. "Oh, I'm delighted to meet you! Is this your first time at the Well of Hope?" She soon found herself sitting next to them in the front row, making small talk with Ana while she wished she was talking to Marlene.

She soon got her wish as more people began filling the seats and Ana left to go meet and greet. Marlene slid over. "I'm glad that part of the job is almost over with anyway. Always liked the hands-on stuff better than dealing with the donors."

Lisa raised an eyebrow and gave her a quizzical look. "Including present company?"

Marlene laughed. "Oh, you're a...friend, not like someone I have to hit up constantly to make the yearly budget."

"Well, that's a relief," Lisa exhaled sharply with a wry smile.

Marlene smiled back. "And how are you enjoying life in the country?"

"Is it that obvious?" Lisa made a face. "The Rapid Tech job was so great, I had to take it. It would have taken years longer for me to move up out East. But yeah, it is kind of a culture shock. I understand the State Fair is a big thing here?"

"Boy howdy, that it is. We like a good livestock and crafts show out here," Marlene's voice took on the local rural accent, and Lisa giggled despite herself. Marlene smiled and added in her normal voice, "Tell you what. Come the week before Labor Day, we'll go check out the Fair. I go every year to see the gardening exhibits. And the seed art. It's a lot more fun than it sounds."

Lisa took a minute to run through a quick list of excuses in her head before she responded. Then she met Marlene's eyes, and the words that she'd been about to say magically transformed themselves. "Sure, that sounds like fun. Food on a stick, you betcha."

After that, they had time to exchange quick smiles before the speeches started. By then, Marlene completely filled Lisa's thoughts. At the tail end of the first speaker's talk, she couldn't help leaning over and whispering, "Do you want to get a drink or coffee after this?"

Marlene gave her a sidelong glance and a half smile. "I'd like to take a raincheck on that. Unfortunately, I'm likely to be wiped out by the time this is done."

Lisa found herself blushing for the first time in years. Of course Marlene wasn't going to be up for drinks after an exhausting evening. "I think I'd definitely like to try and reschedule," she mumbled at last. "Whenever you're up for it," she made herself add.

That, of course, was the moment when Marlene got called to the stage to accept one award and give out another. Lisa watched her, saw the way she glanced around the room, poised and elegant before the large crowd. This was a woman she'd like to have at her side at these events, she realized. Then as she listened to Marlene speak about what WomenServe had accomplished in the last year, she considered that perhaps warm fuzzy jobs were harder than they seemed. Maybe it was the same with gardening.

The awards ended shortly after that. She didn't have another opportunity to talk to Marlene alone that evening, though they often found themselves in the same groups. Once Marlene laughed at one of Lisa's jokes, the lines of strain erased for the moment from her face. Lisa thought she'd like to be able to do that more often. The notion surprised her, almost more than anything else that had happened that evening.

But not quite as much as the next morning when she found herself at the local florist's, buying a houseplant. If someone had asked, she couldn't have said why she did it. Generally speaking, she wasn't a plant and flowers or even pet person. Forget children. All of the above took too much work, took too much time away from what was really important: work.

Still, the plant looked pretty in her condo window, and she followed all the directions so she thought it could survive at least a couple of months in her care. Maybe longer since it seemed to be something that would flower every year. It made her think of Marlene and her garden. But then so did just about everything else right now. She found herself circling the date Marlene was checking into the hospital on her backup desk calendar. "Send flowers and a card," the note said. She wondered if going to visit would be too much.

She pictured Marlene without hair, even though she hadn't said anything about chemo. That was almost a deal breaker, enough to make her walk away from whatever it was between them. But she remembered watching Marlene laugh at the benefit. Surely it wouldn't kill her to make herself useful somehow. Women went into remission from cancer all the time. Why not Marlene?

Wednesday rolled around, and she remembered to pull Marlene's number off the brunch list and call to leave a message. Truthfully, she hadn't thought about much of anything else when she wasn't busy at work. How should she sound? Clingy was bad. So was assuming that Marlene felt the same thing that Lisa felt. Finally she settled on the slightly generic: "Hi. This is Lisa. I just wanted to call and let you know I'm hoping things go really well tomorrow."

Then she ordered flowers and a card from an organic flower company that she found online. Marlene would appreciate that touch when they showed up in her room, or so she hoped.

After that, Lisa found herself searching the Web for gardening information and tips, casually at first and then with the kind of dedication she usually reserved for work projects. At first, she couldn't have said why she did it. It wasn't like she was planning on acquiring a new hobby or something. But she remembered the look on Marlene's face when she looked around the garden, and it made her ache a little.

By Saturday, she violated every dating rule she had by driving past Marlene's house. It didn't look like anyone was home, no cars in the driveway or lights on inside. She debated just going up and knocking but couldn't bring herself to do it. Instead, she went home and called the brunch coordinator to see if she'd heard anything yet.

That got her a second invite to movie night and the information that Marlene was doing reasonably well, at least according to her mother. Lisa declined movie night but ended up going after all. Sunday disappeared in a wave of overtime until the next Wednesday evening rolled around and she found herself driving past Marlene's place again.

Even to her uneducated eye, the yard didn't look too happy. She pulled up outside and went and rang the doorbell. No answer. She scanned the yard. Several drooping flowerbeds stared back at her reproachfully. Well, she could turn on a hose and splash some water around; it wasn't rocket science.

Lisa went around to the side of the house looking for the hose and the faucet. What she found was an intricate and complicated system of hoses and sprinkler heads that left her baffled. Eventually, though, with a certain amount of quiet swearing, she figured out how to turn it on. The nearest head then splashed water all over her suit, and she got one heel stuck in the resulting mud before she got out of range.

Still, once she stopped being irritated about that part of it, she noticed that the garden smelled nice as it got wet. She stood watching the sprinklers for a few moments, oblivious to the fact that she'd acquired an audience. Instead, she slipped off her heels and picked them up before she walked down the path to see if the whole garden was getting watered. There was something peaceful about it, even with the gravel digging into her feet. *And what was another pair of stockings, more or less?*

She turned back to the house and gave a guilty start. Marlene was sitting out on the deck watching her with a bemused smile. "You still have hair," Lisa blurted out. "I'm sorry! I didn't realize you'd be back already and everything looked so dry, I thought..."

Marlene patted the chair next to hers. Lisa trotted obediently up the steps and sat down. For a long few moments, neither of them spoke. "I didn't think gardening was your speed," Marlene's voice was a bit hoarse.

Lisa gave her a sidelong smile. "The muddy heels and the wet skirt give you that impression? I've got to work on my look. So are you contemplating getting a restraining order yet?"

"To complain because you're trying to water my garden? Seems a bit harsh." Marlene smiled. "I'm kind of surprised, though. I could see how uncomfortable you got when I talked about being sick."

Lisa could feel her ears turn pink. "It does. I don't really like to think about illness or dying. Or gardening, for that matter." She looked directly at Marlene. "But I bought a houseplant after the reception. Not like that means much, I suppose."

Marlene laughed. "You're trainable?" She caught Lisa's frown a second later. "I'm sorry, I'm sorry. My filters aren't all back in place yet. I didn't mean that to sound the way it came out."

Lisa stood. "You should probably get some rest. Do you want me to turn off the water before I go?"

Marlene tilted her head back against the chair and gave her one of those looks that told Lisa she was being measured again. "Will you come back and try it again later on this week?"

Lisa gave her a considering look in return. "I'm not sure I'm that 'trainable,' but I could probably be persuaded to bring over a movie or something. For while the garden is being watered." She felt like she had at the benefit. Everything slowed down and focused until the only thing she wanted to hear was the next thing that Marlene might say. The realization panicked her but she rode it out, wrestling the unfamiliar feelings to keep Marlene from guessing what she was thinking.

"I think I'd like that," Marlene said at last. "And thanks. I'm glad I was wrong about how upset you were." She gave Lisa a warm, sensual, and tired smile.

Lisa barely had to grapple with her nerves. "Me, too. See you Friday?" Marlene nodded, and Lisa slipped her shoes on before venturing down the path to turn the water off. The garden had begun to look lush once more, and for the first time, Lisa felt like maybe the Midwest wasn't so bad after all—gardeners, State Fair, and all. She thought about picking up another plant on the way home.

A GHOST
OF A CHANCE

Ariel Graham

Marcy didn't like the basement. Every time she went down there she got another word for it, and every time she got another word for it Samantha argued with her. According to Samantha, the basement of the Victorian they had leased to turn into a party planning, catering, and cake business was not dank, dark, dismal, depressing, damp, damned, or disturbing. It was not unpleasant, unnecessary, or unnerving. It was not repellent or repugnant. But Sam kept laughing at the descriptions so Marcy kept bringing them to her, right up until she said, "Haunted."

Samantha stood at the big, deep double sink that looked out over a backyard gone to hell but in full riotous bloom. It looked like an English country garden, full of wisteria and towering lilac bushes, roses and more roses, and a bunch of tired, twisted, ancient apple trees. Samantha turned her back on the trees where a variety of blackbirds and grackles were eating windfall summer apples. She crossed her ankles and her arms and leaned her hips against the sink. "The basement is not haunted," she said.

Marcy fell out of the game. She ran both hands through her short, spiky dark hair, liberally coating it with grime. "Then you call it," she said, and watched Sam's face turn from anticipation to frowning concern.

"What happened?"

Marcy fumbled for one of the steel and Naugahyde '50s diner-style chairs. "There's something down there. I know I've been kidding about it, but it's not funny anymore. Something—"

Sam waited patiently. She could. Marcy couldn't. They'd been friends forever. Always Sam had patience and Marcy wanted to jump into things. Marcy speculated and Sam researched. Marcy jumped to conclusions, Sam withheld judgment.

It made Marcy a little nuts.

"There's a different feeling in the basement. Something— cold. It's colder down there—" She paused so Sam could say the obvious and appreciated the warm southern sunlight in the apple trees and coming through the filthy window to light Sam's blond curls.

"Basements are colder than upstairs, but you know that," Sam said. "That's not what you meant." But she made it a question so Marcy could keep going.

"It's like it's colder than it should be. And wet. Reno's a desert. We don't get wet. Sweating walls. When I'm down there, I want to be anywhere else. If I stay down there, I get panicky."

"Claustrophobia?" Samantha asked, and turned so she could run a brush along the edge of the sink and tile she'd already made spotless. Really the window was next. Neither of them wanted to do it.

"I don't have it anywhere else," Marcy said.

Sam stopped messing with the sink and moved to the table.

She was thin, graceful, a Michelle Pfeiffer face and a Courtney Cox body. Marcy was all boy muscle, like Starbuck on *Battlestar Galactica*, all shoulders and biceps.

Samantha settled across the table from her friend. "Did something happen?"

Warmth flooded Marcy. It was a relief, really, to be asked. Even if somehow she wanted to pack the experience away and never think of it again. "Something touched me." She said it before she could stop herself. Marcy always stopped herself, rarely coming out at the right time with the right statement, not saying to her father in time, "I wish you loved me," or to her old boss, "But I was trying to help the company" (rather than "But that was the stupid way to do it," which at least had freed her up to pursue her dreams with Samantha). And certainly she'd never said to Sam, "I wish you liked girls."

Sam leaned forward a little. "I don't like that," she said, which wasn't at all what Marcy had expected. She'd expected, "What do you mean?" or "Touched you where?" or "What have you been smoking?" Not "I don't like that."

So Marcy blinked and waited for Samantha to say something she could respond to. But Samantha didn't say anything right away, just drummed her fingers on the table and sat sideways in her chair, staring out the great back window of the fantastic and just possibly haunted Victorian they'd leased where all their dreams were supposed to start coming true if they just both worked very, very hard.

The clock over the old-fashioned, rounded-edge Edsel of a refrigerator ticked loudly and filled the seconds between ticks with an electric buzz. Outside a car went by with the stereo jacked, and a bee buzzed near the back screen door. Marcy found herself staring at Sam's long tan legs where they stuck out from under her low-rise shorts and made herself stop. The silence in the old kitchen was midsummer sleepy. Marcy jolted when Samantha abruptly smacked the table with the flat of her hand.

"Let's find out."

That made so little sense Marcy said, "Let's find out what?"

"What's down there," Sam said. She rose in one fluid motion and paced across the kitchen and back. "We've only got a few days till we open. Flowers coming in, cakes to make, and that idiotic judge's retirement party to cater tomorrow night."

Marcy grinned. "Is the judge or the retirement party idiotic?"

"Take your pick. Either way, let's find out what if anything is in the basement. Where did it touch you?"

Marcy blushed instantly. She'd anticipated the question, she just didn't want to answer it. "Something—brushed me between the legs." Actually it was a long slow caress that had both scared her half to death and made her heart pound pleasantly.

Samantha raised her eyebrows. "So it's friendly," she said, and Marcy laughed without meaning to. "Look, let's come back here tonight—I don't have anything planned, do you?"

Never, Marcy thought, and the thought irritated her. She could date if she wanted to. Anything was better than the unrequited desire for her best friend. "Just a date with a dancing studly— dashing, I mean," and she meant to go on, but Samantha said, "Never trust the dashing sort, they're always in too much of a hurry. I don't have any plans either. Midnight?"

"Isn't 3 a.m. the 'real' witching hour?"

Samantha gave her a look. "You're watching too much *Most Haunted Places* or something. Besides, I'd like to be home and in bed by 3 a.m. if flowers are going to be delivered by eight."

"That's awfully rational of you," Marcy said.

"What do you have against rational?"

"Takes all the spooky fun away."

Samantha pursed her lips. "I promise you spooky. You bring the candles. I'll bring the Ouija board. See you at midnight." And she was gone.

Marcy thought maybe there were other things they'd meant to get done around the shop, but now she couldn't think of them. This was almost like a date. Close as she'd come in months. She wanted to go home, shower, change, eat something. Anticipate midnight. The bee had flown through the back door when Samantha exited. It buzzed desultorily around the cut daisies in the sink.

"Enjoy," Marcy told the bee, and shut and locked the back door behind her.

Midnight creaked through the old Victorian, a series of floorboards sending up protests that sounded like feet running across an upstairs floor. Marcy shivered and wished to hell she hadn't arrived first. Though when did Samantha *ever* get anywhere on time?

She crossed the foyer, and instantly caught the white palazzo pants on a high table standing against the wall, setting it rocking and setting her heart pounding.

"Stop it. You're being silly."

Silly was wearing white to go into the basement, but it *was* almost like having a date. She could be excused. Marcy detached herself from the table and crossed the foyer, heading toward the kitchen—and screamed, hard, loud, and pissed when the basement door shot open.

"Hey," Sam said.

"Where the hell's your car?"

"Didn't mean to scare you."

"Right," Marcy said. "I had no idea you were here."

"I parked out back, like always."

"It's midnight. I figured we could park on the street."

Sam just grinned. "You brought the candles?"

Marcy held out the plastic grocery bag in her hands.

"Then let's go."

Marcy didn't like the basement any better just because Samantha was with her. The florescent lights hummed and seemed to come on at half the light they should have had. And while upstairs wasn't breathtakingly hot, the basement still seemed colder to her than it should have just because it was downstairs.

"Did you really bring a Ouija board?" she asked, and had to force herself not to whisper.

"Yes, I did," she said, turning to display the backpack she wore. It was lumpy, stuffed with things. "If there's something here, don't you want to know what it is and what it wants?"

"Jury's still out," Marcy said, which made Sam laugh again. She hadn't meant to be funny.

The basement seriously bothered her.

One of the selling points—or at least leasing points—with the house had been not only the zoning that allowed residential or commercial or both, should either or both of them choose to live upstairs over their shop, but the full basement. But it wasn't a straight shot, nothing but space; rather, the basement was a cata-comb worthy of 1800s New York or even ancient Rome, Marcy thought. Concrete, appropriately crumbling, supported the upper structure. The staircase from upstairs led down into almost an underground foyer. A tiny concrete room ringed, for no reason, with foot-high concrete that had to be stepped over both entering and exiting the other side, and that would have been a pain in the ass for storing flowers downstairs if there wasn't an entrance from the outside across the basement that didn't have the concrete lip.

There were windows, set high in the walls, thin slats like underground battlements in a topsy-turvy castle. They just weren't much help in lighting the space, particularly at midnight.

From the foyer there were rooms on either side and a straight shot through a narrow passage to the larger entry by the street from outside.

What Marcy particularly didn't like was the small room beneath the inside stairs, a cranny that shouldn't have existed but did. It had been designated the file room, and was where Marcy had been earlier when something had touched her.

"Come on," Samantha said, and headed away from the stairs. The flickering purple fluorescents made her waver and threaten to vanish, and Marcy suddenly wished they'd brought flashlights as well as candles, just in case the power went out. Because the power seemed likely to go out, just to be mean.

You wanted spooky, she reminded herself, but spooky had sounded better in broad daylight.

Samantha led them unerringly to the small, dusty file room under the stairs. Either Marcy had told her that's where she'd been or Samantha just had a good sense of these things. *Or* it seemed the most logical place for spooky, an idea Marcy didn't like. *Or* Samantha had felt something herself in there, another idea Marcy didn't like. *Or* Sam just knew Marcy was afraid of the file room and had determined the best way to break her of it.

"Are you coming?" Samantha asked from the room under the stairs.

"Unwillingly."

Sam laughed. By the time Marcy got herself there she'd spread towels from her backpack on the floor and seemed to be setting up shop. Things kept appearing out of the pack—the Ouija board, the planchette, a flashlight Marcy was very glad to see, a book of notes on Ouija boards, a knife for no good reason

Marcy could think of (would ghosts *care* if they were threatened?), a handful of roses from the bushes out back, a bottle of water, and a dish that turned out to be for the roses to float on.

"How long are we staying?" Marcy asked.

"Not too long. I forgot food."

Which made Marcy finally laugh and crouch to begin divesting herself of the fat pillar candles she carried, and the matches and the lighter and a couple more towels.

She set the candles around them and between them, near the Ouija board that lay between, and lit them so shadows began to dance off the walls. She wanted badly to say "Now what?"—or to just plain run—and wanted equally badly to look like she had a clue what she was doing.

Which was silly, because she didn't, and she didn't think Samantha did either.

"Now what?" Marcy asked.

"Turn off the lights, I think," Samantha said, and the lights failed agreeably.

Marcy blinked several times until she could see Samantha in the dim room. "What did that?"

Sam shrugged. "They've been trying to go out since we got here. Just good timing."

Marcy looked over her shoulder. The door was behind her, another behind Sam. The doors made her nervous. Anyone could suddenly appear behind either one of them. This had been a very bad idea.

"Now what?" Marcy asked again.

"Now we wait," Sam said quietly. She settled across from where Marcy crouched, still wearing those insanely short shorts, and slid effortlessly into lotus position, her legs pretzeled, her hands relaxed on her knees. She smiled across the small room at Marcy, encouraging, and Marcy slid down until she was sitting cross-legged, as close to lotus as her knees were ever going to get. For that matter, as close as she was going to get to Sam's relaxed.

She waited for Sam to close her eyes, but Sam just smiled, her eyes on Marcy's face, almost a caress. Sam seemed relaxed and at ease, her breath soft and regular, and Marcy found she was beginning to relax in the honeyed candlelight. Her shoulders dropped and she eased her neck around in a circle, listening to vertebrae pop and protest. Her hands felt loose, muscles relaxed. Under the flowing white pants, her body betrayed her. Watching Samantha, relaxed and beautiful, her blue eyes in soft focus, lips parted, Marcy felt the longing rise up in her. Her mouth ached and filled with saliva, a sort of hunger, a need to feed or touch or taste. Her pulse sped up, and a second heartbeat started low in her stomach, resonated between her legs where she grew wet, wetter than she usually felt when Samantha was nearby, within touching distance, and they were alone.

Candlelight etched monstrous shapes on the walls around them, but she stopped jolting as flickers made something seem to appear in the doorway behind Sam. Instead she watched the flames flicker over her friend's face, lighting and leaving it in shadow. Samantha's eyes grew heavy lidded. Her breathing deepened, and her lips parted further. Marcy imagined the taste of those lips, the soft, sweet feel of them against her own. She sighed without meaning to, let her body spill a little looser.

Something moved upstairs, sharp sounds like footsteps. Marcy went all hard and tense; her head snapped around to check the door way behind her.

"It's just the house, settling," Sam whispered, and her voice was close, close to Marcy's neck. She started to turn, and something brushed through the room.

The smallest of breezes, as if someone moved past them.

The candles blew out.

In the dark, Marcy fumbled for where Sam had last been. Her fingers brushed flesh, the soft swell of breasts, and she jerked her hand away, said sharply, "Sorry! I—"

Interrupted by a soft laugh. "Stupid. Touch me."

Touch me.

What?

"What?"

In answer, Samantha took Marcy's hand. She didn't fumble or scramble for it. As if she could see in the dark, she took Marcy's hand and pressed it against her breast.

When she could breathe again, Marcy moved her fingers gently, slowly. Her hand slipped down the slope of Samantha's breast until her fingertips stroked the nipple, hard and pebbled under her touch. She heard Samantha sigh, and reached out so both hands caressed and played, finding Sam's hard nipples, her hands going flat over the breasts, pressing hard, pinching down to points, pressing firm against Sam.

Hands came up in the darkness, and cupped Marcy's face. Thumbs rubbed her cheekbones, flicked over her closed eyes. The hands worked down her cheeks, thumbs playing along her mouth, touching her lips, tracing them. Marcy licked out, caught one finger and sucked it into her mouth. She heard a quick sigh before she moved, kissing the palm of the hand, kissing down wrist and forearm, lingering in smells and textures. Hands on her face again drew her forward. Lips touched hers and she fell into sensation, soft lips, sticky, tangy lip gloss, a musty smell, something like a coat taken from storage just before winter.

The lips led her down, and Marcy followed until she felt the spill of woman beneath her, rounded breasts and belly and hips. Legs wrapped around her and pulled her close.

"Sam?"

"Don't stop," Sam's voice said, somewhere near. Somewhere distant.

Sam.

Marcy traced a trail down Samantha's neck, from earlobe to jawline to throat hollow.

The candles had blown out. She hadn't realized. They'd been in the dark for a while. There was the flashlight, but nothing else if they wanted light.

From upstairs Marcy heard the same sound of footsteps, first moving quickly, then running. She jerked in surprise and Samantha said again, "Don't stop."

Kissing down the line of her throat, longer than Marcy had thought all those times she'd imagined kissing just there, behind the ear, or just there, in that hollow between the collarbones. She kissed down the throat, along the hollow, her tongue sliding along dusty-tasting collarbones. Movement, shifting. The hands that had pressed against her, pulling, pushing, stroking, now moved away. There was a scrape, a dry sound of flesh and stone, and Sam said, "Shit," as if she'd scraped an elbow in the dark, and then, "Here, come here," and she pressed Marcy against her. Hands on shoulders, mouths together, and Samantha's naked breasts pressed against Marcy's chest. She ran her hands over Sam's back, tipped her back onto the towels, ran her tongue down, too impatient to play or tease. She just wanted to taste flesh, to suck Sam's breasts into her mouth. Sam gasped, and leaned into her hard, fingers tangling in Marcy's hair, and an odd, random thought floated through Marcy's mind: *It's her, of course. Isn't it?*

And Sam pulled her down, Marcy's mouth still on one breast, sucking, sliding, her hands working down Sam's body to find Sam herself fumbling to get her shorts off and Marcy was still dressed—*worry about that later*. The shorts were hardly a barrier, but they were a pain. Between the two of them they tore them free, and Marcy slid her hands between her best friend's legs and found her soaked and waiting.

Kissing down her flat muscled stomach in a tease that left them both writhing, Marcy wanted to wait now, she wanted to tease, payback for all those years she'd watched Sam from a distance, never knowing what she could have had—and then again, she didn't want to wait, ever again.

Beneath her Sam's hips rose, pressing against her. She kept saying something, "Please" maybe, and Marcy silenced her with one hand over her mouth as she dropped her head and began to lap the inner curl of Samantha's hips, the delicate sheltered concave curl of hip and stomach. Her other hand went down again. Her thumb found Sam's clit hard and full, and she pressed it once, just to feel her friend rise up under her, head thrown back, back arched. Then she slid two fingers inside and began to stroke, thumb brushing clit, fingers seeking inner nerves, tongue ever so slowly winding down along that sweet semi-circle of hip bone. She kissed along the ridge of pelvic bone.

"Don't," Samantha panted.

"Don't?"

"Don't stop. Don't tease."

"Like this?" She ran her tongue back up and away, let her fingers slide out until they just touched the wet, swollen lips.

"I never thought you would be such a bitch."

"Weren't you paying attention?"

Sam laughed, and while she was distracted, Marcy shoved her fingers in, stroked hard just a few times, and then withdrew and replaced her hand with her mouth.

Samantha came off the towels and dusty concrete. Her legs tightened around Marcy's lower back.

Samantha was trimmed short, a feathery divide between

Marcy's lips and tongue and Samantha's clit and cunt. She lapped into her, used her mouth to form a seal over as much of Sam as she could and then darted her tongue inside and around her clit and back inside, faster and faster until Sam bucked beneath her, hips grinding her into Marcy's mouth, hands in fists against Marcy's back, holding tight to the stressed cloth of Marcy's shirt. She said "No" suddenly, as if it were too much. Then, going limp, her breath going fast and shallow, she said a long, drawn out "Yes."

She slid back on the towels, sliding a little away from Marcy, who dropped down from the elbow she'd leaned on and put her head on Sam's leg. It seemed she rested farther down Samantha's body than she should. Darkness danced and whirled in pinpoint colors as her eyes ached for something to see.

"Let me catch my breath," Samantha said. "And reciprocate."

Marcy frowned. "Do you have the flashlight?"

Sam hesitated a minute before she answered. "It's right here." An instant later the beam shone upward at the ceiling of the little room.

They stared at each other, disheveled and now very awake.

Samantha sat, her shorts discarded, bra hooked over one shoulder, her legs sprawled across the towels she'd laid down. Marcy sat across from her on the towels she'd put down, a good three feet away from Sam's.

"Did you move?" Marcy asked, very calmly.

Sam nodded, eyes wide. "But I don't think it was that far."

Marcy nodded back at her. "I don't either." She swallowed. "Must've been, though."

"Of course."

And their eyes met.

Upstairs something skittered across the floors, sounding

nothing like an old house settling. Slowly, and very deliberately, Marcy licked her lips. "You taste like strawberry."

Sam tried to smile, but her eyes kept flicking around the little room. "Do *I*?"

"What else, then?" Marcy asked.

Sam stood, unselfconscious and cinnamon smooth in the rolling light of the flashlight. "One way to find out," she said, and held her hand out to Marcy. "Let's go upstairs."

THE TRAVELER

Olivia Presley

I was taken by Paris. Her beauty broke my heart and mended it at the turn of every corner. I found myself inspired then depressed, lucid yet utterly confused, giddied by what I had found but had to leave. I wanted to make Paris my own.

I started smoking. Little puffs, here and there, as if the smoke I was inhaling gave the air a tangibility I could absorb. I ate too, little bites: sweet and cream filling a place that I could not. Gardens, galleries, churches, lovers: *I* was being consumed, so I ran, back to my garret in the rooftops.

I threw off my clothes and walked naked onto my tiny Juliette balcony, baring all to that magnificent city, begging Paris to take something from me. But I had nothing that Paris didn't have already, so I folded my arms in against my chest and paced, until I fell into bed. When I awoke, hours later, night's cloak had fallen over day and my heart.

I put on a black dress to mourn my last night and a slick of red lipstick to celebrate it. Misery seeks company, so I hailed a cab and asked the driver to take me to a blues bar. But as I got out at the entrance and heard the tinkle of tunes hitting the pavement, something told me it wasn't where I was supposed to be. I turned back to the cab but it pulled away, so I walked around the corner, off the main road and into the back streets of Paris.

Streets and streets passed. It started to rain. A couple ran by, running home to each other. I looked for shelter too, but as it was not a tourist area, most of the shops in the streets were closed, their awnings folded in. A light shone brightly up ahead. A bell rang out through the night as a door opened. I ran toward it and nearly into two women who were leaving. We all laughed and politely swapped places, and for a moment, I felt happy in their company. But they turned and walked away together. So I turned and walked in, alone.

There was no one else in the restaurant, but it didn't feel empty. It was warm with soft, pink light and filled with petite white-clothed tables finished with ornate, glass lanterns. A waiter walked out from the kitchen.

"Est-ce que vous êtes encore ouvert?" I said, asking if the restaurant was still open, in my most perfect phrasebook French. I wiped the wet hair from my brow to appeal to his gentlemanliness.

"Une table pour une personne?" she said in a tone that was as ambiguous as she was androgynous.

"Oui," I faltered. The moment seemed suspended as I looked at the opposition between her angular face and pretty eyes. "S'il-vous-plaît." Indeed.

The corner of her mouth turned up slightly. I couldn't tell if it was with disdain or amusement. My accent was bad. I was embarrassed.

She gestured to a table near the window. As I walked toward it, I read the restaurant's name through the glass. Le Chat

Nocturne. "The night cat," she said in heavily French-accented English, as if she had read my mind.

"Merci," I said, looking over my shoulder at her as she pulled out my chair. She took my jacket, and I sank down into the plush velvet cushion.

"What can I get for you tonight?" She reached into the pocket of her long, starched, white apron for a pen and notebook.

"A glass of champagne, please." I decided against embarrassing myself further with any more attempts at French.

"Nothing else?" she said, dropping her notebook back into her apron without writing anything on it. My eyes couldn't help but drop to the full lips from which her voice had tumbled. I caught myself, just after she had.

"No. Thank you." My skin prickled hot, and that feeling of giddiness came on again.

"As you wish." Her tone was professional, but when I looked up, I saw the glint in her eye wasn't. I reached for a cigarette, but the thought of her leaning in close to light it was too much. I dropped the pack, grasped my hands together, and tried to act normal. Realizing I wasn't, I turned to look out the window, which was frosted with wet and cold.

The table dropped slightly as she leaned on it. So did my heart as I smelt the warm caramely-spice of her body as she reached across me to wipe a clear view out with her hand. I tried not to fidget as she drew back, tried not to dissolve as she looked into me with those brown eyes, before she stood up again. I took a deep breath as she walked away. I hadn't realized I'd been holding it.

I bit my lip and couldn't help but look toward her. She picked up a bottle of champagne out of a nearby ice bucket. I smiled politely at her when she returned my gaze, looked to my fingers, tapped them on the table then managed to pull myself together, just, as she presented the bottle for my approval.

"Merci," I said. She slowly filled my glass.

"Vous avez de trés jolis yeux, je les embrasserais volontiers pour vous souhaiter la bonne nuit," she said, pausing, looking into my eyes.

"I'm sorry, my French is not good," I said, leaning into my hand as I looked up at her.

Her lip curled up at the side again. "I know," she said. Pausing a moment longer than was necessary, she dropped her eyes to my décolletage and then turned and walked away.

A hot French chick was flirting with me. I took a large sip of my champagne then another. *A hot French chick was flirting with me!* This never happened to me in my hometown.

The kitchen lights flickered off. The music followed and moments later the rest of the lights in the restaurant. The kitchen door swung open, and the waitress walked out without her white apron and tie. Her dark curls had been shaken loose, and the top few buttons of her crisp white shirt had been undone to reveal a little of her smooth tanned skin. European. Androgynous. Gorgeous. I downed the rest of my glass.

"I'm sorry to keep you," I said, reaching for my purse. "How much for the champagne?"

"It is with compliments," she said, and held up a set of keys. "Let me show you Paris."

"Oh, thank you. That's very kind..." I hesitated, reached for my scarf..."I have to leave in the morning and it's late...I really should go back to my hotel..." I thought of her there with me: tall, lean, confident, and I found myself without any further objections.

She pulled out my chair, picked up my coat, and held it expertly for me to slide into. I felt myself blush as she watched me pull my hair up from under my jacket.

"Is there somewhere close by I can get a taxi?" My blush deepened.

She held up her keys, and again I saw that glint in her eye. She laughed lightheartedly and, with a casual hand across my lower back, ushered me out of the restaurant and onto her streets.

She locked the door and walked toward a motorbike parked up on the footpath. She looked back at me standing on the door stoop, straddled her bike, and revved the engine.

Now, I'm the kind of girl who knows better than to take a ride from a stranger in a city she doesn't know, where no one knows her. And yet, as I looked up the wet, dark street, the last thing I wanted was to be left standing there alone...watching her drive away.

"Ma cherie, come on," she said, and tapped the back of her seat. I took a step, then ran and jumped on the bike behind her.

"Hotel Langlois, thanks, driver, rue Saint-Lazare, by Opera." She laughed, took off, driving along the footpath, down an alleyway, over a footbridge; through parts of Paris only the locals get to see. Then out onto the main road, the lights, the people, past the Eiffel tower, the Arc de Triomphe.

Suddenly, I felt triumphant: free of myself, free of the rules I'd had to live by as a solo traveler. It felt great to take a risk now, at the end of my long journey, the last destination before I returned home. Here I was, letting caution blow like the wind through my hair, putting myself completely in the hands of this stranger. As I rested my cheek against her back, I realized that was exactly where I wanted to be.

She slowed and pulled over on the side of a dark, tree-lined road. "I booked into a hotel, not a park," I said, my courage deserting me. She got off her bike.

"No, no, no, you can't leave Paris without a midnight walk along the Seine." She smiled, reached out her hand, touched the tips of my fingers with hers. Then she undid her biker jacket. How could I resist? Following her lead, we spiraled down stone stairs and onto the path that ran along the Seine's bank.

I was surprised to see that we weren't alone. There were people all around, each of them as if in place: an old couple waltzing, lovers on a bench, a group of young men sharing a bottle of red and a guitar. "I feel like I'm in a glass menagerie."

"Then let me shake you up," she said and took my hand, spun me around, drew me close, then back-stepped me a short way until I was against the arch of a bridge. The cold stones seemed to meld perfectly into my back. I let my head fall against them.

She lent into me and slid her fingers under my jacket, down my breastbone and under my dress, scissoring my nipple. Her other hand slid from my waist into the small of my back. Her warm lips rested against my ear, and her breath mixed with the sound of a distant accordion. Then she kissed me, and it was like my first kiss all over again.

The eyes of my imagination walked past us and saw the beauty of our embrace.

It was like a dream, what I had traveled the world for. Just one moment like this.

"Joie de vivre," I said to her, understanding in my heart what that famous French saying meant. She took my hand and spun me out from her, and we danced together for a moment or two: just long enough for the magic to swirl through me, just short enough to avoid awkwardness setting in.

"Come, I will show you Paris," she said, and with my hand still in hers, we ran back along the path. I jumped on the back of her bike and we took off up the street. A few minutes later, we pulled around a corner I recognized and then another and drove up the small side street to my hotel.

"I thought there was more to see," I said cheekily as I jumped off the bike.

"There is," she replied sexily, and made a dismissive gesture with her hand to all that lay behind her. "That is for the tourists." She drew me into her hips. I laughed nervously and stepped back, fumbling for the key in my bag.

I turned and unlocked the heavy iron door. Then I turned back to her to thank her for the ride, but her lips were upon me as were her hands, and she pushed me gently backwards into the small foyer. I reached a hand up to her chest to put a little distance between us, but she ran her tongue across my lips, and her strong hands down my back and my crotch ached and belly burned and before I knew it, I was backed against the elevator door. Which I opened, and pulled her in behind me.

"Going up," she said, adopting her professional voice.

"Three, please," I said breathily, and thought of her going down.

I let my eyes roam over her body as she turned to push the button. She turned back to me and pushed me softly against the wall, reached under my left thigh, pulled it up, and pushed herself against me. She breathed hotly against my cheek, bit my ear, and kissed down my neck. The elevator jolted as did she, against me. She pushed up away from me, her mouth slightly ajar, then ran her thumb down my chest and over my erect nipple. Satisfied that she had my attention, she stepped away from me and held the elevator door open.

My knees felt like jelly as I passed her. I didn't look back but could hear her walking behind me down the corridor toward my door. As I put the key into the lock, she ran her fingers down the crack of my ass and pushed between my legs. I breathed in deeply, leaning into the door for more; the door opened and I stepped inside.

I turned to her, undoing the top button of my coat. She undid the rest, pushed it over my shoulders, and let it drop to the floor. She ran her fingers down my neck, down my body, taking her time, watching my face as her hands traveled over my curves.

"Liberty," she said, and slid one strap, then the other from my shoulders. My black dress also fell to the floor. I felt exposed but exhilarated. She reached for my waist and drew me to her, kissed me, calmed me, and placed her hand on my heart, then hers. "Equality," she said.

"Fraternity," I responded, and undid her shirt as sensuously as she had mine. I ran my hands over her shoulders and down her lean firm body. Her skin prickled. My mind popped. I reached for her belt.

"Red, white, and...blue," she said, as her hand slid between my legs. My head tilted back with desire as her fingers grazed under my thong. She breathed heavily as she felt how wet I was. Then she reached both hands under my lower buttocks and lifted me onto her hips. I melted into her as she stepped forward and placed me on the mahogany table in the center of the room. She reached behind me and picked a camellia from the centerpiece and placed it behind my ear.

"There," she said, her fingers skimming my jaw, brushing my cheek. "They say Paris is like a woman with flowers in her hair." She leaned in to smell the camellia in my hair; then she lifted her head and looked into me. "So tonight, ma cherie, you can be my Paris. And I will be your traveler. Because when you wake in the morning, I'll be gone."

The next morning I woke up with a smile. She was gone, and yet, she was everywhere. I reached for the camellia she'd left on the edge of the bed. Underneath it was a note. "Your French is perfect."

SUGAR ON SNOW

Sacchi Green

Powdery snowflakes swirled thick and fast, clinging to our jackets, clustering on woolly hats, even tipping Lea's long eyelashes like a sprinkling of confectioner's sugar. "You're in for it now!" I called back to her. "It's too late to get away, even if your car would miraculously start." I slowed my pace to let her come up beside me, skis swishing rhythmically along the cross-country trail.

"You saw me pocket that distributor rotor, didn't you, Kit." Her face, or what I could see of it through the snow, glowed pink with cold air and exertion. The glint of mischief in her hazel eyes melted away the twenty-five years since we'd been college roommates. It seemed impossible that the smooth hair concealed by a bright knit hat was silver now, and short, instead of the long fall of pale gold I remembered.

"Oh, yeah, I didn't miss that little maneuver," I said. "And then I checked your car while everybody else was indoors packing. Why should I blow the whistle on you if you wanted to stay badly enough to fake an excuse?"

The other two old friends from college had left our mini-reunion two days ahead of schedule, when the morning news had upgraded the weather forecast from light snow to a potential blizzard. They had families and work to consider. My own new assignment with the National Forest Service was right here, in the New England of my birth, after years of moving from region to region. The few relationships I'd managed had been deliberately temporary. Lea was taking a long break from burnout as head nurse in a big-city hospital, and her second marriage had dissolved several years ago. Neither of us needed to be anyplace else any time soon.

We coasted down the incline to my cabin beside the ice-edged river. Her car and my pickup truck were already coated with a thick layer of white as frothy as meringue on a lemon pie.

"I was pretty sure you knew," Lea said, coming to a stop and releasing the bindings on her skis. "But since you didn't say anything right away, I hoped it meant you didn't mind. Thanks for keeping it to yourself. I acted on impulse and then felt silly for not just saying right out that I wanted to stay."

"You *were* silly. What could make more sense than riding out the storm here, where electricity is only one possible option? We have enough firewood and food to last until plowed roads or spring, whichever comes first." I managed to maintain a light tone, no matter how intensely I needed to know what Lea was up to. Once upon a time we'd been close enough to nearly read each other's minds, but that was very long ago. When she had finally understood how much beyond youthful experimentation I wanted of her, and I had realized how much I couldn't have, our friendship had survived but on a carefully superficial level. Over the last decade our communications had dwindled into annual notes on Christmas cards.

"What's sense got to do with it?" Lea flashed a grin, but it faded quickly. "It's not just a matter of shelter from the storm, either. Or...well, in a way, maybe it is, but..."

She paused so long that I picked up my skis and started up the steps. Lea followed into the screened porch. "Well, I'm glad you're here," I said, keeping a firm lid on the hopes and speculations roiling inside. Lea had been under a lot of stress, I wasn't sure she knew herself what she wanted. "We can do some catching up."

She shook her head. Soft snow slumped from her hat across her face, like frosting sliding down a cake still hot from the oven. I reached reflexively to wipe it away, barely stifling the urge to lick it from her cheeks, just as she raised her own hand. When I started to pull back, she wrapped her fingers around my thumb and held tight.

"Not catching up," she said. "Starting over." She let go and gestured toward the white expanse outside. "Doesn't the snow make you think of new beginnings, pristine, untrodden paths, unmarked pages?"

A gust of wind hit us with needles of that pristine snow blowing right through the screens. The flakes were smaller now, sharper, coming down even harder.

"It makes me think of stoking the fire," I said, shaking the snow from my hat and jacket and then opening the door. "And getting in where it's warm. C'mon." She was going to have to be more explicit than that before I could lower my guard against disappointment. But once inside, kneeling to fit logs carefully into the woodstove in the living room, I looked over my shoulder long enough to say, "Lea, you know you made your mark on my pages long ago. Indelibly."

"I do know it, Kit." She was already mixing leftovers from last night's communal feast into some sort of stew. "You don't

know how many times I've wondered, over the last few years...
and wanted to reach out...But we seemed to have traveled so far
apart."

She stood beside me, stirring the pot on the woodstove,
apparently getting into the spirit of rustic living even before
it was necessary. The past three days she'd been cooking and
eating with such enthusiasm that one friend had teased that
her taste buds must have only just recovered from the long-ago
trauma of college meals. She seemed to be making up for lost
time. It did seem to be an irony of nature that Lea, so fixated on
food, was still as elegantly lithe as a cougar, while I, who could
hike all day on a handful or two of trail mix, looked more like
a silver-tipped grizzly.

I stood up stiffly, brushing wood chips from my hands onto
my pants legs. The hell with playing it cool when the heat
building inside me mirrored the flames licking at the wood in
the stove. "We don't seem to be all that far apart now," I said,
beginning to reach for Lea. She turned right into the circle of my
arms. My cheek brushed her smooth hair as she burrowed her
face into my shoulder, and for a moment I thought she might
be crying. But when she raised her head, her lips were curved
into a little smile so delectable that I had to taste it, and then, of
course, a mere taste wasn't enough.

The kiss was so sweet and searing that we couldn't bear to
break it even when the lights went out. Power lines somewhere
had gone down under the snow-laden weight of falling branches.
The glow through the glass front of the stove was enough for us.
The sound and smell of boiling stew beginning to splatter over
and scorch did get our attention, though. We pulled apart, and I
grabbed a holder and moved the pot to the brick hearth.

"I suppose we should eat some," Lea said, somewhat breath-
lessly. "To keep our strength up."

"Definitely," I agreed, and lit a couple of candles from the chimney mantle to place on the folding table close to the stove. Then, while Lea ladled stew into bowls and sliced bread, I opened out the futon couch. I'd been sleeping on it for a few days, leaving the bedrooms to my guests, but tonight I didn't think I'd even need the excuse of staying close to the fire's warmth to keep from sleeping there alone.

"This is so great," Lea said, after about half her meal had been devoured. I'd just dunked my bread a few times and nibbled at it. "So...so..." she waved her spoon as though it might scoop the words she wanted from the air.

"Cozy?" I suggested. "Romantic?"

"Yes, those, but...so *right*, too," she said. "I can't tell you how grateful I am to the storm for chasing the others away."

I shoved back my chair and gave up any pretense of eating. "Lea," I said, "I only invited them to get you to come. So you wouldn't worry."

"Worry about what?" Candlelight flickered across her smile and danced in her eyes. She knew perfectly well what I meant.

"About this." I stood, lifted the whole table aside, and pulled her up from her chair. She raised her face for a kiss, but I resisted, unbuttoning her shirt and spreading it open. "And this." I pressed my lips into the hollow of her throat, savoring its tenderness, getting hungrier and hungrier for more. She shrugged the shirt right off while my hands pushed her sports bra up out of the way so I could cup her small breasts.

"Wait a minute..." Lea pulled the bra off over her head, and while her arms were raised, I caught one taut nipple after the other in my mouth. She gasped, and then tried to keep me from drawing away, gripping my short hair to force me closer. I pulled her hands free and stretched them far apart.

"I need to look at you. It's been so long..."

"And I'm so much older," she said wryly, but didn't flinch from my gaze. There was no need. The set of her head, the curve of cheek and throat and shoulder and peaked breast, had been my standard of desire ever since they had been imprinted on my memory. If I noticed any changes—the very slightest filling out and softening, perhaps, of her breasts?—they just enhanced her appeal.

"And so much more enticing," I said, letting her arms drop so that I could stroke her from shoulder blades downward until my hands slid inside the waistband of her jeans and pressed into the curves of her buttocks. "In the firelight your skin has such a delicious glow, like an apricot glaze." I eased back just a little and bent again to taste her breasts. "Yes, a definite flavor of apricots, but nectarine-sized apricots, sweet and complex." I sucked gently on an eager nipple.

"Ah...Kit...you're making me so hungry...but what I want are soft, ripe mangoes..." Lea's quick fingers tugged my shirt-tails from my pants and got right under to my skin, working upward until she had a firm grip on my flesh. Each lick and suck I gave her was echoed by sharp tweaks that sent tongues of flame streaking through my body. Too soon, of course, sensation overrode both concentration and balance, and we toppled onto the futon in a tangle of limbs and frantically shed clothing.

The wind outside howled down from the mountains through the river valley, making great branches thrash and rattling the damper in the chimney. We scarcely noticed. With my cheek pressed against Lea's breast, I could feel the pounding of her heart and hear the ragged sounds forming in her chest even before they left her throat. I moved my hand insistently, stroking, squeezing, then probing into her slick, hot depths, keeping in time at first with the arching and thrusting of her hips and then increasing my tempo. She kept pace, voice rising, breath coming faster and harder until, with a rough cascade of cries, she clenched her muscles around my fingers in a spasm hard enough to hold them motionless.

I held her close against me until her breathing finally slowed. Even the wind had dwindled almost to silence, and the whisper of falling snow against the windows was as gentle as the stroke of my fingers along her hair.

Lea's soft voice drew me upward through layers of sleep.

"I've been watching you dream," she said. The fire had burned down to bright cherry coals, its light bronzing the silver helmet of her hair.

"Am I dreaming now?" I murmured, still drifting.

She lay propped on one elbow, blankets sliding down her shoulder. The scent of her warm body flooded my senses with memory. Much better than dreaming. I reached out to pull her close, but the goose bumps on her arm reminded me of what the fire's sunset glow meant. I pulled the blankets higher over her shoulders and slipped out from under them myself.

"Time for more wood," I said unnecessarily.

"I was about to do it myself," she said. "I didn't want to wake you. But I'm not quite sure of the etiquette of fiddling with someone else's fire."

"Don't worry. Anything goes in a blizzard." My flesh tingled under her interested gaze as I stooped to the woodpile and knelt before the glass-fronted stove.

When the flames leapt higher, I went to pull the curtains aside and pressed my face against the window. "Over a foot and rising," I reported, not that I could see all that much through whirling snow so thick it might have been a cave wall hollowed out by the heat of our bodies.

"Maybe we'll have to tunnel out," she said. "When I was a kid we used to dig dens and forts under the snowbanks."

Her warmth welcomed me back under the blankets. "I've waited out storms in snow caves a time or two in the mountains," I said, "but this is a whole lot nicer."

"It had better be." She snuggled deliciously closer. "You've got me. And the fire. And plenty to eat."

"Are you sure? I'd better check." My hand parted her thighs to stroke and probe until my fingers were slippery with her responsive wetness. By the time I raised them to my mouth for a taste she was working her own fingers into me with serious intent.

"Mm, yes," she said, sampling the glistening results. "Done just the way I like it," and suddenly she was burrowing under the blankets in a sudden assault on my eager cunt and clit, licking and sucking in a frenzy quickly matched by the bucking of my hips. I had no chance to savor the delicious sensations, to let the tension build; my response came fast, hard, and out of control, leaving me quivering blissfully and totally wrung out.

As Lea untangled the blankets and pulled them back over us, she said, with the satisfaction of a job well done, "Well, if there were any pristine, unmarked bits of these sheets left before this, there certainly aren't now." And she snuggled up against me with a sigh of satisfaction.

The next thing I knew, the white light of a snowy morning was seeping through the curtains. Lea lay sleeping soundly. A tremor stirred her eyelids; I wondered what she saw behind them, and how their tender skin might feel beneath my lips.

Her face was pale, but a faint flush lit the strong, lovely arch of her cheekbones. Her mouth, slightly swollen, was a deeper pink, tempting me to put out my tongue to taste myself there. I resisted, not wanting to wake her yet.

Without interrupting the even pattern of her breathing, I edged out of the blankets and dressed in the back hallway. Then

I filled old water jugs with sunflower and thistle seeds for the birds, and stepped outside.

At least two feet of snow lay on flat areas, more in drifts, but it was coming down only lightly now. As I forged my way to the bird feeders, eager jays and chickadees were already making forays from the shrubbery. Back at the porch I grabbed a shovel and cleared a path to my pickup truck, moving the snow in layers. The road hadn't been plowed yet, which was all right with me; what could be finer than being snowbound with Lea? I contemplated the absurd mushroom of snow on the roof of the truck and decided to preserve it for a while as a natural work of art.

I went back to the house with a childlike urge to show Lea the birds, the snow, the slashes of blue sky emerging between the clouds; to share every smallest pleasure. Just savor the moment, I ordered myself. Don't complicate things. I shook my head, brushed as much snow as I could from my sweater and jeans, and concentrated on the joys of the present.

As soon as the warm inside air hit me, I knew Lea wasn't still curled up waiting under the covers. Regret was muted by my stomach's response to the smell of breakfast cooking.

"I hope you like French toast," she said, flipping the slices in a big frying pan on the wood stove. A pan of maple syrup was heating near the edge. "Not only have I had my way with your fire, I've ravaged your kitchen."

"Feel free to ravage anything you like," I said, admiring her outfit, which consisted entirely of wool socks and one of my old flannel shirts, strategically unbuttoned.

"Which would you prefer, ravishment or eating?" She held me at arm's length with the spatula. Then she tugged at my belt just enough to let a little of the snow clinging to my sweater descend into where I was warmest. I yelped but managed to stay on topic.

"Hey, I can go either way," I gasped. Which, of course, she must have known by then.

"I think I'd better keep my strength up." She flipped food onto plates, carried them to the table, and dug right in. My stomach growled. I leaned over to kiss her, licking syrup from the sticky corners of her mouth.

Laughter interspersed with kisses set the mood for the rest of the day. Something about being snowbound sets the inner kid free, however deeply the decades may have drifted.

After we'd eaten breakfast and hauled in buckets and kettles of snow to melt for water, we worked together on shoveling the driveway. A few snowball volleys were exchanged, a few frosty fingers warmed in moist, tender places, making them all the warmer and moister for the cool touch.

Then, when we'd cleared all the way to the still unplowed road and worked up a fine sweat, Lea climbed up onto the back of the truck and surveyed the enclosed expanse of virgin white. "Snow angel time," she announced.

"There isn't room to spread your arms," I pointed out, but she just grinned and started unzipping her jacket.

"Okay, snow demon, then, if you're going to be picky." Off came jacket, shirt, bra; I watched in awe as she dropped even her trousers and flopped forward into the soft snow, arms curved upward and hands curling out from the top of her head like little crescent horns.

"Terrific!" I said, applauding. "How long do you want to stay there? Incidentally, I hear the plow coming."

"Help!" she spluttered through a mouthful of snow.

I managed to get her up without damaging too much of the very interesting impression she'd made in the snow; even her cold-puckered nipples had left clear dents. Then I half-dragged, half-carried her into the house and dumped her on the futon just as the plow approached. While she struggled to kick off her boots and pants and pull up the blankets, I grabbed the pan of thickened maple syrup still hot on the edge of the stove.

Sugar on snow is a classic tradition in northern New England. I knew just what newly-imprinted snow I could use as a mold.

When I came back inside with my sweet creations, Lea rolled around in helpless laughter once she realized what I'd done.

"You can have one of these if you want it." I held out the plate. "Haven't you sometimes kinda wished you could suck on your own tit?" I bent to lick one sweet, vaguely breast-shaped treat.

She eyed the rubbery forms beginning to lose definition in the warm air. "That wouldn't be my first choice. But if I'm not going to get a better offer, I'll fend for myself." She tossed off the blankets and arched her body upwards. Before I could get rid of the plate and follow my impulse to lay a trail of sticky kisses from her tender belly to her cunt, she had pulled up her pants and rolled off the bed.

"Wait a minute," I pleaded. "You can have anything you want!"

"What I want now is lunch," she said, rooting around on my pantry shelves and choosing a few cans. "Don't interrupt while I'm in domestic mode."

My major hunger was situated well south of my stomach, but I cleaned off the syrup with snow water as well as I could and kept out of her way. She was still shirtless; I enjoyed the scenery, the brisk grace of arms and hands, the subtle movements of naked breasts.

The savory aroma of her concoction reminded me that I'd used a lot of energy shoveling. Food might not be all that bad an idea. I consumed my share of a soup somewhere between chili and minestrone, and then asked, hopefully, "Apricots for dessert?"

Lea glanced down at herself. A faint flush spread across her skin as her nipples hardened into exquisitely tempting tongue-candy, but she pushed away from the table and grabbed a shirt.

"That," she said, "might be better by firelight. And anyway, there's still snow to clear, where the plow shoved it into the driveway." She scooped up her boots and shirt and headed toward the door, slipping her hand briefly but effectively between my thighs as she passed. "Plenty of time to build up tension."

So she was planning to stay at least another night. My tension hit levels even shoveling couldn't release.

The plow had left a huge bank of snow across the driveway. We cleared away most of it, leaving a narrow strip along the road by mutual consent to signify that we were still "snowed in." Then there were other paths to be cleared, to the woodpile and toolshed, and looming mounds to be raked from the eaves of the house. Finally, after consulting with my knees and deciding that a little more wouldn't make much difference, I strapped on snowshoes and went along the ski trail for a mile or so to check for fallen trees—and to give Lea a chance to rest.

When I came back through the dusk, lights were visible down the river valley. My nearest neighbors, at least, had their electricity back, and my house must have it too. I figured Lea would be cooking in the kitchen now, free to use the modest amenities of modern life it offered, but she was still tending to a kettle on the woodstove. The cabin was lit only by the fire and an oil lamp I always kept handy on the mantle. I could see that the electric wall clock was running and had been reset, so Lea must be deliberately prolonging our adventure.

The soft light made the room seem all the warmer, more intimate, although Lea's presence cast the warmest glow. Something spicy was cooking, and there was still a lingering scent of maple syrup. Or—wasn't that the syrup pan heating again on the edge of the stove?

"What are we having?" I asked, trying to warm my frosty hands by the fire before daring to touch Lea.

"You'll see, when it's ready," she said, "but first you'll have to earn it by providing an appetizer."

"I'm all for that!" I leaned close to kiss her, and she responded with enthusiasm, but broke off too soon.

"That's fine, but not all I had in mind. You'll have to forage for it." She handed me the jacket I'd just hung on a peg by the door. "Bring me a basin of the whitest, most pristine snow."

I grinned, snatched another kiss, and got right to it. Her general plan was clear, although she'd certainly aroused my curiosity as to just how it was going to take shape.

Lea stood for a moment, long-handled pan in hand, surveying the smooth white surface I'd provided. "Y'know," she said thoughtfully, "some folks say the only thing men can do that women can't is to write their names in the snow standing up. Although you certainly wouldn't want to eat that yellowed snow afterward." With deft, swift movements she poured out a thin stream of hot syrup in curving lines. The heart shape was only slightly lopsided, and the names "Kit" and "Lea" within were clearly distinguishable to an eye eager to see them.

"It's too beautiful to lift out and eat," I said in awe.

"You're right," Lea agreed. "And that wasn't my original plan, anyway. How about taking it out on the porch and letting it freeze? And then you can bring me some fresh snow."

I returned in minutes, warmed by a tingle of anticipation—and stopped in further awe. Lea waited, entirely naked, with the lamp dimmed and the firelight caressing her body.

You didn't think you were going to get off without some very chilly personal contact, did you, Kit?" she said, trying to sound severe. "Put your hand in it. No, not there! In the snow!"

So I did, without flinching, and held it there, fingers spread, until Lea pulled me away. Silently, steadily, she poured a thick stream of amber syrup into the mold I had left.

"Now," she said, "you may warm your hand anywhere you'd like—aagh!" Her voice rose at least an octave as I took her up on the offer. She tightened her warm thighs around my fingers, though, even while she reached into the basin of snow to lift out the congealed shape there and raise it to her lips.

"So sweet…" She tasted each distinct finger before drawing it all over chin and throat and breasts, and lower. I sucked at her irresistible lips until she urged my mouth down the sticky trail, all the way to the truest, warmest sweetness, eager to flow.

Dessert came first that night, and the next night, too, complete with the savoring of apricots. Lea had to leave eventually, to tend to the other aspects of her life, but in a month, when the maple sap was rising, she was back to sample a new crop of syrup.

Soon summer will be on us, with wild strawberries ripening in clearings along the trails, followed by raspberries and then blackberries. I'm sure we'll think of some way to incorporate the tangy intensity of their flavor with our own; but nothing will ever warm me more than sugar on snow.

MÉLANGE

Allison Wonderland

If she's dead, I'm going to kill her.

My fingers tug at the telephone coil, winding the coral-colored cord around my hand like a bandage. I stare at the rows of buttons and digits and letters and listen to the insufferable drone of the dial tone.

I can't call Irene's boss, because the fabric store has been closed for three hours.

I can't call the community center where Irene takes a ceramics class on Wednesdays, because today is Sunday.

I can't call the police, because even though I miss Irene, my missing her doesn't necessarily mean that Irene is a missing person.

I can't call Irene, because she is trapped in a time warp and doesn't own a cell phone. *I don't believe in them*, she asserts, as if denouncing a deity.

Replacing the receiver in its cradle, I slump to the couch and begin to thumb through the rolodex of worst-case scenarios.

This is standard procedure. Rarely are people optimistic when they don't know the whereabouts of a loved one. No one ever says, *Oh, I'm sure she's fine. There's nothing to worry about.* At least not sincerely. Instead, they become perturbed and petrified and panic-stricken.

This is probably how my parents felt every time I (dis)missed my curfew as a teenager. I think I will apologize the next time I see them.

Damn it. Where is she?

Why didn't she leave a note? She always leaves a note. She should have left a note. She should have left a note where she always leaves a note: in washable marker on the skin of a banana.

I heard that snicker. I snickered, too, the first few times. But once I adjusted, once I learned to decipher her one-note missives, they didn't seem so silly anymore.

Every morning, without fail, I eat a banana for breakfast, so she knows that I'll get the message. And, she reasons, since I'm going to discard the peel anyway, it's an ingenious way to preserve trees and the money that doesn't grow on them.

Here's how it works. If Irene writes a number on the peel, like a five or a seven or a nine, that means she will be home by five or seven or nine o'clock. If she writes a word on the peel, like *milk* or *tampons* or *deodorant*, that means we have run out of milk or tampons or deodorant and that she has gone to the store to get what we have run out of. Once, Irene wrote the word *lube* on the peel, and I was dismayed when I found out that she intended the lube for her bicycle and not for our bedroom.

I get up off the couch and trudge into the kitchen, pausing when I reach the wastebasket. I pluck the peel from the trash and peer at the shiny yellow surface. But there is neither a number nor a word. There is only an oval-shaped sticker of a woman with an enormous basket of fruit strapped to her noggin.

As I drop the peel back into the basket, I catch sight of my nails, nibbled down to the nub. Irene used to scold me for this, eventually breaking me of the habit. I had been in remission for seven months until my relapse this evening.

Damn you, Irene. What am I going to do without you?

There is something intrinsically selfish about the loss of a loved one, whether that loss is real or feared. How will *I* live without her? How will *I* cope with *my* loss? Everyone else in Irene's life, even her life itself, seems secondary, incidental, to the anguish that I will feel if I lose her.

I return to the couch, accidentally sweeping the TV remote to the floor as I tuck my legs underneath me.

Irene didn't really care for television. She only watched a few select shows.

Didn't? Watched?

The resurgence of Worst-case Scenario Syndrome. I'm already thinking about her in the past tense, reminiscing as if I'm writing the first draft of her eulogy.

I've known Irene for seven years and lived with her for three. We met at the fabric store where she works. Irene says that even though I took up with her, I wasn't exactly taken with her. And she's right, I wasn't. When I approached the counter with a bolt of glittery blue organza, Irene waved her scissors at me and stretched her face into an absurdly broad smile.

As she sliced the fabric, I scrutinized her appearance. She wore slacks that were identical in color to a glass of orange juice and a sweater she had no doubt swiped from the closet of Heathcliff Huxtable. Her accessories consisted of silver thimbles suspended from her earlobes and glasses with chunky cheetah print frames and a slew of smiley-face stickers affixed to their stems. *I'm trying to scare away all the superficial people*, Irene informed me as she handed over the fabric—and her phone number. A test, she confessed later, to determine if I were really as shallow as I seemed.

A smile twitches at my lips. There are so many things about Irene that I would miss. I would miss her eyes, with their voluminous shape and turquoise irises. I would miss her body, with its sugar cookie skin, creamy and comely. I would miss the way her clothes mingle with mine in the hamper. And the way her lashes graze my cheek when she gives me butterfly kisses. And the way her Star of David becomes entangled in my hair when she hugs me, which hurts, but it prolongs our embrace, so it's worth it. And—

"I'm home!"

I spring from the couch and careen around the corner like a speeding car. My socks skid across the waxed hardwood, and I crash right into her, knocking us both to the floor.

"You take that welcome mat very seriously, don't you?" Irene quips. "Well, you've certainly got my vote for homecoming queen."

I inhale her words, with their sweet scent of butterscotch, and make no attempt to get up.

"Sorry I'm late. I kind of dozed off at the bookstore. I guess now I can say that I've slept with Dorothy Allison." She laughs, seemingly content to stay sprawled on the floor. "Anyway, I know I should've called, but…well, I would've if I could've, but I couldn't, so…I didn't. But I did ask the saleslady—the one who I bought the book from, because of course I had to buy it now that I got caught sleeping with it—anyway, I asked her to write me a note, and she just looked at me like…I don't know, like I was a few encyclopedias short of a full set or something. So, no note, but you trust me implicitly, so…no worries."

I stare at her, unblinking, undecided about whether I want to kill her or kiss her but slowly leaning toward the latter.

"Are you okay?" she asks, concern coloring her voice. "You didn't throw your back out, did you?" She studies my face, her eyes oscillating like the pendulum of a grandfather clock.

"What happened to the banana?" I want to know.

"What? Oh. I was feeling spontaneous this morning," she shares, "so I wrote the note on the bathroom mirror instead, after I took a shower, when it was all steamed up. I guess by the time you got up"—she shrugs—"it had already evaporated."

I lift my hand, bring my finger to her lips, outline the ellipses of her mouth. "If you were dead, I was going to kill you," I confess.

She giggles and coils her arms around my neck. "You worry so much," Irene says, and it isn't a complaint or a reproach. It is simply a statement of fact.

I continue to gaze at her. This mélange of wit and wile and whimsy. Our lips unite, motivated by instinct and impulse.

I feel a familiar warmth diffusing through my body, surging through the labyrinth of nerves and veins and arteries, before returning to its place of origin.

My heart.

PLACE, PARK, SCENE, DARK

Elspeth Potter

After I broke up with Angie, sometimes women would hit on me. I'd tell the truth: "Sorry, can't. Werewolf."

Only tonight, instead of the answers I'd gotten used to ("Freak!" or "What the hell is *your* problem?"), she smiled and slid onto the stool next to me. "Really?"

"Yeah, really." She was too femme, like a model in a magazine. Her sleek Asian skin looked like she exfoliated every five minutes. Her hair hung to her butt, black like used motor oil; she wore slut-red lipstick, slick and shiny as patent leather, that matched her miniskirt and snug jacket. Her knee-high boots, also red, had heels that could poke out an eye.

She crossed her legs and I glimpsed inner thigh, creamy as ice cream. I licked my lips. Apparently, tonight femme could be my type. She asked, "What kind of a werewolf?"

I swigged my beer to hide surprise. The kind who wished someone would bite her and put her out of her misery. I said, "The biting kind."

"Really," she purred, leaning forward. Her jacket gaped, of course. She wasn't wearing a shirt underneath. I could see the upper slope of tits, a bit of rounded shoulder where it curved into her delicate neck, and that hard line of collarbone that always makes me want to trace it between finger and thumb. She smelled like leather and pussy, and I'm not kidding about how I could smell her. Hell, I could've told you how she tasted from her smell. In a couple of days, when I Changed, I would've been able to pick her out by smell at the New York Pride Parade.

Ms. Femme looked like she could smell me, too. She said, "I like it rough."

"Where'd you get your dialogue, a porn movie?" I asked, looking away from her collarbone and then trying not to look at her ass. "You're bothering me, little girl."

She smiled, slow and dangerous. "I'm here to bother you. I'm Xia," she said. "Hong Xia. You can have that as a present. You're Ellery Carver. Your old friend Angie said you needed me to tie you down and"—she leaned forward again and breathed into my ear—"fuck your little bitchy brains out."

If I hadn't sworn off killing, I would have killed Angie. Didn't she remember this was our anniversary? Of the last time. Or did only pitiful fuckers like me remember things like that? "Sorry," I said. I tossed a ten on the bar and thumped my glass on top. I reached for my jacket.

Before I could straighten up, a lot of warm woman stretched against my back. Xia's thigh lifted and rubbed the side of my leg. I could feel her flex through my jeans. Exfoliating obviously didn't hurt her muscles.

She said, "Don't be a spoilsport. The moon's two days from being full, babycakes. It's safe. Let's go to the park and play." She pinched my ass hard enough to hurt.

The pinch did it. I don't like games, but at least I knew Xia wasn't afraid, and it had been a long time, because even when I masturbated I remembered that last horrible time and what I'd done to Angie. I pulled away from Xia's grip, shrugged into my denim jacket, and plunged my hands into my pockets. "In the grass," I said, half-hoping she would refuse.

Xia looped one manicured hand through my arm. "Let's go," she said. She sounded businesslike. Was she really a friend of Angie's, or a professional? I decided it didn't matter. I would go with this woman, and I would get off in a public place, and I would like it. Hell, everybody else seemed to do it. Why not me? Maybe then I could forget Angie. For ten minutes or so.

Xia led me into the park like a dog on a leash. It was fall, the air just beginning to get that crispy apple edge, the leaves waiting to let go. The concrete path ran in a circle around the park, with rays leading in to the King Tree, oldest tree in the city, now circled by its own weatherworn bench. Each path was lined with old-fashioned lampposts that cast a yellow gleam, to my eyes not as bright as the silvery moonlight.

We stopped and Xia casually balanced on one foot. She unzipped her boot, flashing bare calf and thigh while she yanked it off. Wrapping her thigh was black webbing, not a garter but a harness for something, probably a knife. She meant to let me see it. I wasn't too excited. If she planned to hurt me, I would smell it.

Xia didn't stagger or even waver in her posture as she set one boot on the sidewalk and took off the other while I watched. No harness on that leg. She folded the tops of the boots and tucked them under her arm, explaining, "I don't want to tear up the turf."

"How socially responsible of you," I said.

Walking backwards, she beckoned me onto the damp grass.

I followed, because I'd followed this far, and if I backed out now, it'd be embarrassing. And...because I was intrigued, just a little. Women like Xia didn't turn up in my corner bar every day. In fact, women like Xia never turned up in my corner bar. Wasn't it strange—no, Angie must have told her. I'd been trying to forget Angie'd had a hand in this. Nobody normal would want to—then again, Xia wasn't what you would call *normal* if, say, you saw her in my local Stupidfresh.

I said, sarcastically, "Are we there yet?"

"Behind the King Tree," Xia said, grabbing my wrist and dragging me. I let her. Someone was there, waiting. A figure clad head to tiny feet in black leather—motorcycle boots, snug trousers, zipped jacket, gloves, and form-fitting mask—slowly stood up from the encircling bench and strolled toward us.

I sucked in my breath, floated on her scent for a second, and then blew it all out again. "Not fucking funny, Angie!" I growled. I wanted to scream, but that would bring the cops down on us. Sending Xia was one thing. Showing up herself was another.

Angie unzipped the mask and tugged it off. Her hair was shorter than it had been, short as velvet and dark as shadow. I could clearly see the vivid scar slicing down her high cheekbone, a raised pink line against her dark skin. It gleamed accusingly.

Angie said, "This isn't a joke. I asked Xia—"

"You can both fuck the hell off," I said, and whirled to stomp away. The only thing that stopped me was Xia's taloned hand seizing my wrist. If I wrenched loose, I would hurt her, and I never wanted to hurt anyone again, ever.

"I want you back!" Angie said.

Very carefully, I tried to pry off Xia's fingers. When I couldn't loosen her sharp grip, I took a deep breath, then another, like I'd learned in meditation class, before I spoke. "I hurt you," I said. "I fucking bit you in the face. One day either way and you would've been like me, trying to chew the chains off your own fucking feet every month. If you think I'm going to risk that happening again, then fuck you, because you don't know me at all." I tugged harder at Xia's hand, without success. Fuck, she was strong.

Angie moved closer. Overwhelming about a million other things, I could smell her. She'd touched an engine sometime that afternoon, not her bike but another one, and had eaten Chinese food, and drunk too much black coffee. But she'd stopped smoking, long enough ago that the stench had faded from her leathers. She said, "I know you too well."

I said, "It's over, Ange."

"I refuse to let it to be over. That's why Xia is here."

I said, as roughly as I could, "Some bimbo is supposed to give me the hots and I'll fall face first into your pussy?"

Xia laughed. "Bimbo, huh?"

Angie lifted her chin. "You're worried about hurting me. Well, Xia will make sure you don't. She's a professional bodyguard."

I looked at Xia. She grinned back at me and did something to my wrist that made me gasp. Still, neither of them seemed to understand. I said, "I. Am. A. Werewolf."

Xia said, "Not tonight you aren't."

"I'm still stronger than both of you." Or would be if I was ruthless enough to attack them.

"Will you at least try?" Angie took one more step and laid her hand on my shoulder. I could barely feel it through my layers of denim and flannel, but at the same time I flushed, because she was so close, because she dared to touch me. Because she trusted me.

Normal people might not understand that. I mean, how many people know a werewolf, and if they do, how many of them know what it's really like? Even our families, even our lovers? How many of them *can* know?

Like I explained to Angie one time, it's like we have a contagious disease. We *do* have a contagious disease, even though it's really difficult to pass on—there has to be a bite, at the right time of the month, and the bite has to puncture deeply enough, and there has to be enough spit. I just didn't trust myself not to lose it one day. I couldn't.

"Come on, El," Angie said. "Do you want me to spend the rest of my life alone?"

"Stop guilt-tripping me," I snarled. I tried to remind myself why I couldn't do this, but the reasons wouldn't come. It was the wrong time of month for me to be contagious, and creepy as it seemed, we had a safety monitor, and damn it, I still loved her.

"Let me go," I said to Xia, and when she did, I walked over to Angie and kissed her.

I barely touched her lips with mine, just brushed back and forth, showing her I could be gentle, showing her I was sorry. She turned her head a little and opened her mouth, and then I felt the barest tip of her tongue touching me before she drew back. She smiled.

Then Xia jumped me. Her hand slapped my neck and I felt a tiny sting. After that, nothing.

I woke up, pissed as hell. I was still outside, still in the park, from the smell of green plants and a hundred dogs who'd marked their territory. It was still night, the same night; I knew because I can always feel the moon's phase. My wrists were cuffed behind my back. The bar between the cuffs was attached to an oak; they'd used one of those chains that's sheathed in plastic. I wrenched at it. No good. I growled, hurting my throat, which wasn't the right shape for growls yet.

Angie stepped into sight; I'd been able to smell her lurking behind a bush, waiting for me to make a move. She had the leather mask back over her face. Xia stood behind her, at her shoulder. Angie said, "It's for your own good, El. And it had to be when you're this close to Changing, so you'd know for sure I can keep you safe."

"I trusted you," I said. "What's this about? You wanted to get some wolf pelt while it was in season?"

She didn't say anything. She sauntered up to me, her scarlet avenger backing her up. She grabbed my ears and shoved her tongue down my throat.

I was angry but I was horny, too. I was always crazy for sex right before I Changed; we'd made a lot of jokes about Pre-Lupine Tension. I kissed her back and then, to show I was pissed off, tried to nip. She jerked back before I could catch her lip in my teeth.

Xia stepped up and, still with that perfect balance, pressed her long, bare foot into my crotch. "Hold still, honeybunch," she said. "Angie's not through playing with you."

I snarled and lunged. This didn't get me much further from the tree, but it did drive Xia's clever foot into my pussy. She grinned, grinding a little before she lowered her leg and took up a guard position by my shoulder.

"She can't hurt me like this," Angie said to her. Of me, she asked, "Can you?"

She was right. In a way, this was what I'd wanted. I was still mad, though. Nobody had asked me. Well, not about being chained to a tree. I had consented to sex. With both of them, if you wanted to be anal-retentive and insist.

"She wants this," Angie said. "Ellery, I've won."

Xia began humming something. I knew the song. It's called "You're the Top." What a smartass.

I asked, "Won what? Me being pissed at you?"

Angie didn't say. She shoved my denim jacket off my shoulders, letting it help tangle up my arms. She unbuttoned my flannel shirt the rest of the way, then shoved my tank top above my tits. "Xia, hold her," she said.

Angie was still wearing leather gloves. When she grabbed my bare tits, the gloves abraded and I twisted away from her. Xia forced me back and held me immobile. Angie hadn't hurt me accidentally. Her palms rotated hard against my nipples until they were swollen and painful prickles shot into my belly.

"Does that hurt?" she asked, shoving her face into mine.

When I spoke, I could feel her scar against my lips. "Not as much as I hurt you," I said. I reached out my tongue and touched her scar with the tip. "I don't like being hurt. But you can hurt me. You deserve it."

"Damned right," she said. Then she sank her teeth into my cheek.

I have a pretty high pain tolerance, more since I was Changed, but her teeth hurt enough to tear a sound out of my throat before she stopped as suddenly as she'd started. She shoved me into Xia, and staggered backwards, away from me, her hand over her mouth.

"Holy shit," Xia muttered. If she was sympathetic, it wasn't enough for her to let go of me; instead she twisted one of her arms more firmly through one of mine. I appreciated the support. My whole face throbbed, radiating out from where Angie had bitten me. The air was cold on the dampness she'd left behind. Gradually, the cold numbed it. It was going to bruise for sure. I tried to tell myself I didn't want her to do it again.

I wanted to touch the spot. I wanted her to hurt me again, because when she had, the pain that lived coiled in the pit of my belly felt a little less. She'd been mad, mad enough to hurt me. That meant she still cared.

I couldn't see Angie's face, but I could tell whatever she was feeling, it was fucked up. Probably not as fucked up as me wanting her to bite me again, though.

Angie said, "When you bit me, did you want to hurt me?"

"No," I said. "I wanted to bite you. I was—"

"—turning into a wolf, I know—"

Angie kept talking, faster and faster. The sound of her familiar voice, the smell of her, Xia's hot grip, and the sweat that had sprung out on her were making me restless and twisty inside. I squirmed and tried to focus on Angie's face, which sometimes worked when I wasn't too far gone. It worked better than I'd expected. Her scar shocked me back from the wolf again.

She was saying, "I never would have gotten you here tonight if you hadn't been close. And see, I took care of you. I knew you were close, and I made sure you couldn't hurt me. You can trust me to take care of you when you're like this. You want me to do that, don't you? Don't you, El? Because you don't want to live without me, either. If I could be safe, you'd want us to be together again. And I can make that happen. Just trust me. Just let me take care of everything."

She kept talking, and I was making a sound in my throat, and it sounded like an animal whimpering. Begging.

Because she was right. I wanted that. I wanted her to take care of me, to be the one in charge, the one who made sure everything was all right. I wanted to be her bitch. I already was, after all. I'd proved that tonight.

And I wanted her to bite me again, and I wanted not to be able to do a damned thing about it. That was the only way I could make it right.

"Ellery!" Angie said. Xia gave me a shake. I shook my forelock out of my eyes and lifted my head. "Say *yes*."

"Yes."

"Let her go, Xia."

I didn't want Xia to let me go, but Angie hadn't meant for her to unchain me, just to release the lock she had on my arms. Xia tidied up my tank top, making sure it was folded neatly above my tits. Then she undid my fly and wrestled my jeans down my hips until they tangled at my ankles. She didn't bother taking off my work boots, just reached back up and peeled my underwear down. Then she stepped back, flashing a grin and a salute.

Angie didn't even unzip her jacket. She said, "From now on, I'm in charge. Right, El?"

"Right," I said. I turned my head just enough to show my throat.

Angie leaned in and closed her teeth on my pulsepoint, gently. Heat blossomed across my skin. She licked the place on my cheek she'd bitten, then slid her tongue into my mouth, tasting inside my lower lip, and flicking along the edges of my teeth. One of her gloved hands held my head still while the other one rubbed my tit and then skated down my belly. I let her do what she wanted. That was what *I* wanted.

Xia slid behind me again, only this time with her hands gripping my hipbones, massaging my lower back and ass, teasing me with her nails, and pressing me open for Angie's gloved finger. Xia pressed scalding kisses to my neck and ear. Her long hair swung over my shoulders and draped my tits, tickling and carrying her scent. I could smell myself now, too, my own cream wafting into the air, and I smelled hot leather and Angie.

I felt surrounded by more than two women. I shuddered, straining against their leather, the clothes that bound my arms and ankles, the cuffs. I writhed around the rawness of a gloved finger working its way into my pussy and a gloved thumb digging into my clit until I spasmed hard, and twisted up on my toes to force Angie's hand into me again, and again. This time the spasms kept coming, jerking out of me with each breath until I slumped between them, my knees hitting the cold wet grass.

It was over, and I hadn't bitten anybody. I hadn't even wanted to bite. They'd kept me safe, just like Angie had said.

Xia uncuffed me. Angie kissed me. I kissed her back. For the moment I was content. I said, to both of them, "Thanks."

Angie smiled. "Next time, we'll even chain you to a nice comfortable leather couch."

MUSIC ON
THE WIND

Radclyffe

Anna woke in the dark to the sensation of a cool, damp
wind blowing across her face. She reached for Graham,
and when she didn't find her, shot upright, her heart racing. The
cabin glowed with the eerie blue-gray cast of moonlight in the
midnight sky, and it took her only a second of glancing frantically around the strange space to realize that the doors to the
balcony were open and she was completely alone.

"Oh, my God." She lurched from bed, grasped her robe in one
hand, and hastily pulled it on as she ran outside. "Graham!"

Graham Yardley turned her face away from the ocean and
toward the sound of Anna's voice. "Anna? What's the matter?"

"I couldn't find you," Anna gasped, pressing her hands to
Graham's chest. With the moon and ocean behind her and her
face in shadow, Graham's chiseled profile and blade-thin form
appeared like a rent in the fabric of a dark and dangerous
painting. Searching for something to say that wouldn't betray
her terror, Anna said, "Darling, your shirt is soaked."

"I'm surprised at how much spray there is all the way up here." Graham covered Anna's hands with hers and bent to kiss her. "We're quite high up, aren't we?"

Anna shivered, thinking just exactly how high above the water their suite was situated. From the balcony where Graham had stood alone, it was at least a hundred feet to the surface of the ocean. Had she fallen…Anna pressed her face to the curve of Graham's neck and wrapped her arms tightly around her waist. "How long have you been out here?"

"Not long. Ten minutes." Graham stroked Anna's hair and gathered her close. "You're upset. Why?"

"I wish you wouldn't take midnight tours without me, darling," Anna said lightly.

"After five years you don't trust me to walk around by myself?" Graham tilted Anna's face up with a finger beneath her chin and kissed her again, skimming her tongue lightly between Anna's lips before drawing back.

"There's no one in the world who knows as well as I how independent you are," Anna murmured, resting her cheek on Graham's shoulder. "But it's our first night and we've never been on a ship like this before. Graham, you can't realize what it's like out here—it feels as if we're a tiny city adrift in an endless, uninhabited universe. There's nothing around us except the stars overhead. The seas are quiet right now, but if there were turbulence and you lost your footing, you wouldn't be able to—"

"Anna, love," Graham whispered, "I've seen the ocean. I've even seen oceangoing ships." She reached beside her and curled one hand around the balcony railing. "And I can hold on quite adequately."

"I know, but you haven't seen *this* one, and I'd feel better if you got acquainted with it a little more before you started investigating on your own."

"Well then," Graham said, "let's take a walk and you can show me."

"Now? It's the middle of the night." Anna laughed, realizing she was the only one exhausted by four months of nonstop touring on three continents. Graham never seemed to tire of the hectic concert schedule, and performing only seemed to invigorate her. "You're not tired at all, are you?"

Graham smiled. "Excited. We haven't had a vacation together in a very long time."

"It seems to me that we've been in every major European city in the last few—"

"It's not a vacation for you when I'm touring, I know that. I'm distracted and self-absorbed, and you worry that I don't eat enough." Graham slid her hands inside Anna's silk robe and caressed her breasts. "And I'm not very attentive."

Anna caught her breath, ambushed by the sudden swelling of her breasts. Every part of her responded to Graham's touch, as if her body were as precisely strung as the strings on Graham's concert grand. "Graham, darling, you are very attentive when you're touring because all the passion that wells up in you when you play is still there after the performance." She kissed Graham lingeringly. "And I'm always waiting."

"I still don't feel like I take enough time with you." Graham clasped Anna's hand. "Let's explore."

"I need to change." Anna skimmed her fingers over Graham's shirt. "And so do you. I'll find you something."

"I'll wear my jeans," Graham said, following Anna's gentle lead back into the cabin. "Then I'll know I'm really on vacation."

Anna smiled to herself as she opened the suitcases they hadn't yet unpacked. She found a pair of black denim jeans and a soft cotton navy V-neck sweater. Graham had never worn casual clothes off the rack before they'd met. Her wardrobe had been custom-made all of her life, because she'd been performing all of her life. She'd only stopped playing after a car accident left her blind and she'd gone into seclusion for a dozen years. But now she had returned to the concert stage and to life. Their life.

"Here," Anna said, turning with the clothes in her hands. She stopped, startled despite how many times in their years together the same thing had happened. Graham held out one of her favorite lounging-around outfits, a pale green, scoop neck sweater and tan cotton slacks. "I don't how you do that."

Graham grinned, momentarily softening the austerely handsome planes of her face—a classically beautiful face marred by a diagonal scar across her forehead that extended into one eyebrow. That mark of past tragedy only made Anna desire her more.

"I know the way they feel from touching you in them," Graham said. "And I plan on spending a lot more time touching them this evening."

Anna's legs felt suddenly shaky and she laughed self-consciously, as if they weren't longtime lovers but newlyweds on their wedding night. "Stop," she said softly.

Graham cupped Anna's cheek and smiled. "You're blushing."

"I was just thinking that there's something about being here, away from our normal lives—if anything about our life can be called normal—that makes me feel as if it's our first time together. I can't…" She feathered her fingers across Graham's mouth. "I can't wait for you to make love to me."

Graham grew suddenly still, her clear dark eyes focused unerringly on Anna's. She parted Anna's robe and skimmed it off her shoulders, dropping it behind them on the bed. Then she curved an arm around Anna's waist and pulled her close, caressing her breasts as she kissed her. Anna moaned and leaned into Graham's embrace.

A moment later, Graham glided her lips along the rim of Anna's ear. "Perhaps the tour should wait until morning."

Anna's heart pounded and her stomach tingled in that "wanting to be touched" kind of way that always made her long for Graham's talented hands. Shaking her head, she gently disengaged. "I want to walk with you for a while and think about how wonderful you're going to make me feel later."

"It's a clear night, isn't it? A little bit cool."

"Yes," Anna said, slipping the sweater over her head, loving the freedom of having nothing against her skin except the soft, familiar fabric. "How can you tell?"

"The air is very sharp and crisp, despite the salt spray. It feels as if there's nothing between my skin and the stars except the night."

"There isn't. When we go up on deck, I'll point them out to you. The stars."

"I'd like that."

Anna brushed a lock of dark hair back from Graham's forehead and smiled to herself as it promptly fell back. Graham's hair, though carefully styled for the concert stage, was still casually roguish. Traces of gray streaked her temples now, and although she was naturally pale and slender, she radiated vitality and passion with every breath.

"I love you," Anna whispered. Not that long ago Graham had nearly slipped away, and Anna would never forget the agony of almost losing her.

Graham looked up from buttoning her jeans, and as always, Anna felt her gaze. Graham couldn't see her, had never seen her, but she had never felt so known in all the ways that mattered.

"I love you." Graham held out her hand. "Are you prepared to be my tour guide?"

"Always." Anna threaded her fingers through Graham's. "We

are in the center of the main room of the suite right now. The bed—a queen size, very nice—is behind us. To your left are—"

"Two sets of double doors to the verandah, which faces the bow and overlooks the port side of the ship. We're on deck nine—Pegasio, which is the highest level containing passenger cabins. To our right is the sitting room and the door to the bath."

"I told you all this earlier, didn't I?" Anna said, laughing.

"You did. If you hadn't, I wouldn't have gone out onto the verandah."

"Uh huh," Anna said with a hint of disbelief. She tugged Graham toward the door and opened it. "The hallway is ten feet wide with cabin doors opening every twenty feet or so along it. We're at the very front of the ship, so if we walk down the corridor to the central foyer, we'll reach the elevators."

Anna waited while Graham closed the door, her right hand on the handle, and pivoted to face the direction in which they would walk. Although Graham had not been born blind, she had developed an unerring sense of herself in relationship to her environment and adapted very quickly to new surroundings. Still, she could not see and that made her vulnerable, and Anna was intensely attuned to that fact every moment of the day. And every moment of the day, she worked hard so that Graham would not sense her worry.

"Ready?" Anna asked.

Graham took Anna's hand as any lover would upon embarking on a stroll. "Yes."

"The ship is almost 900 feet long, which is almost..." Anna hesitated, working on the math as they walked.

"A little bit over an eighth of a mile." Graham tucked Anna's hand in the bend of her arm.

"Something like that." Anna laughed. "Now, this deck actually overlooks one of the main restaurants two decks below."

They reached the end of the passageway and Anna stopped. "Have you been counting?"

"Yes. To the right are the elevators?"

"That's right. And to the left is the open balcony that rings the restaurant below. Halfway around in that direction are the doors to one of the outside pools. There's also a cabana and bar out there, but they're closed tonight, of course." Anna wanted to tell Graham not to attempt navigating anywhere in this area by herself, but she refrained. In all likelihood Graham would not go anywhere without her. As independent as Graham might be, she wasn't foolhardy. "We can go down to the lounge now, or check out the decks where the health spas and casinos are located, or we can go outside and see the stars."

"We'll have plenty of time to explore the rest of the ship tomorrow," Graham said, draping her arm around Anna's shoulders. "I opt for stars tonight."

"Good." Anna encircled Graham's waist and tilted her head against Graham's shoulder. "Let's find a deck chair to cuddle up in."

Once outside, Anna chose a deck lounger out of the wind and away from the few couples who stood at the rail on the far side of the pool, apparently taking in the view. She tilted the back of the lounger so that it was nearly reclining and said, "You lie down first."

Graham stretched out and Anna settled between her legs, her back to Graham's chest. When Graham's arms came around her, she clasped them and nuzzled her face against Graham's neck. "Perfect."

"Are you cold?" Graham murmured with her lips against Anna's ear.

"No, not with you holding me this way."

"Can you count the stars?"

Anna laughed. "There are thousands."

Graham eased one hand free from Anna's grip and slid it underneath the bottom of Anna's sweater, spreading her fingers over Anna's stomach. "How many can you see directly above us?"

"Oh," Anna mused, realizing how many small stars there were between the bright points of the constellations. "Hundreds."

"Even the wind is different out here," Graham said, tilting her head to one side. "It ebbs and flows as if the sky itself were breathing. Or playing for us."

Anna closed her eyes, hoping to capture the refrain that Graham heard in the night sky. The stars still sparkled beneath her closed lids and her skin tingled, stirred by Graham's fingers moving rhythmically on her bare stomach, recreating the wind-song on her skin. Graham did that unconsciously when a melody formed in her mind, her pianist's fingers playing chords as the music came to her. Anna had fallen hopelessly in love watching Graham play and had lost her heart to the woman whose music was life. Now, years later, she fell in love with her all over again every time Graham played. Tonight, she *felt* her play.

"Your hands are so warm." Anna shifted her hips between Graham's legs, feeling the heat spread from Graham's hands throughout her stomach and settle deep, deep inside.

"Your skin is so soft." Graham skimmed her other hand beneath Anna's sweater, this hand cooler than the first had been. When Anna tensed, Graham stilled. "Too cold?"

"Mmm, no. It feels wonderful." Anna kissed Graham's neck, then, eyes still closed, she arched one arm back and slid her hand behind Graham's neck, tugging Graham's head lower so she could find her mouth. She kissed her, exploring her lips and inside her mouth as if her tongue were all she could see or touch her with. When Graham lightly sucked on the tip of her tongue,

Anna moaned. "I think we should go back to our cabin."

"I think you should let us play for you, the wind and I." Graham cupped Anna's breasts and rippled her fingers over the nipples, scoring the melody, note by flowing note. "Listen, Anna," Graham breathed. "Listen."

Anna strained to feel what Graham heard, her body electric with silent sound. A sliver of cool night air licked her belly where Graham's wrists tented her sweater, and she tightened inside. Or was it Graham's fingertips, as soft and clever as her mouth, gracefully tracing a phrase over her breast, striking a cantabile deep in her flesh, that ignited the familiar ache? Anna couldn't tell. Like a counter-melody, elusive and sweet, she felt Graham's hands in places beyond her body and her blood. Her passion brimmed and pulsed, as fluid and graceful as the chords that flowed beneath Graham's hands on the concert stage. Pleasure pierced her nipples and converged in a single point between her legs. She floated on the music flowing in and around her—the distant rush of water, Graham's heartbeat, her own breathless moans. So much beauty to hold, too much pleasure to contain. She ached to spill into the night, onto the wind, over Graham's hands.

"Graham," Anna gasped, trembling in the curve of Graham's body, "what you're doing to me. I can't keep it all inside. I need to...oh, god I need to let go. Will you make me come?"

"Yes," Graham breathed against Anna's ear. "Anything. Always."

Anna fumbled to open her slacks. "It won't take very long. I'm so ready for you."

"Don't hurry." Graham slid her hand down Anna's stomach, beneath her shorts, and cupped her tenderly. "Tell me what you see."

"Lights sparkling everywhere. Endlessly." Anna arched her

back and pressed herself to Graham's palm. She was wet and open, aching to be filled. "Please put your fingers on me. I love when you touch me…"

"Is the moon very bright?"

"Yes, very…oh, that's perfect…just keep touching me there and I'll—"

"What else?" Graham caressed her lingeringly, then fleetingly, now harder, then softly, coaxing every note from her flesh.

"Wisps of clou…there, touch right there…" Anna whimpered when Graham's fingertip circled the spot on the underside of her straining clitoris that always made her come. She needed to come so badly she couldn't think, couldn't speak, but still she tried. She wanted Graham to see. "Clouds…like a veil obscuring the face of a beautiful woman…I'm going to come soon, darling."

Graham stroked faster, massaging the place that made Anna moan. "You're my night sky, Anna," Graham whispered, "and the light of all my days."

Anna's orgasm played in her depths, a teasing melody she couldn't quite grasp. "Inside. I need you inside me, darling, please."

"Do you hear it, love?" Graham entered her, one finger after the other until Anna tightened around her and tossed her head in wordless pleasure. Groaning, Graham pressed harder. "You will always be the music, Anna."

"You'll make me…oh, god, I can't…" Anna pushed down against Graham's hand, forcing her deeper. "More. Bring me, darling…I'm so close now."

"Listen, Anna," Graham urged, thrusting smoothly, her movements a glissando that carried her lover toward climax. "Listen to the…"

"I'm coming," Anna cried softly, burying her face against Graham's chest. She sobbed her joy into the night, and the wind carried her song to the stars. "I love you. I love you with all I am."

Graham held Anna tightly, her mouth skimming Anna's. "I love you. When I touch you, I..." Her voice drifted off as Anna kissed her throat and worked a hand inside her jeans.

"You what, darling?" Anna cupped and squeezed with a slow, steady rhythm, the last notes of her own orgasm still drifting through her body. Graham was hot beneath her hand, her slim form vibrating with tension. Graham always needed release right after she made Anna come, needed Anna to finish her quickly and hard. "Can you still hear the windsong?"

"Yes," Graham groaned, covering Anna's hand and guiding Anna's fingers to the hard ache between her thighs. "Anna... Anna..."

"What, my love?"

Graham cupped Anna's cheek as the first surge of release broke through her. "The sky," she gasped, shuddering helplessly in Anna's embrace, "the sky is beautiful out here, isn't it."

"So beautiful." Anna took care that her tears did not fall on Graham's face. As much as her heart cried for the hurt that even her boundless love could not heal, she rejoiced in knowing that their love song was eternal.

ABOUT THE
AUTHORS

KATHIE BERGQUIST is the coauthor (with Robert McDonald) of *A Field Guide to Gay and Lesbian Chicago* (Lake Claremont Press). Her writing has been published in *Best Date Ever: The Lesbian Edition* and the *Harrington Lesbian Literary Quarterly.* She holds a B.A. in Creative Writing from Columbia College Chicago, where she is currently pursuing an M.F.A.

RACHEL KRAMER BUSSEL is senior editor at *Penthouse Variations,* hosts In The Flesh Erotic Reading Series, and wrote the popular "Lusty Lady" column for *The Village Voice.* She's edited a dozen anthologies, including Lambda Literary Award finalists *Up All Night* and *Glamour Girls: Femme/Femme Erotica;* as well as *First-Timers; Ultimate Undies; Sexiest Soles; Secret Slaves: Erotic Stories of Bondage; Caught Looking; She's on Top; He's on Top;* and *Naughty Spanking Stories from A to Z 1* and *2.* Her erotica has been published in more than 100 anthologies, including *Best American Erotica 2004* and *2006,* and she's contributed to *Bust, Curve, Diva,* Gothamist,

Huffington Post, Mediabistro, *New York Post, On Our Backs, Penthouse, San Francisco Chronicle, Time Out New York,* and *Zink.* Her website is rachelkramerbussel.com.

ANDREA DALE's stories have appeared in *Screaming Orgasms, Yes Ma'am, Hide and Seek, Naughty or Nice,* and other collections. Her novels include *A Little Night Music* (with Sarah Dale) and *Cat Scratch Fever* (with Sophie Mouette). "In Flight" was inspired by a daylong falconry course she took in Wales. Her website is at cyvarwydd.com.

SHANNON DARGUE is a carpenter living in Calgary, Alberta, with her partner of six years and their eleven-year-old daughter. This is her first published story.

JENNIFER FULTON is the author of eighteen romance and crime novels under the pen names Jennifer Fulton, Rose Beecham, and Grace Lennox. She is a recipient of the Alice B. award, Lambda Literary award finalist, and GCLS award winner. Jennifer lives with her family in Colorado.

SHANNA GERMAIN is a poet by nature, a short-story writer by the skin of her teeth, and a novelist in training. Her work, erotic and otherwise, has been widely published in places like *Absinthe Literary Review, Best American Erotica 2007, Best Bondage Erotica 2, Best Gay Romance 2008, Best Lesbian Erotica 2008,* and *Salon.* Visit her online at shannagermain.com.

ARIEL GRAHAM lives and writes in Reno, Nevada, with her husband and cats. Her work can be found on Pink Flamingo and Fishnet and in the anthologies *Beyond Love, Bound to Love,* and *Sacred Exchange.*

SACCHI GREEN writes in western Massachusetts and the mountains of New Hampshire. Her stories have appeared in a hip-high stack of books with inspirational covers, including multiple volumes of *Best Lesbian Erotica, Best Women's Erotica,* and *The Mammoth Book of Best New Erotica.* She has also edited or co-edited three anthologies of lesbian erotica (with a fourth in the works), and an upcoming speculative fiction anthology of queer alternative history.

KAY JAYBEE has had a number of stories published in Cleis anthologies, including *Lips Like Sugar, Best Women's Erotica 2007, Lust,* and *Best Women's Erotica 2008.* Her work has also appeared in the collections *Sex and Music, Ultimate Sin,* and *The Mammoth Book of Lesbian Erotica.* A regular contributor to the erotic website *Oysters and Chocolate,* Kay is very much looking forward to the publication of her first solo work of erotica, *The Collector* (Austin & Macauley).

KARIN KALLMAKER's writing career began with the venerable Naiad Press and continues with Bella Books, spanning more than two dozen novels in print. Her novels of lesbian romance, lesbian erotica, and lesbian science fiction/fantasy include the Goldie and Lammy award-winning *18th & Castro, Just Like That, Maybe Next Time,* and *Sugar.* Translations include Spanish, French, German, and Czech. More than sixty short stories have appeared in anthologies from publishers such as Alyson, Circlet, Bold Strokes, and Haworth.

MAGGIE KINSELLA's erotica has previously appeared in multiple editions of *Best Women's Erotica, Mammoth Best New Erotica, Best Lesbian Love Stories,* and in *Best Lesbian Romance 2007; Best Lesbian Love Stories: Summer Flings;*

Foreign Affairs: Erotic Travel Tales; Rode Hard, Put Away Wet: Lesbian Cowboy Erotica; After Midnight: True Lesbian Erotic Confessions; Erotic Interludes 3: Lessons in Love; and many others.

CATHERINE LUNDOFF's stories have appeared or are forthcoming in more than sixty publications including *So Fey: Queer Faery Stories; Time Well Bent: GLBT Alternate History; Periphery: Erotic Lesbian Futures; Farragos Wainscot; Khimairal Ink; The Mammoth Book of Best New Erotica 6; Stirring Up a Storm; Garden of the Perverse; Sex and Candy; Amazons;* and *Best Lesbian Erotica 2008.* She is the author of two collections of lesbian erotica: *Crave: Tales of Lust, Love, and Longing* (Lethe Press) and *Night's Kiss* (Torquere Press), and editor of the fantasy and horror anthology *Haunted Hearths and Sapphic Shades: Lesbian Ghost Stories* (Lethe Press). Her website can be found at visi.com/~clundoff.

EVAN MORA is a recovering corporate banker living in Toronto who's thrilled to put pen to paper after years of daydreaming in boardrooms. When not writing erotica, she's busy penning her first novel.

ELSPETH POTTER's upcoming publications include "Poppies Are Not the Only Flower" (*Lipstick on Her Collar*) and "Silver Skin" (*Periphery: Erotic Lesbian Futures*). Her work has previously appeared in *Best Lesbian Erotica, Best Women's Erotica,* and *The Mammoth Book of Best New Erotica.* Her erotic romance, *The Duchess, Her Maid, the Groom, and Their Lover,* will be published by Harlequin Spice under the name Victoria Janssen.

Born into a bevy of brothers, **OLIVIA PRESLEY** comes naturally to the part of cat amongst the pigeons. She traveled far and wide throughout her twenties, relishing jobs as diverse as dominatrix and fraud analyst. On the eve of her thirtieth birthday, tired of new places and faces, Olivia returned to Australia to study writing. She now dreams of living in a sailboat off Turkey.

TERESA NOELLE ROBERTS's erotica has appeared or is forthcoming in *Best Women's Erotica 2004, 2005, and 2007; Ultimate Lesbian Erotica 2007; Lipstick on Her Collar;* Fishnetmag.com; *The Mammoth Book of Lesbian Erotica;* and many other publications.

KI THOMPSON resides in the Washington, DC area with her partner and two very spoiled but much loved cats. Her novels include *House of Clouds,* a romantic saga set during the Civil War; and the romances *Heart of the Matter* and *Cooper's Deale,* all from Bold Strokes Books. She has short stories in the *Erotic Interludes* series, *Best Lesbian Romance 2007,* and *Fantasy: Untrue Stories of Lesbian Passion.*

Called a "trollop with a laptop" by *East Bay Express* and a "literary siren" by Good Vibrations, **ALISON TYLER** is naughty and she knows it. Her sultry short stories have appeared in more than eighty anthologies including *Rubber Sex, Dirty Girls,* and *Sex for America* (Harper Perennial). She is the author of more than twenty-five erotic novels, most recently *With or Without You* (Virgin), and the editor of more than forty-five explicit anthologies, including *J Is for Jealousy* (Cleis), *Naughty Fairy Tales from A to Z* (Plume), and *Naked Erotica* (Pretty Things Press). Please visit alisontyler.com for more information or myspace.com/alisontyler if you want to be her friend.

RAKELLE VALENCIA, when not cowboyin', has co-edited four erotic anthologies including Lambda Literary Award finalist *Rode Hard, Put Away Wet.* She has published many erotic short stories, which can be found on the bookshelves of the most excellent bookstores. Her nonfiction, technical articles on natural horsemanship, have been printed in the most discriminating rags. Her photos and freelance artwork have appeared on puzzles, advertisements, and logos. This year's motto is to "always keep the hairy side up."

ALLISON WONDERLAND has a B.A. in women's studies, a weakness for lollipops, and a fondness for rubber ducks. Her favorite sound is Fran Drescher's voice, and her cocktail of choice is a Shirley Temple. Allison's writing has been published at FortheGirls.com and is anthologized in *Wetter, Island Girls, The Longest Kiss, Hurts So Good,* and *Visible: A Femmethology.* See what she's up to at aisforallison.blogspot.com.

ABOUT
THE EDITOR

RADCLYFFE is the author of numerous lesbian novels and anthologies including the Lambda Literary Award winners *Erotic Interludes 2* and *Distant Shores, Silent Thunder*. She has selections in *A Is for Amour; H Is for Hardcore; L Is for Leather; Rubber Sex; Hide and Seek: Erotic Stories; The Taste of Him: Oral Sex;* and *Best Lesbian Erotica 2006, 2007,* and *2008,* among others. She is the president of Bold Strokes Books, an independent LGBT publishing company.